THE ROCKSTAR

THE ROCKSTAR

g. glass

iUniverse, Inc.
New York Lincoln Shanghai

The Rockstar

iUniverse books may be ordered through booksellers or by contacting:

iUniverse
2021 Pine Lake Road, Suite 100
Lincoln, NE 68512
www.iuniverse.com
1-800-Authors (1-800-288-4677)

Cover design: g.glass & Giulia Nuccitelli
Cover by: Giulia Nuccitelli

ISBN: 0-595-34298-1

Printed in the United States of America

It amazes me that the more I write, the more my friends and family rally around me.

Mom and Pop, your support means the world to me!

Marilyn, Denise, Audra, and Tonya. Thank you for taking the time to read and being such wonderful friends.

Giulia and Cathy, thank you for your support! It's an honor to stand behind you in line!

Anita, You Rock my world! You are an inspiration!

To my best friend, lover, soul mate and partner. You inspire me to be the best I can be in everything I do! I love you!

To all of you that are about to read this novel, find the true Rockstar inside of you and let it shine!

CHAPTER 1

Sonata made her way into the Red Lion Pub.

The smoky small club was packed like sardines.

Wherever the Travelers played, they packed them in. The five member all girl band had a huge following.

She couldn't believe that her boss K.C. Reynolds sent her to England to look at this band. Were they that hard up for new talent in the states? Yes, in fact, she could believe it. Sonata had a three-month sex fest with her boss. She really thought that she would get the ax, but K.C. made it very clear that if she kept her mouth shut, she would still have a job. Sonata chuckled. She was so paranoid about her sexuality that she was willing to do anything to keep it hidden. The funny thing was, everyone knew. Come on. This is Hollywood and the record business. No one much cared. But, if it kept Sonata in the groove and her job, then she was game. Sonata knew that K.C. was seeing Val Morrissey now, and that was fine. Who knew? Maybe she would find her true love in jolly old England. Stranger things have happened.

Sonata looked near the stage and spotted the reserved sign. She made her way to the table.

The lights started to dim, and the crowd became restless. The band ran out and took their places.

"One...Two...One two three four!" the drummer called out.

The band broke into a wonderful version of Heart's Barracuda. Sonata took out a note pad and began to jot things down. What she liked, what needed to be changed, what they wore onstage. She was interested in how the crowd reacted to them. After an hour of note taking, she finally sat back and watched. They were all such great musicians.

"Thank you." Lisa the keyboard player said. "The Travelers thank you. Now we're gonna feature our drummer Eddie. Give her yer luv."

The crowd went wild as the tall sleek drummer climbed out from behind her equipment. She moved to the piano and sat down. She looked up and smiled. The crowd started to scream and whistle.

Sonata sat up. Their eyes met and held a stare.

Eddie Sutcliffe's raging blue eyes burned deep into Sonata.

"Ah, I'm gonna give it a go here on a Joan Armatrading song." Eddie said shyly.

The crowd went crazy as Eddie started playing the piano and singing "The Weakness in me." Sonata was amazed how Eddie was able to draw the crowd to her. She held them in the palm of her hand.

Eddie looked up and once again caught Sonata's eyes. She was different, Eddie thought. Not the normal type of groupie that hung around her because of what she did for a living.

Before she hooked up with Lisa and the Travelers, she would sleep around a lot. But, she got tired of wham, bam, here's my demo tape ma'am. She longed for he one true love. She made a commitment to Lisa, but still thought something was missing.

It was so refreshing to see this beautiful redhead sitting in front of her. She smiled looking at her once again.

❦   ❦   ❦

After the show, Sonata made her way backstage to meet the Travelers. She was impressed with the group as a whole. But, there was something about Eddie's presence that stood out. Sonata felt a definite attraction.

The small backstage area housed only one dressing room for all five girls. They were used to it. They had dressed in their van as well as at gas stations.

Sonata was amazed by how many women were hanging around. Most were holding drinks and CD's to be signed.

Hmm. Sonata thought. They already have a fan base. This was a good thing in England maybe, but would they hit in the states?

Lisa, the keyboard player, and manager of the group came out first. A slew of crazed women rushed over to her begging for autographs and photos. She worked the crowd by winking, flirting and posing for pictures. She spotted Sonata and came over.

"Let me guess. You're the American?" She held out her hand.

"Guilty." Sonata smiled and shook Lisa's hand.

"I'm Lisa. The founder and manager of the lot. You liked what ya saw tonight then?"

"Yes I did. I wonder if we might go somewhere and talk?"

"Sure. Let me get rid of these stragglers, and we can go to the pub and have a pint and a chat."

"Great." Sonata smiled. She watched as the rest of the group came out and mingled with their fans. Eddie was the last one to immerse from the dressing room. She was clearly the fan's favorite. She came out wearing black leather pants with boots, and a white silk shirt.

Sonata was turned on by her look. She definitely had a way about her.

Eddie happily signed autographs and posed for pictures. Some of the women had flowers and stuffed animals. Eddie loved this part. Fans were cool. She looked up and caught Sonata staring. She grinned. Eddie had never seen someone so beautiful with red hair and hazel eyes. This was simply a vision that stood in front of her.

Eddie quickly excused herself from the adoring public and made her way over to Sonata.

"Well now. I can tell by the looks of you, you are not one of 'em." Eddie said.

Sonata laughed. "No, I'm not."

"Well not to good for me then, eh?" Eddie smiled.

"Well, not yet anyway." Sonata was taken by the tall drummer's kind smile. She was so serious in her photos and on stage. Still, Sonata couldn't help but see some sadness in her eyes. "Hi, I'm Sonata Williams."

"Eddie. Eddie Sutcliffe." She juggled the flowers and stuffed animals in her arms; she took Sonata's hand and held it.

Sonata didn't want her to let it go.

"So, you're the one who wants to take us to America?"

"Yes, I hope to."

"I hope so too. Excuse me a moment." Eddie grinned again as she turned and sat her gifts down, to sign a few more autographs.

Sonata was entranced. All she could see was herself wrapped in the arms of Eddie Sutcliffe. She wondered what it would be like to make love to her. She felt things stirring inside her that she hadn't felt in a long time. Even K.C. Reynolds didn't make her feel the way Eddie's touch made her feel. She thought about what K.C. told her. Never mix business with pleasure. It won't work. Still, there was something about Eddie that Sonata felt deep inside. She had to be with her.

After an hour, the groupies had all left. Sonata got the chance to meet the rest of the group. They were all really nice girls.

Eddie came back up to Sonata. "Can I ask you something?"

"Sure." Sonata smiled.

"Where are you from, exactly, in America?"

"Venice Beach." Sonata looked at Eddie. "Why?"

"No reason, really."

Lisa came up and gingerly put her hand on Eddie's ass. "You two ready?"

"Yep." Eddie took Lisa's hand.

Sonata felt like a fool. She didn't even stop to think that Eddie might be with someone, let alone Lisa.

The pub was crowded and loud. Sonata sat across from Eddie and Lisa. She wanted so much to be able to have some time alone with Eddie. But with Lisa always hovering, it didn't look like that was going to happen.

Lisa ordered gin and tonics for herself and Eddie, and talked Sonata into a pint.

"So, when do we leave for the States?" Lisa asked frankly.

"Well, first we need to get you into the recording studio and make a demo, and take some publicity shots. Then, Reynolds Records, back in the States, will take it from there."

"What about money? Demos and shots don't bloody come fer free ya know."

Eddie shot Lisa a look. She could be so rude sometimes. She looked at Sonata.

"You don't pay for a thing. We will compensate you for your time as well and all expenses."

"Well now, that's more like it then." Lisa took a swig of her drink.

"We would, however, like one of the songs on the demo to be the cover Eddie sang tonight."

Eddie looked up at Sonata. They locked into each other's stares. Lisa caught it and was not pleased. She would deal with Eddie later.

"That's fine and all, but Eddie ain't the lead. I am." Lisa stared at Sonata. "She only sings, when I need to rest me voice."

"We need to showcase the whole band's talent. If more than one of you can sing it only benefits the entire group."

Lisa was just about to say something when her cell phone rang. "Yeah?" she smugly said into the phone. "What? You tell that bastard he better pay up if he knows what's good fer em."

Sonata took a sip of her beer, and smiled at Eddie.

"Sounds like he doesn't want to pay." Eddie said.

Lisa reached over and slugged Eddie on her arm. "Shut the fuck up, Eddie. I'm on the fuckin' phone!"

Eddie quickly clammed up and sank down into her chair.

Sonata couldn't believe it. Why would Eddie take that from her? Lisa didn't just tap her. It was a hit. Besides, they were in a loud noisy bar. She watched as Eddie winced in pain. She was rubbing her arm.

"You don't let that prick out of your sight! I'm coming now." Lisa growled into the cell. "Well, that's just rich. Look, I have to go, can we do this tomorrow?" Lisa looked at Sonata.

"Ah, yeah sure, tomorrow is fine." Sonata looked at Eddie. She could tell that Eddie didn't want to go.

"Move yer arse, Eddie. I don't have all fuckin' night."

"Would you mind if Eddie took me back to the hotel? My first time in England, and I know I'll get lost."

Eddie smiled.

"Yeah. Well, good luck to ya. Eddie couldn't find her way out of a market sack!" Lisa laughed at her joke, and took the last swig of her drink before heading to the door.

When she was gone Sonata turned to Eddie. "She has some temper."

"Yeah. She's got lots of pressures, managing and such." Eddie sipped her drink.

"Eddie, I really liked your solo tonight. You play piano beautifully."

"Well, thanks. It's me favorite song. So tell me, with the name Sonata, that must mean you play as well?"

"The guitar. But I always wanted to learn the piano."

"I'll teach ya if ya like. If and when we get to the States." Eddie smiled.

Sonata put her hand on Eddie's. "I'd like that." She said.

Eddie looked down at Sonata's hand. Heat rushed through her and took her by surprise. This was going to be a problem, especially with Lisa. Eddie knew that Lisa cheated on her. She called her on it once and ended up with a black eye and a busted lip. Eddie wanted to get away from Lisa, and maybe, now, Sonata held her ticket to freedom.

"You fancy a game of darts?" Eddie asked, pulling her hand away.

"Sure, why not?" Sonata smiled. "As long as I'm not keeping you."

"Naw. It's early fer me yet. You know us rock and rollers. The whole lot of us are vampires. Besides, how often do I get to play darts with a beautiful American such as you?"

Sonata blushed as she followed Eddie to the dartboards.

They laughed and drank and played darts for over 2 hours. It was the best time Eddie ever remembered having.

Sonata looked at her watch. "Eddie, it's 1:00am. I'm sorry I kept you out this late."

"It's fine, luv, but I should be getting you back to the hotel. Lisa will be wondering why I'm not back at the flat."

The walk back to the Savoy was great. Eddie was a fabulous tour guide. Sonata didn't want the evening to end.

"Here ya are. Safe an sound." Eddie smiled.

"And, it didn't rain." Sonata said, looking around.

"That's cause you brought the sunshine with ya from the States."

Sonata looked into Eddie's eyes. She had to be with Eddie, plain and simple. She didn't care what would happen. All she knew was what was in her heart, and in her heart was Eddie Sutcliffe. All of Sonata's morals were being put to the test. This was a musician. And she knew all about musicians. Once the Travelers hit in America, all hell would break loose, and Sonata could kiss any chance she had with Eddie goodbye.

"Would you like to come up? Maybe have a cup of tea?" Sonata asked hopefully.

"Thanks, but I need to get going. Maybe a rain check?" Eddie smiled.

"Ok. I will see you all tomorrow. Thanks Eddie, for walking me back."

Sonata stood on her tiptoes and kissed the blushing drummer on the cheek.

Eddie was flustered. She never met anyone like Sonata. "Ah, have a good one then." Eddie watched as Sonata walked into the Savoy. It would have taken an act of God to remove the smile from Eddie's face.

Eddie looked at her watch. It was now 2:30am. Lisa would be livid. But, after all, she was doing it for the band.

She opened the door slowly and walked inside. It was dark and quiet. Maybe she lucked out and Lisa wouldn't be home yet. She walked into the bedroom to see Lisa waiting up.

"Where the fuck ave you been?" Lisa growled.

"At the pub and then I walked Sonata to the hotel."

"Did you get lost on the way to the flat?"

"Lisa, it's nothing to get riled about. We just talked and played some darts. I thought it would be good for the band."

"There ya go again! How many times do I have to bloody well tell you? I am the reason we are where we are. Not you. Where do you get off telling shit to the record lady?"

"It was just talk, Lisa." Eddie knew where this conversation was heading. She could tell by the smell in the room that Lisa had been using. She always got like this.

"Just talk?" Lisa stood up and pulled out a knife from her robe pocket. She walked over to Eddie. "Did you fuck her?"

Eddie started to back up slowly. "Don't be crazy, Lisa."

"Oh, so now ya say I'm crazy? Is that what ya told her?"

"Sod off, Lisa. You are half pissed and stoned. Go an sleep it off." Eddie tried to make a stand.

Lisa lunged forward and caught Eddie on the arm. The blood permeated her shirt. Eddie grabbed her arm. "Fuck Lisa, you cut me!" She ran to the bathroom and slammed the door.

Lisa dropped the knife and went to the door. "Why did you get in front of me Eddie? It was a joke, and ya had to step in front of the bloody knife."

"Sod off!" Eddie yelled. Who was she kidding? Eddie grabbed a towel and wrapped it around her arm. She was hoping she wouldn't need stitches. She looked at herself in the mirror. The four years with Lisa were beginning to show. She was tired of the hell Lisa put her through. After a year on coke, and other miscellaneous drugs, Eddie went clean. It was hard, but she was determined to do it. She did smoke a little pot every now and then, but she had it under control.

She slowly unbuttoned her shirt and peeled it off. The pain was bad. The cut was fairly deep. She turned on the tap and ran her arm under it.

She had become numb to the pain that Lisa had inflicted on her. Most of it was mental, but as of late, more physical.

When she finally got the bleeding to stop, she patched up her arm and walked out of the bathroom.

Lisa was on the bed passed out in her drug-induced stupor. Eddie threw on her sweat pants and T-shirt. She grabbed the comforter and her pillow and went into the living room. She lay down on the couch until sleep finally came to her.

CHAPTER 2

The morning was cold and damp. Sonata looked at the clock on the night-stand. It was 10:20am. Did she really sleep that long? She rolled over and stretched and smiled as she thought of last night and Eddie. When she got into her room she had three messages from K.C. She quickly phoned her back and told her that she thought the Travelers would be a huge asset to Reynolds Records, especially the drummer. KC gave her the green light to go forward, but with caution until the company gave the final word. They ordered up a demo and a photo shoot. KC also gave Sonata full responsibility of the group. From now on, Sonata was to be in charge of the Travelers.

Sonata sat up in bed and picked up the phone. She had a lot of work to do. She ordered room service and then looked for her organizer. She had the numbers for a recording studio and a photographer. She made her calls. If all went well, the Travelers would be in the states by the end of the month.

Eddie woke up to the smell of coffee and a joint. Lisa was sitting in the living room staring at her.

"Glad you're awake." Lisa tried to smile at Eddie.

Eddie sat up holding her arm. The blood had soaked through her bandage, and she was still in pain. "Didn't think you felt that way last night." Eddie said bluntly.

Lisa moved to the couch and sat next to Eddie. "Look Eddie, about the cut. I'm sorry. I just got a wee bit mad. That prick shorted us pay, and then I come back to the flat and you ain't here." She put her arm around Eddie. "Ya know

I'm doing this fer us Eddie. We're going to be huge when we get to the States, luv. We'll drink champagne, and live in a mansion."

"What about the drugs, Lisa?" Eddie looked at her.

"What about em?" Lisa smiled. "I got it under control. Ya got to trust me, Eddie."

"You call this under fucking control?" She held her arm up. "Look what you did Lisa."

"I know. And, I said I was sorry." She looked at Eddie with her puppy dog brown eyes. She could always get to Eddie.

Eddie looked at Lisa. Why did she have this affect on her?

Lisa took Eddie's face into her hands and kissed her. She pushed Eddie back down on the couch and climbed on top of her. Her hands started to expertly roam over Eddie's body. She kissed her neck and started to suck hard on it. She would leave her mark clearly so that any bitch would know that Eddie belonged to Lisa O'Brien, especially that American. She needed to know who was running the show and Lisa had no problems telling her how it was going to be.

❦   ❦   ❦

Sonata looked at her watch. The band was thirty minutes late. That was one pet peeve Sonata had. It was very unprofessional and she would clearly set the record straight once they showed up. KC would be pissed. Time is money. They had England's top photographer sitting around drinking mimosas with his five member crew, a stylist, a hairdresser and a make-up artist, all getting paid to do nothing.

Finally, Sonata saw the van drive up. It was Linda, the bass player, and Annie and Pamela, the guitarists. They were all smiles, ready and willing.

"Hey guys." Sonata tried to smile. She looked around. "Where are Eddie and Lisa?"

"They'll be along." Pamela smiled. "They had a productive morning."

The girls giggled.

Sonata knew what that meant. Her heart sank. "Well, you three go on inside and get started with hair and make-up."

The girls went in. Sonata looked at her watch again.

What seemed like hours later, a taxi came up. Eddie and Lisa got out. Lisa quickly took Eddie's hand and started to walk past Sonata.

"The driver needs some money, luv." Lisa smirked at Sonata. "Remember, expense is no object."

Sonata looked at Eddie.

Eddie quickly looked away.

Lisa tugged on Eddie's hand, then preceded to go in.

Sonata couldn't believe it. She thought she had read her right. She thought there was something between her and Eddie. Musicians…she should have known.

The honk from the waiting taxi brought her out of her thoughts. She walked over to pay him, wondering what she was going to do.

The girls were having a blast. They had been a band for five years and had never been treated like this.

Sonata had brought in a video camera and was filming the antics. It would be great on a concert DVD. She watched Eddie who seemed to take a back seat to the rest of the band. She sat quietly. Sonata caught Eddie looking at her twice. After make-up and hair the girls got to pick out some clothes. Lisa chose first. The other girls seemed to know their place in what was Lisa's world.

Eddie took her jacket off and started to look through the wardrobe.

"Can I keep me trousers on?" Eddie looked at Sonata.

"Please, wear what you feel comfortable in. We want to see the real you." She looked at Eddie and smiled.

The smile from last night returned to Eddie's face.

Sonata felt an ease come over her. She knew something was going on. She looked down and saw the cut on Eddie's arm.

Eddie are you ok?" She moved closer to inspect her arm.

"She's a klutz. You should know that about Eddie Sutcliffe." Lisa laughed.

The other's started to chuckle.

"What happened Eddie?" Sonata looked deep into her eyes. She saw the hickey on her neck.

Eddie looked at Lisa who stared at her. "It's just a scratch Sonata. I'll live."

The photographer's assistant walked in. "Joseph wants to start with solo shots. Who's first?"

"That'll be me." Lisa grinned. She grabbed the jacket and walked out the door.

"The rest of you are welcome to come and watch." The assistant offered. The girls checked their make-up one last time and followed the assistant. Eddie stayed behind.

Sonata closed the door. She walked up behind Eddie. "Are you ok?"

Eddie turned to Sonata. "Yeah, I'm a tough bird." She chuckled.

"Eddie, did Lisa do this to you?"

"I told you, Lisa is under a lot of pressure." Eddie turned away.

"And this is how she handles it? By hurting you?"

"Lisa loves me Sonata. You'll see." Eddie looked at herself in the mirror. Who was she fooling?

"For your sake, Eddie, I hope I do." She put her hand on Eddie's shoulder. "I care about what happens to you. If you ever need anything, you let me know."

She turned and walked out of the dressing room.

Tears started to well up in Eddie's eyes. How she wanted to tell Sonata what happened. She liked her, and felt that she could trust her. Maybe she would tell her. Maybe she could help her finally be free.

The photo shoot was a headache. Lisa had to have control of everything. Sonata was just about to call the whole deal off. She excused herself and went to call KC. She was about to dial, when Eddie came in. She put the phone down.

"Just came to check on ya." Eddie smiled.

"Eddie, I am going to be real honest with you. I have a problem. A big problem."

"Lisa, I bet." Eddie said.

"She is a monster Eddie. I'm sorry. But I just don't know if it's gonna work."

Eddie moved up to Sonata. She put her hands on her shoulders. "Please…. Don't give up on us."

Sonata melted into those deep blue eyes. How could she say no to Eddie?

"I know, I'm not one to say this, Sonata, but I think you were sent here for me, I mean, for us."

"Oh Eddie. I want to see you succeed more than anything. I think you are a wonderful talent and you have a beautiful soul. But, I have to tell you, I think Lisa will hold you down."

Tears started streaming down Eddie's face. Sonata was right. Lisa did hold her down, but she didn't know what else to do. Lisa was all she knew.

Her mother died when she was two and her father abused her until she ran away from home when she was fifteen. She was in and out of back packer's shelters. She found a job in the local music store. She would stay late after everyone left and practiced the drums and piano. She also played guitar and the violin. She met Lisa one day, when she came into to buy an amp. Lisa fell madly in love with the tall lean drummer. She was perfect for her band. Eddie followed her around like a little puppy dog. Lisa had her move in and took control of her life.

"Eddie where the hell are ya." Lisa shouted.

Eddie quickly pulled away from Sonata. She wiped the tears from her face and looked in the mirror.

"Look at me. You must think I'm a bleedin' idiot." She tried to chuckle.

"No Eddie, I think you're terrific." Sonata said.

"You do?" Eddie looked at Sonata.

"Yeah, I do." Sonata reached for Eddie's cheek. She carefully brushed a tear from it.

Eddie felt the heat rush through her again. She had never felt like this before.

"Eddie!" Lisa's voice rang through Eddie's thoughts.

"I better go." She opened the door and turned to Sonata. "Thanks, Sonata." She smiled and left.

Sonata looked at her self in the mirror. She was falling hard for Eddie Sutcliffe, and now, there was no turning back.

After the photo shoot Sonata had a limo waiting for the girls. She made special reservations for lunch at the Savoy.

The girls couldn't believe it. They had never been in a limo, let alone the Savoy.

"Now I know I died and went to heaven." Pamela squealed.

"Can you bloody believe this?" Linda chimed in.

"Well ladies, if we play our cards right, and you're all willing to work hard as a group, then, I think you will have a lot of limos in your future." She looked at Lisa. "We are a team ladies, now more than ever we need to act like one."

Lisa didn't care what Sonata had to say. She was the star of the Travelers. She hand picked the girls and brought the group together. Lisa was positive that once she got to America, she would be singled out as a superstar. She knew that a solo career was inevitable.

The restaurant at the Savoy was glamorous. Sonata arranged for a private room. Lisa took Eddie's hand and sat on the other side of Sonata. Linda sat next to her and Pamela and Annie each took an end.

The waiter came and took drink orders. Sonata reached into her brief case and grabbed a stack of papers.

"First things first ladies." She passed out the papers to each one of the ladies.

"This is a standard option contract. Sign it now, if you wish, or look it over. I need them in my hands in forty eight hours."

"What happens in forty eight hours?" Annie asked.

"We go in to a recording studio to cut a demo. I can't let you sing for us until these are signed."

"How do we know ya don't ave yer foot in both camps? Ya could be yankin' our chains with this?" Lisa looked at Sonata.

"I don't make up the terms of the contract. Like I said, if you want to look it over or have your attorney look it over, that's fine."

"What does the option part mean?" Eddie looked at Sonata with interest.

"It means they can fuck you over if they want to." Lisa said as Pamela and Annie laughed.

"Eddie, it means that if Reynolds Records finds you worthy, they will option you for a full CD. They will market and promote you. If the CD hits, then, I suggest you re-negotiate. The simple truth is, if the demo is good, you get a one record deal. If that is good, then the sky is the limit. If it bombs, you get sent home to England." Sonata said, very business like.

Eddie grinned. She loved learning about the business end of music. Lisa never let her in on anything.

"Ok, I have a question." Linda said. "What about our families?"

"Well, that's what we are doing right now. I need to know from you, about you. If your option is picked up, we need to know if you want to live in the US, or stay here in England."

"Well, Pammy and I have a son, and we need to bring him with us." Linda looked at Sonata as she made notes. "This won't botch it for us will it?"

"No, of course not." Sonata smiled. "Your family is your family."

"And, I am sure you are well aware that the lot of us are dykes." Lisa said.

"Lisa." Eddie mumbled.

"Ok, that is your personal life. Frankly, we don't care who you sleep with, but the tabloids might. I think you should be up front with it, then they will leave you alone." She looked at Eddie. "And since we are laying our cards out on the table, I am also a lesbian."

You could have pushed Eddie over with a feather. Sonata? This was incredible, Eddie thought. There was a reason Sonata was here.

"So you'll be in our corner?" Annie asked.

"All the way." Sonata smiled. "I really think you all are special. You have a lot to offer."

"Hold it." Lisa looked up from her contract. "There's nothing in here that says we can bloody well be ourselves. You'll tell us what to sing an how to act. We won't be the Travelers no more. Just some American manufactured piece of shit."

"C'mon, Lisa." Pamela said.

"Sod off, Pammy!" Lisa looked at her. "You didn't put every ounce of yer life into this band."

"Lisa, the record company would have control of your look and your song choice. But, I can assure you, we don't fix things that are not broken." Sonata said.

"And that should make me feel better?" Lisa looked at Sonata.

"This is a new group. You need to have the backing of the label. Like I said, if you sell, then you can call the shots. Until then, we do."

Lisa frowned. This was all bullshit. She brought this group to where it is now. She didn't need any two-bit Americans to become a star. There were plenty of British record labels that would want them.

"Would ya give us a few to chew the cud?" Lisa looked at Sonata.

"Sure." She grabbed her cell phone and left the room.

"I don't like this." Lisa said to her friends.

"Why not?" Annie looked at her. "America is the place to be, Lisa. We sure as hell can't get there without 'em."

"This is a pig in a poke. Don't ya see? If we go, then we won't be us."

"I trust Sonata." Eddie said.

"Well the dead has risin'." Lisa looked at Eddie. "And how would ya know to trust her? Ya only just met her yesterday."

"I can just tell. There is something about her. She wants to help us."

"I agree with Eddie." Pamela said. "She's got a good heart."

"And she's one of us." Linda chimed in.

"Will you listen to ya? Have you all just gone off?"

"Maybe Lisa has a point." Annie smiled.

"Look, all I'm saying is we are the Travelers. I want to stay the Travelers."

"Sonata wants us that way too." Eddie said. "That's why she came to see us. I want to sign it."

"I want to." Pamela said.

"Me too." Linda added.

"C'mon, Lisa. Give it a go." Eddie smiled.

Lisa looked at the contract again. She looked at Eddie and then to the rest of her friends. She knew she had no choice. Maybe Eddie was right. Maybe

Sonata did care. If she felt that they were stringing her along she would simply make the worst CD of her life and call the deal off. Besides, she knew after she got to America, she would be going solo.

"Go get her." She said to Eddie.

Eddie bounced up and ran out the door. She saw Sonata looking out the window.

"Second day and still no rain. Told ya you were good luck."

Sonata smiled. She turned to Eddie. "Let's hope that everyone's luck is about to change."

"I came to fetch ya. I think you got a deal." Eddie smiled.

"Great. Let's go."

"Wait a sec. What if Lisa don't sign? I mean can I still sign and go." Eddie asked hopefully.

"Well Eddie. I'd like to say yes, but it is a group deal."

"Oh." Eddie looked down.

"But I'd do my best to get you there."

Eddie smiled. "Yeah?" She was falling for Sonata. She was just so much everything Lisa wasn't. She wanted to be with her, but she couldn't. Lisa was a force and she would never put Sonata in harms way.

"Yeah." Sonata smiled. "Let go back in."

The rest of the lunch went off without a hitch. The girls all signed their contracts. Sonata informed them that there would also be a mandatory physical for insurance purposes. None of them seemed to mind. She told the girls that tomorrow they would be in a rehearsal hall to go over the song choices for the demo.

Eddie was thrilled. She loved where Sonata was taking them. She wanted to learn every aspect of this business.

"Well ya did it." She smiled at Sonata.

"One down." Sonata said as she gathered her things.

"Ah, listen, if ya have any time to spare, could we go over a couple things on the contract?"

"Sure, Eddie, is there a problem?" Sonata looked at her.

"No…No. Well it's just that…Well I want to…"

Lisa came up to them. "Well Sonata, ya got us by the balls now. Hope yer happy."

"I hope you're happy. I think this will be a good partnership." Sonata said.

"Yeah, right. Look Eddie, me and Annie are gonna go and grab some sheet music. We are gonna kick around an idea fer a new song. I'll see you at the flat later."

"Ok." Eddie said.

"Don't be buggin' her all day neither. We don't want her yankin' the papers back cause of you." Lisa looked at Eddie.

"You ready?" Annie asked Lisa.

"Sure thing, luv." Lisa smiled.

"Remember to keep all receipts so you can be reimbursed." Sonata said.

Eddie watched as Annie and Lisa left. Pamela and Linda followed suit.

"Well that's that then." Eddie said. "Guess I should get out of your hair."

"Wait a sec, Eddie, what were you going to ask me?"

"It was nothing big."

"Well, I have nothing to do for the rest of the afternoon, would you like to come up?"

"For that spot a tea you owe me?" Eddie grinned.

Sonata chuckled. "Yes."

"I'd like that." Eddie grabbed Sonata's brief case and they walked to the elevator.

"So, Eddie, what do you think about all this?"

"It makes me head spin. It's all going so fast. But, I love it."

"Well if you have any questions, please ask."

The elevator door opened and they got off on the 10th floor. They walked to the end of the hall to the suite. Sonata unlocked the door and held it open for Eddie.

"Wow." Eddie said as she walked inside and looked around.

"Pretty nice, huh? I still can't believe it myself sometimes."

Sonata picked up the phone and dialed room service. "Hi, this is Ms. Williams in suite 1012. I'd like to order the tea & cookies for two, please."

Eddie smiled as she watched Sonata.

"Great thanks." Sonata set the phone down. "It'll be here shortly."

"So, can I ask you something?" Eddie blurted out.

"Anything you want." Sonata smiled and sat next to her.

Eddie wanted to ask her a ton of things. *Was she single? Could she ever go for a gal like her?* "Would you teach me about the business end of music? I mean if time is there for it?"

"Are you serious, Eddie?" Sonata looked at her.

"Forget it. It's stupid." Eddie frowned.

"No, sweetie, it's not. I think it's great. I think all musicians should know about the business part. It's just that most don't care."

Eddie only heard one thing Sonata said. Sweetie.

"Eddie? Eddie?" Sonata said.

"Wha?" Eddie came back to earth.

"I'd be happy to teach you anything you want to know."

"For reals?" Eddie smiled.

"For reals." Sonata laughed.

They stared into each other's eyes. Sonata wanted to kiss Eddie, but she held back. She needed to make sure that Eddie was safe from Lisa before she could go any further.

❦   ❦   ❦

Annie came out of the bathroom. She followed the path of clothes that led to the bed. Lisa lay waiting for her to come back.

They had been sleeping together since day one. Annie was kinky and Lisa thrived on that. Eddie wanted romance and love. Annie wanted sex and lots of it.

Lisa lit up a joint and took a big draw. She passed it to Annie. "From now on babe, it's the good stuff fer us, no more off the street shit."

"It will be good." Annie chuckled. She slid into bed and kissed Lisa's stomach.

"Yep in me mansion with a pool an the works!" Lisa smiled.

"Yeah? And what are you planning to do about Eddie?" Annie said. For the past year and a half, Lisa had promised Annie that she would leave Eddie. But, she never did. Annie couldn't figure it out. Lisa didn't love Eddie. So why stay?

"Don't fuckin' get on me about Eddie, Annie. I told ya I'd take care of things."

She put the joint out and went back to kissing Annie. Her hands started to find their way around Annie's curvy body. Lisa loved being with Annie. She was up for anything. And they had tried it. Lisa knew that Annie wanted a commitment. Lisa wasn't going to commit to anyone. As soon as she got to Hollywood there would be countless women waiting to get in her pants, and she wanted to accommodate every last one of them.

❧   ❧   ❧

Sonata had the contract all laid out. She took Eddie step by step over it and explained everything to her. Eddie was smart, and she picked up on everything quickly.

"It's pretty simple, really." Eddie smiled. Lisa always told her that she wouldn't understand anything, so, she stopped asking.

"I told you, but you're smart Eddie."

"That's somethin' no one's ever told me."

"Well, they should have, cause it's true." Sonata smiled.

Eddie looked at Sonata. "Have I said how happy I am that you're here?"

"Yes, cause it isn't raining."

Eddie laughed. "No, silly. It can pour for all I care. You are just real special Sonata. Yer partner is a lucky bird."

Sonata looked at Eddie. She wanted to kiss her. It was getting harder by the minute to stay away from her.

"I don't have a partner, Eddie. I'm single."

Eddie looked deep into Sonata's eyes. They were so safe and full of love. Eddie wanted to be with her. But she had to hold back. She made a commitment to Lisa and she had to see it through.

Sonata leaned in to kiss Eddie as the phone rang. She moved to answer it.

"Hello…Yeah, Lisa she is, hold on." She held the phone up to Eddie.

Eddie frowned. It was like Lisa had radar on her. She took the phone from Sonata. "Hey Lisa…. Nothing just chattin'…How come…what time? Right, I got it." She handed the phone back to Sonata.

"Lisa says I need to leave you be." Eddie started to stand.

"Do you have to go?" Sonata asked.

"Well, she said I can't go back to the flat tonight. I'll just have a sit in the pub." Eddie looked down.

"Wait a sec. She is kicking you out of the house?"

"She said she had an idea fer a song. It's best to leave her be." Eddie started to put her jacket on.

"Eddie. Please. Stay here. There is plenty of room. We have a meeting tomorrow. You don't need to be sitting in a bar all night."

"Aw, you are sweet, Sonata, but I can't impose. If Lisa found out…"

"Then we won't tell Lisa." Sonata looked at Eddie. "It's settled."

Eddie laughed. "You're crazy, Sonata Williams. You know that?"

"I want you to be happy, Eddie."

"Sonata, you need to be careful. Just don't cross Lisa."

"Eddie, I'm not scared of her." She took Eddie's hands. "I don't want you to be either."

Eddie knew what Lisa was capable of. She was scared of her. She didn't need Sonata getting mixed up in that.

"Well, the night is young. What do you say we make a go of it?" Sonata smiled.

"What did you have in mind?"

"Oh, I don't know. Surprise me, Eddie Sutcliffe."

Eddie smiled. She knew exactly where to take Sonata. "Get your jacket."

Sonata complied. Eddie opened the door for her and they left.

🍁   🍁   🍁

Lisa carefully tied the band around her arm. She picked up a syringe and looked for a vein.

"Don't be shootin' up luv till we get the money." The sandy blonde guy said.

"How do I know what I'm getting' then?" Lisa looked at him.

"We've been dealin' to ya fer over a year. Ain't nothin' changed."

Annie came up behind Lisa. "Get rid of 'em, so we can have our own party." She whispered in her ear.

Lisa looked at Annie and grinned. She reached into her pocket and pulled out a wad of cash. She tossed it to the guy as he smiled and left.

"Remind me to give Sonata Williams the receipt for that." Lisa laughed.

Annie came around and straddled herself over Lisa's lap. She picked up the syringe and held it up. "Let the fun begin." She smiled.

As she felt the cold metal pierce her flesh, and the hot drug entering into her, Lisa tilted her head back. When Annie pulled the needle out, Lisa took the band and wrapped it around Annie's arm. She reloaded the needle and shot it into Annie.

Lisa kissed Annie. She cupped her hand around Annie's breast and roughly kneaded it.

Annie arched back. She loved Lisa's hands when they were on her. She was starting to become jealous of Eddie. She was in bed with Lisa every night. The fact that Lisa got the best drugs only made it that much harder. Eddie was stupid. She should never let Lisa out of her sight. So, Lisa was a little wild. She was young and smart and talented. Lisa was a great catch in Annie's eyes.

"C'mon." Annie cooed. "Let me show you how I feel about you."

She pulled Lisa to her feet.

The doorbell rang.

"Who the fuck is that?"

Annie grinned. "That's your surprise."

"Oh yeah?" Lisa smiled as she walked to the door and opened it.

There stood three women. They were scantily clad. They had bottles of booze, and were ready to party, a blonde and two brunettes.

Lisa remembered them from the other night. The groupies. She grinned.

"Ladies, welcome." Lisa said.

The three women walked in. The blonde came up to Lisa and started to kiss her. She shoved her tongue deep into Lisa's mouth.

Lisa grabbed the blonde and held her tightly against her body. She loved women with big tits.

The blonde reached down and started to rub Lisa's crotch.

Lisa pulled away. "Easy there, luv, we have all night for that."

"Then, why wait?" The blonde kissed her again.

Lisa grabbed her bottle of gin and staggered down the hall holding the blonde's hand. Annie already had the other two girls in the bedroom. She had lit up a joint and was passing it around. Lisa came in the room and jumped on her bed. Oh how she loved the music biz.

Eddie opened the door to the restaurant for Sonata.

It was nice and cozy. It catered to mostly lesbians. Eddie always felt comfortable here. When Lisa kicked her out in one of her writing moods, Eddie always came here.

The Hostess sat them at a nice quiet corner table. Eddie pulled out the chair for Sonata.

She took a seat, and watched as Eddie sat across from her.

"Eddie this place is great." Sonata said looking around. "Do you and Lisa come here often?"

"Well, I do. Lisa ain't never been. Not her thing really. She stays at home a lot."

"Can I ask you something, Eddie?"

"Anything."

"You really love Lisa, don't you?"

Eddie didn't know how to answer that. She made a commitment to Lisa. At one time she thought she was in love with her. But now she just wanted out of her living hell.

CHAPTER 3

The room was lit by candles. Lisa poured herself a gin. *The blonde knew how to go down on ya.* Lisa thought to herself. Annie was in the shower with her now and Lisa was aiming to feast herself on the second brunette. She had such a buzz from the heroin and the gin. She was flying high and it was only 9:00pm. This was gonna be a good night. She drug herself out of the bed and into the bathroom. She watched as the blonde was on her knees sucking and licking at Annie. She needed to keep the blonde around, Lisa thought. She opened the shower door and got in.

Annie came hard. She always thought that heroin pushed the intensity of her orgasms.

The blonde stood up and turned toward Lisa. She pushed her against the wall of the shower and kissed her hard. She slowly moved down and started kissing Lisa's already erect nipples.

Annie moved to Lisa and started to work her hand between her thighs. Lisa had died and gone to heaven. She was going ride the waves all night long.

Eddie and Sonata laughed. They were having such a good time. Dinner was wonderful. Sonata had fish and Eddie steak. Sonata told Eddie about her childhood. Eddie sat and stared. She wanted to hear every word that she said.

"Oh gee, Eddie, I'm boring you."

"No, Sonata, please. I love to hear ya talk." She smiled.

"Well, I can safely say that is the first time anyone has said that."

"Well then, they should say it more." She put her hand on Sonata's.

Sonata looked down. She wanted to kiss Eddie. She wanted to make love to her. She wanted Eddie in her life forever. She turned her hand up and held Eddie's.

"Your hand is soft." Sonata said.

"Naw, I have drummer hands, see." Eddie flipped her hands up for Sonata to see.

"Hey, how is that cut?"

"I'm gonna make it, I think." Eddie chuckled. "So are you ready?"

"For?"

"The rest of our date?" Eddie smiled.

"Sure." Sonata said.

Eddie stood up and took out her money and tossed it on the table. She walked over to Sonata and pulled out her chair. She held out her hand and Sonata took it. Eddie grinned as they walked to the exit and out onto the street.

"Thank you for dinner, Eddie." Sonata kissed the tall drummer on the cheek.

Eddie blushed. "Thanks fer the grand company."

"So, where to now?" Sonata looked at Eddie. She knew where she wanted Eddie to take her.

They walked hand in hand through the streets of London. Eddie didn't care who saw them, not even Lisa. She had a new mission in life. She was going to break free from Lisa and start a new life. She hoped that the new life included Sonata Williams.

They walked down Viller Street until they reached Heaven.

"This here is me favorite pub. You like to dance, Sonata?"

"Sure do."

"Great." Eddie smiled and opened the door to the club. "It's an old club but it's the best."

The club was packed with men and women and some Sonata couldn't make out. There were five dance floors, and they were all packed. Eddie took Sonata's hand and led her to the floor. Abba's "Dancing Queen" was playing. Eddie and Sonata started to dance, while their eyes locked into each other's.

Sonata couldn't believe what a great dancer Eddie was. She was smooth. She only wished Eddie could be this free when she was around Lisa. The song faded out as Gloria Estefan's "Here we are" started to play.

Eddie started to leave the floor when Sonata stopped her. She took her hand and pulled her back. Eddie took her into her arms as the music filled their souls.

Sonata closed her eyes and melted into Eddie. She could stay there forever.

The song ended. Eddie looked down into Sonata's eyes. She took her face into her hands, leaned forward and softly kissed her.

Her lips were warm and soft. Sonata could have kissed her forever.

An older lesbian couple came walking past. "Nice to see two people so in love." One of them said.

Sonata stepped back. She looked at Eddie. "Eddie;" was all that would come out.

Eddie was a rush of emotions. Not only did she kiss another woman, she kissed her boss! *Did she just ruin what she and her friends worked so hard to get? She had to kiss her. She was glad she did. What about Lisa?* Eddie was so confused.

"Sonata. I'm so sorry."

"Don't be, Eddie." Sonata smiled.

"I think I should get ya back."

"We don't have to go."

"I think it's best."

The walk back was quiet. It started to rain, and Eddie wouldn't say a word. They reached the Savoy, and stopped.

"I'll see you tomorrow Sonata."

"Wait, Eddie, I thought you were staying here?"

"After what's happened, I don't think I should."

Sonata's heart dropped. "Eddie, please."

Eddie reached over and gently stroked Sonata's cheek. Sonata took Eddie's hand and kissed it.

Eddie grabbed Sonata and kissed her. She quickly pulled away. "I'm sorry, Sonata, but I made that bloody commitment to Lisa." She took off down the street.

Sonata watched the tall lean figure disappear as it rounded the corner. Tears came to her quickly. She had fallen in love with Eddie Sutcliffe and couldn't do a damn thing about it.

Sonata reached the rehearsal hall early. She couldn't sleep at all and it showed. She needed to talk to Eddie but she knew that it would be impossible unless Eddie was early. She sipped on her strong coffee as she took out her note pad and went over a few things. The door opened and Eddie came in. She smiled shyly at Sonata.

"Mornin', Sonata." Eddie said flatly.

"Well, you look as bad as I do." Sonata said.

Eddie smiled. She walked over to the coffeepot and poured herself a cup. Sonata walked up to her. "Eddie, I think we need to talk."

"About?"

"About last night. About us. I am sure you felt something in that kiss too."

Eddie did. She sat up all night thinking about what a life with Sonata would be like. It was the brass ring. She also knew Lisa O 'Brien. Unless Lisa broke things off, Eddie was stuck. "Ah, it was a nice kiss Sonata." Eddie looked away.

"Was that all it was to you, Eddie? Just a kiss?" Sonata's voice shook. "I get it, big shot rock and roller. Love them and toss them to the curb."

Sonata turned away as Eddie grabbed her and spun her around. She took her in her arms and kissed her.

"Listen to me Sonata. I am absolutely mad about you. You have me feeling things that I never knew I could. But you don't know Lisa. She is a dangerous woman. I won't have you in harms way."

Sonata smiled. She was in heaven hearing those words come out of Eddie's mouth.

"We'll work it out Eddie. I promise. Just don't give up on us." She stood on tiptoe to kiss Eddie again. The door opened and Linda and Pamela walked in.

Eddie quickly turned away and went on to get her coffee.

"Good morning." Sonata smiled.

"And how are you today, Sonata?" Linda asked.

"Just peachy." She giggled.

Pamela knew Eddie well. She once had slept with Lisa, and was well aware how she treated women, especially Eddie. But today Eddie looked different. More at peace, and extremely happy. She wondered if Sonata was the reason.

"So, what needs to get done today?" Eddie asked.

"We need to come up with 8 to 10 songs to record for the demo. I want a mix of originals and covers. We just need to wait for Lisa and Annie." She looked at her watch.

"Sonata, our son will be along a bit later. The sitter can't keep him long today." Pamela said.

"That's fine. I can't wait to meet him." Sonata smiled.

"Yeah you can." Linda said.

Pamela hit Linda. "Don't say that to er Lin."

Sonata laughed. "It's ok Pamela. I know she was kidding."

Three hours went by. Sonata went to the phone and made a call to Lisa. The phone was busy. She tried Annie's and got the message machine. She knew that Lisa was going to be a big thorn in her side, but where was Annie?

Annie rolled over. She was sore but man what a party. She looked at the clock. It was noon. She rubbed the sleep from her eyes and looked around. Lisa was next to her and the blonde next to Lisa. She tried to sit up. Her head was spinning.

"Lisa. Lisa get up. We need to be at rehearsal."

There was no answer.

"Lisa!" Annie raised her voice. "Move yer bum."

"Sod off." Lisa moaned. She was in no mood.

"C'mon. We are late. Sonata's gonna ave our heads." She rolled out of bed. She staggered to the bathroom.

Lisa looked at the clock. "Fuck." She said under her breath. She knew she had to get moving, but her body had other ideas. She looked at the blonde sleeping next to her. She definitely remembered her. Lisa grinned as she thought of everything she did last night and part of the morning. She leaned over and kissed the blonde's back.

The blonde stirred.

"Hey ya need to get movin'." Lisa told her. "I need to be gettin' my arse to rehearsal."

Annie came out of the bathroom. She smiled as she went over to Lisa. "You look worked." She giggled.

"Yeah…. Well I have somethin' left fer ya." She grabbed Annie and pulled her to the bed. She kissed her.

"Later. We need to get." Annie said.

"You go. I'll be along. We can't show together anyway."

"Lisa. When are you goin' to break it off with Eddie so we can be together?"

"I know, Annie, stop fucking my brain up with that shit."

Annie grabbed her shoes and struggled to put them on.

Lisa knew that Annie was pissed. She had to do damage control. "C'mon, bird. Don't be this way. Yer me gal now." She pulled Annie to her. "No one makes me feel like you. When we get to the States it will be different. You'll see." She kissed Annie.

Annie smiled. "See you in a bit. Don't dottle." She grabbed her bag and left.

Lisa took a deep breath. She bought herself some more time. She looked at the blonde lying naked next to her. "Just enough time fer another go I say." She started to kiss her guest's back.

❀   ❀   ❀

Eddie was at the piano playing different songs for Pamela's little boy. Linda and Sonata were looking through songs, and Pamela was filing her nails.

"Ok, I like this set." Linda smiled. "It works well. Eddie should sing more anyway."

Sonata smiled. Her thoughts exactly. And when all was said and done, Eddie would be the star of the Travelers.

Annie came in trying to look her best. She smiled. "Ey everyone."

"You're four hours late." Sonata looked at her watch. "Where's Lisa?"

"Don't know." Annie tried to cover up.

Sonata could tell she was lying. She went up to Annie. "Here's the songs for the demos, I suggest you learn them." She handed Annie the list.

Annie looked at it. They were mostly cover songs that featured Eddie. Lisa would not like it.

"I thought we were gonna do Lisa's song?" Annie looked at Sonata.

"Listen up ladies. You all signed contracts. You put your faith in Reynolds's Records. We know what we are doing. There will be changes made to the group. But they are more superficial. But we won't tolerate attitudes. I can assure you that our boss will up and dismiss every one of you. I believe in your group and your music, so let's just not blow it." She looked at Eddie.

Lisa came staggering in. She smelled of smoke and alcohol. She looked at Eddie. She plopped in a chair next to Annie.

Sonata walked over to her and handed her a list. "These are the songs we are using on the demo."

Lisa looked at the list. "We ain't singing this crap." She looked at Sonata and threw the list down.

"Really? Well, I can't imagine that you much cared, since you are over four hours late. Oh yeah, I remember now. You were held up in your house writing that smash hit. Well, let's hear it." Sonata looked at Lisa.

Lisa let out a deep sigh. *This bitch obviously didn't know whom she was dealing with.* She looked at Eddie, and turned away.

Sonata grabbed her cell phone and walked out. Linda and Pamela looked at each other. Lisa stood up. "Eddie, let's move." She grabbed her backpack.

Eddie didn't want to go. She knew what was going to happen. Lisa was angry. She would only get worse and lash out. Eddie was going to get the end result.

"I'll go talk to her. Maybe I can fix things." Eddie offered.

"Don't you move." Lisa warned her. She walked out the door.

Sonata was talking to her boss when Lisa came walking up.

"We need to talk."

Sonata looked up. "I'll call you back KC." She hung up. "What could you possibly have to say that might interest me?" She looked at Lisa.

"Eddie and I want out. Break the contract." Lisa said.

"What?" Sonata looked at Lisa. "She said that to you?"

"Yeah. She can't handle being around Americans."

Funny, Sonata thought. *She didn't seem that way last night when she had her tongue down my throat.* "So that's it huh? You just want to walk away?"

"It's not the Travelers no more. You are turning us into a bunch of bloody wimps. We have good songs and we should sing em. Not this cover pop shit that you are choosing."

"Lisa, whether you have a point or not, you are forgetting something. You no longer rule the roost as far as the Traveler's go. You signed a contract giving us the control. I liked what I saw at the pub that night. But all this shit that you are bringing with it. The attitude and coming in whenever you feel like it. You are only hurting the band. And if it continues, then it's over." Sonata looked at Lisa, then turned and walked back inside.

Lisa pulled out a cigarette and lit it up. "We'll just see about that now won't we?" She laughed and took a big drag. She walked back inside.

The rest of the afternoon was pretty peaceful. The group came together and sang. Sonata was impressed. This was the band she wanted to put out in the mainstream. She also noticed how close Lisa was keeping tabs on Eddie. She was next to her at every turn. They went out to smoke together, sat next to each other during lunch. Sonata caught Eddie staring at her a few times. She was sad. Lisa left them not one second to talk.

Linda walked over to Sonata. "Sonata, if you have no plans tonight, Pammy and me would like ya to come by the flat. We'd like to get to know you better."

Sonata smiled. She wanted to spend this evening with Eddie. But she knew that Lisa wasn't going to let her out of her sight. "Sure Linda. Thank you. That would be nice."

"Say about seven then?"

"Seven it is." Sonata said.

"Are we done here? I need to get some rest." Annie said.

"Yes, we are. Do you all feel we can go into the studio, or do we need more rehearsal time?"

"Let's just record the bloody demo and get going." Lisa said. "We're as ready as ever."

"Ok, then, tomorrow we record. Rest your voice ladies, and FYI you still do have a club date this weekend. We are going to have some papers and news shows there for a bit. So let's be on our best behavior." Sonata looked at Lisa. "Ok, have a great rest of the day."

They started grabbing their things. Sonata noticed that Annie had Lisa in a corner talking.

"Ah, Eddie? Can I see you a second please."

Eddie walked over to Sonata. "What can I do fer ya?"

"I need to see you." Sonata whispered.

"It's not safe. Not now."

"Eddie, I told you, I'm not afraid of her."

"C'mon, Eddie, I'm waiting." Lisa growled.

"Look, I have to get. If I can, I'll come by." She winked at Sonata and walked to Lisa.

"Annie is coming over for supper tonight." Lisa said. "Ya need to make something good. In fact, we have a few friends coming over to wish us well."

Eddie smiled. She was sure that Lisa would send her out. Anytime she had her friends over, she would make Eddie get lost. This time Eddie wouldn't mind a bit.

"And you need me to get lost right?" Eddie asked.

Lisa put her arm around Eddie. "Yer my gal, Eddie. I want you by my side."

Sonata watched as Lisa kissed Eddie. It turned her stomach.

Annie was none too happy, either. She scowled at Lisa and stormed off.

"What's eating her?" Eddie asked.

*Me...Later...*Lisa thought. "Who knows. Come on, babe." She took Eddie's hand. "Have a good one, Sonata." Lisa grinned. She opened the door and led Eddie out.

Sonata knew that Lisa could tell her feelings for Eddie. She only hoped that she hadn't put Eddie in danger.

Linda came up to Sonata. "Here is our address, and how to get there from the Savoy."

"Great. Thanks." Sonata said less than enthused. She took the paper from Linda.

"You ok?" Pamela asked as she came up.

"Yeah, fine." Sonata smiled. "I'll see you guys later." She grabbed her things and walked to the door.

Sonata stopped. Was it written all over her face? She turned to Linda and smiled. She opened the door and left.

CHAPTER 4

Eddie stirred the pot of stew she made. She turned it to simmer. All she wanted to do was see Sonata.

Lisa walked into the room. "Hmm smells grand, babe." She came up behind Eddie and put her arms around her.

"So what time do I need to leave, Lisa?" Eddie asked.

"I told you before, I want ya to stay and party with us." She kissed Eddie's shoulder.

"Lisa. You know I don't like the parties. I'm not into that stuff anymore. You need to stop too. We're about to go to the States, we need to have our wits about us."

"Eddie, perhaps if ya partied with us, ya might lighten up a bit."

"Sonata said…"

"Sonata can sod off fer all I care. What is it with you Eddie? You starting to have feelings for the American?" Lisa looked at her.

"She's nice Lisa. And she's me friend."

Lisa laughed. "Ya known her fer five days Eddie. She's not yer friend. She's using you and me and the whole lot of us. They are gonna stand to make a pretty penny off us Eddie, and yer precious Sonata is one of them. Stick to yer own Eddie. You belong down here with us." Lisa laughed as she left the kitchen.

Eddie didn't want to hear what Lisa said. She knew Sonata was different. She saw it in her eyes. She felt it in her kiss. Lisa was wrong. She had to be.

❦   ❦   ❦

Sonata showed up right at seven. Linda and Pamela's house was nice. More like a cottage. She knocked on the door.

"Eddie! Eddie!" A voice said from behind the door. The door opened and Sonata looked down. Little Oliver stood in the doorway. "Yer not Eddie." He said.

"No, I'm not, Oliver. But, we met today. I'm Sonata. Remember?"

"Yeah." Oliver said in disappointment.

Pamela came to the door. "Oliver, let her in, luv." She smiled as she opened the door wider. "He loves Eddie. C'mon in."

"Thank you. What a charming place." Sonata said as she looked around.

"Linny! Sonata's here." Pamela yelled.

Linda walked out and hugged Sonata. "Can I get ya a drink?"

"Ah, a diet soda would be nice." Sonata smiled.

"One diet soda commin' your way." Linda said. "With ice I suppose?"

"Please." Sonata giggled.

"Come, take a load off, Sonata." Pamela moved to the living room.

Linda came in with Sonata's drink, and sat next to Pamela. "One diet soda iced up for the American." She laughed.

Sonata smiled. "Thanks, and thank you for inviting me, this is a treat to have a home cooked meal for a change."

"Well, don't be saying that till ya eat and wake up the next day." Pamela said. Linda wanted to cook tonight.

Sonata laughed. Linda and Pamela had such great personalities. They were perfect for one another.

"So, how long have you two been together?"

"Six years next month." Pamela smiled.

"That's great." Sonata smiled. She wished she had a relationship last six weeks let alone six years.

"So no one special in your life, Sonata?"

"Well, yes, there is someone special. But it doesn't look too good right now. Too much baggage. You know how that is."

Linda and Pamela exchanged glances.

"Really?" Pamela said.

"What?" Sonata asked.

"The only baggage Eddie Sutcliffe has is Lisa O'Brien, and I bet she is willing to give that up at anytime." Linda said.

Sonata was stunned. Was it that obvious? "Huh?" Was all that she could say.

"C'mon now Sonata, we aren't blind, luv. We can see how you two look at each other."

"Look. I am sure you may think that Eddie and I have something going on, but I can assure you…"

"Sonata, stop. This isn't gonna go nowhere. We want Eddie to be happy. We know she's not with Lisa." Linda said.

"Since you've come aboard, Eddie's all smiles for once." Pamela added.

"Please, I don't care about me, but you can't say anything for Eddie's sake." Sonata looked at them.

"No worries, Sonata. We're not like that." Linda said.

"I will say that you didn't waste any time, did ya?" Pamela laughed.

Sonata smiled. "It was only a couple of kisses, but she is something so incredible."

"She'd be even more incredible if she'd lose Lisa." Linda frowned. "She's a great rock and roller, but a lousy partner."

"She is gonna leave Lisa, right?" Pamela said.

"Well it isn't a question of wanting to, it's more like being too scared to."

"Yeah. Lisa can be this side of evil when she wants to." Linda said.

"You need to be careful Sonata, I've known Lisa longer than most. She can be unpleasant." Pamela said. "When I met Linny, she gave us a hard time cause I wouldn't sleep with her no more."

"Enough garbage talk, Lisa is a waste of good breath. Let's eat." Linda smiled.

Pamela and Sonata stood up and started to follow Linda.

"I've got to run to the loo. I'll join ya in a moment." Pamela said as she ran to the bedroom. She picked up the phone and dialed.

Lisa sat the phone down. She smiled.

"Who was on the telephone?" Eddie asked.

"Pammy. She wanted us to come over for supper." She looked at Eddie. "Maybe I should just send you eh?"

Eddie wanted to go. She knew that Sonata was there. She also knew that Lisa was in a mood. She only hoped that Lisa would send her out when the others got there.

The doorbell rang.

"I'll go." Lisa said.

She walked over to the door and opened it. She smiled as she saw Annie standing before her. She was dressed in tight jeans and a tank top. Her braless efforts paid off as Lisa grinned and touched Annie softly on her breast.

"Not out here ya fool." Annie giggled. She came inside and kissed Lisa.

"Who's here Lisa?" Eddie said from the kitchen.

Annie pushed Lisa off. "What the bloody hell is she still here fer?" Annie said.

"Will you relax. I ain't gonna row with ya." Lisa winked. "Trust me…. It's Annie." She yelled.

Eddie came out of the kitchen. "Oh, hey ya, Annie. Care for some stew?"

"No thanks." Annie said smugly.

Eddie smiled and walked back into the kitchen. What was Lisa up to? She wanted to call Linda and Pamela's. She wanted to go over. She wanted to be with Sonata.

Linda stoked the fire until it was raging. Oliver brought out a bag of marsh-mallows and wire hangers. Pamela came in with a tray of tea.

"This has been so nice." Sonata smiled. It was nice. But all her thoughts were with Eddie.

"Want a marshmeller, Sonata?" Oliver asked.

"Why thank you, Oliver. He is a doll." She said to Pamela.

"Yeah, he's a good egg, now that Linny's in his life. He was wild there for a bit."

"Well, he is just a kid." Sonata smiled.

"A kid acting twenty five." Linda laughed.

Pamela looked at her watch.

"Am I keeping you? Sonata asked.

"No, not at all." Pamela said. "I'll be frank. Sonata, I phoned Eddie. I tried to get her to come over, but Lisa answered the phone."

Sonata tried to smile.

"Here's yer marshmeller." Oliver handed Sonata the warm gooey treat from the hanger.

"Thank you Oliver. Are you looking forward to going to America?" Sonata asked, trying to change the subject.

"Yes, I can hardly wait." Oliver beamed. "But me mum says I have to finish me studies here, and she and Linny will call for me when they get settled."

"Well, Oliver, I'll tell you what. You do well in school and when you come over I'll take you to Disneyland. How about that?"

"Oh man! Mum did ya hear that?" Oliver squealed.

"I sure did, luv." Pamela smiled.

"Hey now, what about me?" Linny said. "I cooked ya supper too."

"Aw. I'll take you too." Sonata giggled.

"Awesome!" Linda shouted.

"Can Eddie come too?" Oliver looked at Sonata.

"I would like that a lot Oliver." Sonata smiled. *She would also like to see her right now too.* She thought.

❦   ❦   ❦

The party was in full gear. Eddie hated it. She didn't know any of the guests. They were all slobs. A bunch of street rats, smoking pot, doing coke and drinking. Eddie wasn't into the drug scene anymore. She had to stop. She grew up and had to live her life. Lisa said she would stop too. She did for a few months. Then it was a little booze here, just a joint to relax, some blow at a friend's party. Now, Eddie thought, Lisa was shooting up. She saw some needle tracks on her arms, but never asked. She knew that she was also sleeping with Annie. She was always around. They always hung out after a gig. Lisa always said that they were writing but she never heard anything new from Lisa in quite sometime. Why didn't she just call it off with her?

Eddie grabbed some empty bottles and walked back into the kitchen.

Lisa, Annie and a blonde were snorting coke on the kitchen table. A smelly guy wearing shorts and nothing else watched on with a dazed smile on his face.

"There ya are luv." Lisa stood up and walked over to Eddie. "Come and meet some friends, maybe have a line."

"Lisa, no. You know I don't do that no more. I'll just go get lost fer a bit, and you can have yer fun."

"The fun begins with you, Eddie Sutcliffe." Lisa kissed her.

Eddie hated her like this. "Lisa, stop it."

"Come on, do a little line fer old time, sake." Lisa said.

"It's grand shit, Eddie." Annie said as she did another line.

"Look here, Eddie. You don't embarrass me in front of me friends. You get that?" She glared at Eddie. "I suggest you get rid of that holy attitude of yers, and sit the fuck down."

Eddie didn't want to start anything. She walked over to the table with Lisa. She sat next to her.

The blonde smiled at her. "Well now, who have we here?" Her glazed eyes drooling over Eddie.

"This is me gal, Eddie." Lisa said.

Annie frowned at Lisa.

The blonde looked at Eddie. She slowly put her hand on Eddie's thigh. "Yer a sexy one there." She giggled.

Eddie quickly removed the blonde's hand as it started to slowly creep up her leg.

The blonde laid out a line for Eddie. "Here ya go, Eddie. Goes up smooth."

Eddie looked at Lisa.

"Do it." Lisa snarled.

Eddie slowly took the hollowed out pen from the blonde. Flashbacks came to her. The parties. Waking up in a stranger's bed. The endless nights of blacking out. She promised herself at her mother's gravesite that she would never go back there, no matter what the cost. The cost now could be her life at the hands of Lisa.

"Fuckn' run the pigs are here!" The guy in shorts yelled.

The commotion was loud as people were running all over the place. Glass was breaking and chaos was all around. The police entered and started rounding up people.

Lisa grabbed Annie's hand and started to run. Eddie moved to the kitchen door. People were running in all directions. Some had possessions of Eddie's as they ran for the door. She looked back as she saw Lisa being grabbed by an officer. She quickly headed out the door. Eddie quickly climbed the chain link fence. She ripped her shirt on the way down and reopened her cut.

"Bugger!" She said but she kept moving. She had a lot of ground to cover before she could put distance between herself and the house.

❦   ❦   ❦

"This was such a great evening. I thank you both so much." Sonata hugged Linda and Pamela.

"We were glad you could make it." Linda smiled.

Pamela opened the door. "Looks like we're in fer a wet night."

Eddie came running up the walk. She was cold and wet and bleeding from her arm.

"Oh my God, Eddie." Sonata said.

"Get in here, you're a wet mess." Pamela said.

"Eddie, what happened?" Sonata asked.

"It's" Eddie panted and tried to catch her breath. "It's Lisa and Annie"

"Are they hurt?" Linda asked.

"What did they do?" Sonata asked.

"Lisa had some friends over. The cops came. I ran here."

"That arm looks bad." Pamela said.

"Where are they?"

"Last I saw, they got em." Eddie took a deep breath.

"Ok, first we need to get you cleaned up and dried off. Then you need to see a doctor about this arm. It's gonna need stitches." Linda said.

"Sonata, I gotta tell ya. It ain't gonna be good fer 'em. They had drugs." Eddie looked at her.

"Shit." Sonata said. "This is perfect. Just what we need. Damn her! Why didn't you tell me she had a drug problem?" Sonata said harshly.

The girls looked at each other.

"What are we gonna do?" Eddie asked.

"Just sit tight while I call K.C. and find out what to do." Sonata pulled out her cell phone and started to dial. "Linda, will you help Eddie clean that cut up?"

"Sure thing. C'mon ya stooge. Fer the life of me Eddie Sutcliffe, I will never understand how you get yer self in these predicaments."

Eddie rolled her eyes and followed Linda to the bathroom.

Sonata listened while K.C. yelled at her on the phone.

"I had no clue K.C."

"Sonata, I swear." K.C. said. "Look here's the thing. I am moving to Nashville, to start the new country division. Lee and Kenny are heading this one up."

"Kenny? Are you serious?"

"Yeah, I know. Don't do anything till you hear back from me. I'll see if we can pull some strings."

"Thanks, K.C." Sonata sighed.

"They better be worth it." K.C. said.

"They are, especially the drummer."

"Shit, Sonata! You fell for the drummer? Didn't anything I tell you sink in?"

"K.C., I don't need a lecture right now. Just see what you can do and get back to me." Sonata hung up. She hated when K.C. scolded her. She walked into the bathroom where Linda and Pamela were trying to patch up Eddie.

"Ouch, Linny! What ya pourin' in there, ey? I'd like to save me bloody arm thanks." Eddie frowned.

"Well, what did K.C. say?" Pamela asked.

"We need to sit tight until she calls us back."

"We can't bloody well leave 'em in the clink." Eddie said. "We have to do something."

"Eddie, she's done enough already." Sonata snapped. *How could she still care what happens to Lisa?* "I think our bigger problem now is convincing Reynolds Records to still take a chance on you."

"You mean that Lisa might have ruined it?" Linda looked at Sonata.

"They are not real happy with us right now."

"Damn her to bloody hell if she messes this deal for us." Pamela said.

Eddie's heart sank. She never thought she wanted something so bad. She wanted to go to America and sing. She wanted to be with Sonata. Now it all hung in the balance. She stood up and walked to Sonata.

"You gotta get them to keep us, Sonata." Eddie looked at her.

Sonata's cell phone rang. "I'll do my best." She gave Eddie a quick smile, and answered her phone.

Linda, Pamela and Eddie waited holding their breaths, as Sonata begged and pleaded.

Sonata listened as Lee Reynolds told her that she as well as the Traveler's were now on in house probation. They were to make the demo, finish their last engagement at the Candy Bar, then sit tight and wait to hear if the were to come to America. If there were any other altercations, it would be over for the Travelers.

"Thank you, Mr. Reynolds." Sonata said, as she hung up her phone.

"Well?" Eddie asked.

"They were able to persuade the officials to drop the drug charges to disturbing the peace. They have been fined, with timed served, so they can come to the states."

"Yes!" Linda screamed.

"Wait, there's more. We are all on an in house 30-day probation. We are to make the demo, finish the gigs and sit tight until we hear from them. If there is trouble, they drop the Travelers…and I lose my job."

Eddie put her hand on Sonata's arm. "I won't let that happen to ya. I promise. You'll see, Sonata. We will straighten Lisa and Annie out."

Sonata smiled. Eddie was a Godsend to her. "First things first. We need to get you to the Emergency room and get that arm looked at."

"I'm ok." Eddie said. Even though her arm was killing her.

"No you're not. Don't argue with me Eddie Sutcliffe!" Sonata looked into the drummer's steel blue eyes. "First we get that arm taken care of, then we'll deal with Lisa and Annie. Linda can you drive us?"

"I'll get me keys."

🍁   🍁   🍁

The holding cell was damp and cold. Annie was cuddled in Lisa's embrace to keep warm. There were a few other women in the cell with them. They stared at Lisa and Annie.

"I'm freezing me arse off in here." Annie shivered.

"I hope Eddie got away and got us some help. She's so senseless, she's most likely sitting in the cinema bout now."

"Are you still in luv with her?" Annie said as she pulled away from Lisa.

"Annie, not now." Lisa said.

"It's always not now with ya. Piss off, Lisa O'Brien. I knew you were playin' with me." She walked to the other end of the cell. Lisa walked over to her.

"Look, Annie. I told ya, things will be different in America. But now, Eddie needs me. I can't bloody well throw her out of the flat. I am all she has. We're friends, but it's you, Annie Sullivan, that I want to be with."

"Don't fuck with me, Lisa." Annie said. She wanted so much to believe Lisa. She was in love with her and wanted a commitment. But, with Eddie in the way, she knew she wouldn't get one. She would just have to work hard to get the problem out of the picture.

❦   ❦   ❦

Eddie winced as the doctor finished stitching her wound.

"Ya did yourself a good one here." The doctor said.

"Yeah, caught it on a stupid fence."

"Really? Looks more like a knife got to you."

Eddie looked away. Damn! Why didn't she have the nerve to just tell the world? "It was a sharp fence there." She said.

"Well, it looks a tad infected. I'll write you a note for some medication. Should clear it up."

"Thanks." Eddie smiled and took the prescription. She walked back out to the lounge, where Sonata and Linda were waiting.

"All sewn up." Eddie grinned.

"How many ya get?" Linda said.

"16." Eddie laughed. "It's me lucky number."

"It is?" Linda said. "How so?"

"It's when I met Sonata." On the 16th. She looked into Sonata's eyes.

Sonata grinned.

"Well now, I hate to get in the middle of yer bliss here, but ya think we should be gettin' to the jail?" Linda said.

"Yeah, we should get going." Sonata said still looking into Eddie's eyes.

❦   ❦   ❦

The guard came and unlocked the cell.

"You two. Yer free to leave." She said to Lisa and Annie.

Lisa nudged Annie. "C'mon, we need to go."

Annie rubbed her eyes. "What's wrong?"

"C'mon luv, move yer bum." Lisa stood up.

Annie stood up and groggily followed Lisa.

Sonata, Eddie and Linda stood in the waiting area. The guard on duty came up to them.

"Hey there, you're the Travelers!"

Eddie and Linda smiled. They loved to be recognized.

"That's us." Linda smiled.

"My lil sis is simply mad about you all. Especially you." He smiled at Eddie.

"Yeah?" Eddie grinned. She looked at Sonata. She loved this part of the job. This was her drug, the fans.

"She'll have me head if I didn't bring yer signature home. Would you?" He handed Eddie a piece of paper.

"A pleasure, as always." Eddie said, "What's her name?"

"Tammy. Oh man, this is fantastic."

Eddie signed the paper and passed it to Linda who also signed it.

Sonata watched as Eddie and Linda handled their fans so perfectly. This would benefit them greatly.

"Is your sister going to their show on Saturday?" Sonata asked.

"She wanted to but ya can never get into one of their gigs." The guard said. "The Candy Bar has been sold out fer weeks."

"Tell you what. Here's my card, have her ask for me at the door and I'll see that she gets in, and comes back to say hi to the girls." Sonata handed the guard her card.

"Wow, she won't bloody believe this. I got to call her. Thanks." He ran off.

"You handled that one rather nicely, Sonata." Linda said.

"Well, they are the ones who pay your bills. And beside, one nice gesture is worth about 1000 fans I say."

Eddie laughed. "You are one of a kind, Sonata."

Lisa and Annie came down the hall. They looked terrible. Neither had slept and they were coming off their high.

"What are you doing here?" Lisa looked at Sonata.

"Lisa, Sonata and the record company are the ones who sprang you." Linda said.

"She got yer charges down to a minor disturbance." Eddie added.

"Yeah, well where the hell were you Eddie? You ran and left us fer the coppers." Lisa hissed.

Eddie didn't want to get into it with Lisa.

"Look, it's very late. We need to be in the recoding studio tomorrow. Why don't we all just go home and get some rest." Sonata looked at Lisa.

"C'mon Lisa. Let's go." Annie begged.

Lisa looked at Eddie. "Don't show yer face to me. Yer fuckin' dead in my eyes right now" She grabbed Annie's hand and walked out.

Eddie looked at Sonata. She walked over to her.

"It's ok, Eddie. You can stay with me." She whispered to her.

Eddie took Sonata's hand and walked out followed by Linda.

❋   ❋   ❋

Sonata got out of the shower. She had been in England a little over a week now. She was in love and her ass was now on the line with her job. She looked at herself in the mirror. How could such a few days change her life so drastically?

She put on her robe and walked out of the bathroom. She stopped to see Eddie sleeping on the couch. She was out cold. Completely exhausted.

Well there's my answer. She thought as she watched Eddie sleeping. She thought of waking her but decided against it. She went into her room and came back with an extra blanket. She slowly covered Eddie. She leaned over and kissed the drummer gently on the lips. Eddie stirred but didn't wake up.

Sonata smiled. She turned the light off and went into her room.

CHAPTER 5

Linda and Pamela walked into the recording studio. As always they were on time. Linda made sure she was never late to anything. She would rather be early and wait around, than ever think about being late. Pamela on the other hand was always late. When she brought Linda home to meet her family, Pam's father pulled Linda aside and told her that the women in their family were always late.

"You want Pammy there early, then ya tell her to be ready at least an hour earlier." He told her. "Her mum and sis, the whole bloody lot of them are that way."

Linda thought it was the endless pints that Pam's father consumed. But after dating, then moving in, Linda soon found out how right Pam's father was. She also became a positive image in Pamela's life. When she met Pamela, she was with Lisa. She was doing drugs and partying every night. Linda fell hard for Pam, and they became close friends. Eddie joined the band and Pamela saw Lisa make moves on her. She turned to Linda and fell in love with her best friend. Lisa was less than pleased and threatened Linda. Linda stood her ground and gained the respect from Lisa, who was now heavily involved with the new drummer, Eddie.

"Where's yer head, luv?" Pamela asked as she kissed Linda's cheek.

"Nowhere really. Just thinking of what we did to get here." Linda smiled.

"It's incredible. Because of you." Pamela smiled.

"We're a good go together." Linda kissed Pamela.

"I think so too."

Lisa and Annie walked in. They were well rested and looked no more worse for wear than usual.

Linda frowned as she saw Annie holding Lisa's hand. Lisa was such a bitch! She didn't have the decency to break up with Eddie before she flaunted her newest flavor of the month. And Annie should be ashamed too. She knew Lisa was with Eddie. It was the likes of them that gave lesbian's a bad name Linda thought.

"Where's Eddie?" Lisa said looking around.

"Not here yet." Pamela said.

"Oh? And I suppose our American isn't here either?" Lisa looked at Linda.

"Leave it alone, Lisa." Linda looked back.

"Sod off, Linny. You don't know shit about what's going on."

"I know a lot more than ya think I do."

"C'mon you, two. We need to be focused here. No rows today, please." Pamela looked at Linda.

"I'm gonna go grab a smoke." Linda said and walked outside.

"Let's go in and get settled babe." Annie said to Lisa.

Pamela watched as Annie hung all over Lisa. She shook her head. "Pitiful lot they are." Pamela turned and went outside.

"Why didn't you wake me?" Sonata said as she rushed to put her makeup on.

"You were at peace. You needed the rest." Eddie said.

"I'll rest when we get you all to America and signed to the label."

Eddie walked over to her. "Then we can be together?"

Sonata fell into Eddie's open arms. "That would be a dream come true."

"When it's safe Sonata, I promise." Eddie kissed the top of her head.

"I hoped you would have come into the bed last night." Sonata said holding on tight to the drummer.

Eddie laughed. "Serves me right for nodding off eh?"

What she didn't tell Sonata was that she was in fact in the room last night. She sat and watched as she slept. She wanted to get in the bed and hold Sonata. Wanted so badly to make love to her. But the sound of Lisa's voice rang in her ears. The threats if she left. The doubt that Lisa put into Eddie's mind. It was all still there and it stung hard. Eddie had to make sure that she and Lisa were through. She wouldn't put Sonata in danger.

"We're late. We need to jet." Sonata looked at her watch.

She grabbed her briefcase and put her shoes on.

"You ready?" She looked at Eddie.

"Oh yeah." Eddie smiled as she opened the door for Sonata.

❦   ❦   ❦

Sonata smiled as she sat in the production booth. The Travelers were "On" and things were perfect. Lisa's vocals on her original tune, "Time Will Tell" were great. Sonata thought it would be a good song to be the first single. Eddie sat at the piano and sang. Sonata thought it was going to be "The Weakness in Me", but Eddie surprised her and sang The Carpenter's "Superstar", one of Sonata's favorite songs. Eddie's voice was brilliant. Sonata could tell that everyone was hanging on every word that came out of Eddie's mouth.

"Damn, she is incredible!" the sound mixer said.

Lisa even stopped and listened to Eddie. She grinned slightly. Eddie was a grand singer. It was at times like these that Lisa really liked having Eddie around. She thought about what it would be like settling down with Eddie. Playing it straight and boring. No parties, no other women. Lisa then thought about the wild adventure Annie had taken her on the last three months since they started sleeping together. It was what ran through Lisa's blood. She liked living on the edge and being the center of attention. Annie worshiped her; Eddie wanted to be her equal. There was no equal in Lisa's world. She was the one that stood above the rest. Maybe it was time to move on from Eddie.

Sonata wiped a tear from her eye as she noticed the goose bumps that came from Eddie's sultry voice.

After the producer yelled cut. The studio burst into endless cheers and applause.

Eddie blushed as she sat at the piano. The girls and Sonata came into the studio.

Lisa frowned. She was the star of the Travelers, and Eddie needed to realize it.

"That was awesome buddy." Linda said as she high fived Eddie.

"Thanks Linny." Eddie smiled.

"I always knew ya could sing anything, Eddie, but shit!" Pamela laughed. "Ya bloody well blew me away." She kissed Eddie on the cheek.

"Yeah, Eddie that was insane." Annie added in.

Eddie looked at Sonata. "I hope you didn't mind I changed up on ya?"

Sonata smiled. "No." She said as she squeezed Eddie's shoulder.

"So are we done now?" Lisa asked.

Eddie frowned. She knew Lisa was pissed.

"Do you have everything you need Steve?" Sonata asked the producer.

"Yeah, I am all set. I'll have the copies to ya in a bit. Not much to do after that." He smiled.

"Ok, here's the deal. Tomorrow you have the day off. I suggest you get your things in order. We have another show to do and hopefully we will have some news by then. If its what I think it will be, we'll be on a plane and off to America in no time."

"Lisa. Can I talk to ya a sec?" Eddie said, as walked over to Lisa.

"Yeah, what?" Lisa said.

"I need to pack up me stuff."

"Yeah."

"Yeah, so I'll be over later on." She tested Lisa.

"Take what ya want Eddie. The flat is trashed after the cops got done with it. I'm staying with Annie."

"About that." Eddie said. "Where does that put us?"

Lisa chuckled. "It puts us nowhere Eddie. Yer a band mate ta me now. Nothing more. Annie does it fer me. Take a lesson. If ya think ya got it made with Sonata, think again. You are just dollar signs in her eyes. You'll never be anything more." Lisa stared at Eddie. She could still see that she had an effect on Eddie's mind. "Just remember." She leaned into Eddie and whispered in her ear. "I'll always be inside your head. Ya'll never be rid of me." She turned and walked over to Annie.

"Let's go, luv." She said softly as she took Annie's hand. "See ya birds later."

They watched as Lisa and Annie left. Sonata walked over to Eddie.

"You ok?"

"I think so." Eddie said. She still needed to be cautious.

Sonata smiled.

Eddie wasn't sure of what it meant. Lisa was a master of pulling the rug out from under you. She didn't want to fall for it.

"I'm gonna go to the flat and pack some things." She looked at Sonata.

"Great, I'll get us a cab."

"No, wait." Eddie looked at her "I'll catch up to you. I need to do this by me self. Do you mind?"

Sonata smiled. "Not at all." She hugged Eddie. "I'll thank you for my song later."

Eddie gently stroked Sonata's cheek and walked out.

"Things are looking up there, Sonata?" Pamela asked.

"I hope so."

"I'll believe it when I see it." Linda said. "Lisa O'Brien doesn't give up that easy."

Eddie's mouth dropped, as she walked through the open the door. She looked around, not believing her eyes.

The place was totally ransacked. She carefully stepped across the mess that lay before her feet. She walked back to her bedroom where the door had been kicked in. She picked up a few of her things. Most of her possessions were either destroyed, or gone. She walked to the closet and opened it up. Most of her clothes were piled on the floor. She pulled them out of the way in a frantic search. There underneath the clothes, she found the small wooden box. She took it out and went and sat on her bed.

Lisa walked into the room.

"I'm glad the bastards didn't get that." She half smiled.

"Yeah. What brings you here?" Eddie asked.

"I came back to see what was left. And to see you."

"Me? What fer?" Eddie looked confused.

"Well, we never get the chance to talk. There is usually a lot hangin' around us an all."

"Yeah."

Lisa looked at Eddie. She leaned over and softly kissed her on the lips.

Eddie was stunned. A rush of emotions overtook her.

Lisa kissed her again. This time it was longer more intense.

Eddie pulled away. "This is no good Lisa. Stop."

"Why, Eddie? You used to like it."

"Before you started messin' around Lisa. What about Annie?"

"Eddie, you need to turn your head on. We are rock n rollers. Birds are part of it."

"Lisa, that's just not me. I don't want an endless stream of women in me bed. I just want one. One who will luv me fer ever."

Lisa laughed. "Yer so stupid, Eddie. That shit never happens. Yer head's in a bloody fairytale. You'll see what I mean. Yer gonna be so famous, every woman's gonna want to go down on ya. Yer not gonna wanna settle yerself down with just one."

"Yer wrong, Lisa. You can have it. But it takes work. I want it that bad. I'll fight fer it."

"Then why didn't ya fight fer us?" Lisa snapped.

"Cause, you didn't want us, Lisa." Eddie looked at her. "You never felt fer me like you do fer Annie. Holding her hand, calling her luv. You never wanted that with us."

Lisa knew she was right. She made Eddie Sutcliffe. Brought in a nobody music store clerk and turned her into a rock star! Eddie was Lisa's creation. She was in love with an image she created.

Lisa stood up and walked to the doorway. She turned to Eddie. "Just know Eddie Sutcliffe, when yer make believe walls come crashing down, you'll come back to me. You can't let me go."

Eddie didn't look up as Lisa walked out. She fingered the wooden box as the harsh words from Lisa bounced on the walls of her brain. Tears came streaming out as the doubts created by Lisa started to pour out. She opened the box up and took out a picture of her mother and a gold wedding band. She looked at the photo searching her mind for some bit of remembrance of her mom. She had flashes of her now and then, but was never sure of what she was like. The one person who could give her answers was in a drunken stupor at some sleazy bar.

Eddie quickly put the photo and ring safely in their hiding place. She grabbed a duffle bag and quickly shoved some clothes in it. She looked around the room and grabbed her box.

"I won't be missin' this place." She said. "They should ave burnt it to the ground."

She turned around and walked out, telling herself never to look back.

❧   ❧   ❧

Stuart Sutcliffe sat on his bar stool, just like he did every day. His face was whisker ridden and his un-washed hair tousled about as always.

"Keep 'em comin'." He slurred, as he jiggled his remaining ice cubes at the bartender.

"You're on yer way to pissed again, ey Stu?" The bartender said as he refilled his glass.

"Better to be pissed off than pissed on." Stuart raised his glass and took a swig.

Eddie walked in and looked around. She saw him sitting at the bar and froze. She swallowed hard and took a deep breath. She slowly walked over to him.

"Stuart Sutcliffe?" Eddie's voice cracked.

"Who wants to know?" Stuart said as he turned around.

"It's me…Eddie."

Stuart turned back to his drink.

"I'm yer daughter." Eddie said flatly.

"I know who you bloody well are. You look like a spittin' image of yer Mum."

"That's why I'm here. I need to know about me Mum."

"Yer Mum is gone and buried. That's all you need to know."

"Please, I just want…"

"Let the woman rest." Stuart snarled.

"Look, I'm leaving fer America soon and I need to get some things in order."

Stuart turned to his daughter. She was the image of her mother. Her eyes were beautiful.

"Fer what, a holiday?" He asked.

"No, me music. We are gonna be signed to an American record label."

"Gonna be?" Stuart looked at his daughter. "Ya don't know fer sure?"

"It's not set in stone, but it will be soon."

"Really now?" Stuart looked at Eddie. "Why are ya here Eddie?"

"I wanted to know if you could tell me about me mum before I left."

"Jack, get me girl a pint." Stuart told the bartender.

Eddie took a seat at the bar. She smiled.

"What ya want to know kid?" Stuart took a drink.

"Well, anything. I don't remember much." Eddie said.

"Don't be painting' a pretty picture of her. Yer mum was a whore."

"Don't be sayin' that!" Eddie's eyebrow narrowed.

"Why the hell not? It's the bloody truth. Why do you think she was never around?"

"Working, I guess." Eddie offered. "Like I said, I don't remember much."

"I was out working me ass off fer you and your brothers, and all that bitch did was sleep around. I was the fucking laughing stock of the city." Stuart downed the rest of his drink.

"Yer lying!" Eddie's eyes were on fire. "You were a mean ol bastard to her the way you were to me, Ryan, and Denny."

"Shut yer trap!" Stuart turned to his daughter. "Don't be spoutin' off that mouth unless ya know what's good fer ya."

"I didn't come here to get into it with ya. I just want to know about me mum." Eddie's voice cracked.

"Well ya came to the wrong place." Stuart turned back to the bar.

"Yeah, I sure did. I can see that now." Eddie stood up. "No worries though, I won't be bugging ya no more." Eddie stormed out.

Stuart stayed focused on his drink "Give me another one." He said, as he shook his head.

Sonata sat in her hotel room the whole day. She sent the CD to the states and was waiting for their reaction. She was also waiting for Eddie. It had almost been twenty-four hours since she last saw her, and she was starting to get worried. She called Linda and Pamela, but they hadn't seen or heard from her. Sonata didn't know where to even start looking for her. She could only wait and hope that she was okay. She paced around the room and decided to call Linda and Pam back.

"We still haven't heard from her, luv." Linda said.

"This is crazy, Linda, where could she be?" Sonata asked.

"I called Lisa and she was no help. Just said she better be at the gig tomorrow."

"Please, if you hear from her will you let me know?"

"Will do. Try not to get yer knickers in a twist. Eddie has always wandered off when things get tough fer her. Maybe she needs Ollie's sitter."

Sonata chuckled. "Trust me, when we get to the states I'll put a leash on her."

"You know yer welcome to come here and wait if you like." Linda offered.

"Maybe later. I'll call you."

Sonata set the phone down. It rang again.

"Hello."

"Hey luv, it's me." Eddie said.

"Where have you been, Eddie? Are you ok?"

"Yeah…"

Sonata could tell that something wasn't right. Eddie was listless, very monotone. "Where are you?" She asked.

"Just hanging 'round." Eddie said.

"Do you need to talk about it?"

"Nope, nothing that a couple hits and a few pints can't fix."

Sonata didn't like what she heard. Eddie had told her of her past with drugs, and Sonata believed her when she said she was clean.

"Eddie, I can assure you that is not the way to go. Whatever it is can't be that bad."

"Really? Well Sonata Williams, maybe it is that bad fer me!" Eddie started to cry.

"Eddie, where are you? Let me come pick you up."

"I don't know where I am anymore."

"Eddie, you're scaring me. Please, please tell me where you are?"

There was silence. Sonata could hear Eddie sobbing on the other end.

"Eddie…I want to help you sweetie…why don't you come here. Get a nice hot shower, and some rest…"

The phone went dead.

"Eddie? Eddie?"

Sonata set the phone down and hoped that they were just disconnected and that Eddie would call right back.

❧   ❧   ❧

Sonata sat by the phone. The rain was coming down steady. Sonata called Linda and Pamela. Linda had driven around to all of the spots she knew Eddie would go when she needed some alone time. She called Sonata to let her know she came up empty. Sonata's heart sank. She didn't care about anything else. Her job, her life in the states, nothing mattered except Eddie Sutcliffe. She couldn't sit around any longer. She grabbed her coat and her cell phone and ran for the door. She opened it and found Eddie standing there wet and trembling.

Sonata flew into Eddie's arms. She held her tight. Eddie started to cry. Sonata walked her into the room and shut the door. She held her again, and felt her heart racing against her ear. She looked up at the drummer.

Eddie pulled Sonata up to face her and kissed her. It was a hard passionate kiss. They stared into each other's eyes.

Sonata took Eddie by the hand and led her to the bedroom. She slowly started to peel off Eddie's wet clothes.

Eddie stood watching Sonata as she unbuttoned her top. She liked what she saw. She led Sonata to the bed and took off the rest of her clothes. She lay Sonata down on the bed and stood over her, watching Sonata like a cougar looking at its prey.

"Eddie." Sonata said.

"No words luv." Eddie said as she knelt on the bed next to Sonata.

Eddie slowly started to trace Sonata's frame with her finger.

Sonata felt the heat starting to stir deep within her.

Eddie slowly started to kiss Sonata. Her lips were intense and determined. She made her way down Sonata's body, stopping to look at her. *She is so beautiful,* Eddie thought. She slid her hand between Sonata's legs and caressed the inside of her trembling thighs.

Sonata moaned at the pleasure she was feeling and what was to come.

"I wanted ya from the moment I saw you." Eddie said.

Sonata tried to answer but lost her breath as Eddie's long, lean finger entered her. She arched her back. Eddie slowly moved in and out of Sonata and slowly entered her with two fingers.

Sonata was ready to explode. "Eddie…" She gasped.

Eddie moved down and spread Sonata's legs apart; she started licking the sweet juices from her lover.

Sonata was over the top, her thighs started to tremble, "Don't stop Eddie." Sonata got out.

Eddie entered Sonata with her tongue, sucking and licking, until Sonata came hard and fast.

Sonata couldn't believe the release she had with Eddie. No other lover had touched her that way.

They made love the entire afternoon it was passionate and secure. They showered together and ordered room service. They sat in bed and ate.

"Eddie, I'm so happy." She kissed her lover.

"Me too, luv…about earlier. I didn't mean to give you a fright."

"Shhh. It's over, Eddie. Unless you want to talk about it?"

"I kind of do, if ya don't mind?"

"Of course not."

Eddie looked into Sonata's eyes. She kissed her passionately.

"You're gonna make it difficult to talk." Sonata giggled.

"Just a peck fer luck." Eddie grinned.

"Well then." Sonata kissed Eddie.

Eddie ran her hand through her hair and took a deep breath. "Where to begin?" she said. "I went back to the flat to gather me things, you should have seen it, Sonata. I hardly knew I lived there. Everything was scattered about and broken. I found me important things. I was just about to leave, when Lisa came in. She started kissing on me and telling me things. I needed to get some answers, so I went to the pub and saw me father." Tears started to run down Eddie's face.

Sonata wiped the tears from Eddie's cheek, and took her into her arms. Eddie slid down and laid her head on Sonata's breast. The rhythm of Sonata's heart calmed her.

"Did you get the answers you needed?" Sonata asked softly.

"Hardly. That bastard cut me mum down."

"I'm sorry."

"I should have known. He's done nothing but hurt our family. He would come home pissed, and beat on me brothers. They were the lucky ones though. They only got the beatings."

Eddie started to cry harder.

Sonata knew what was coming. Tears started to well up in her eyes.

"Did he?" Sonata asked.

"Fer three years. Until I was old enough to get out." Eddie said, as she wiped the tears from her eyes."

"How did you get away?"

"He came home pissed as usual, I knew what he wanted. But I knew I wasn't gonna take it no more. He came into my room late one night and started talking about how much I looked like me mum, and now that she was gone, it was me he wanted.

"Oh God." Sonata said.

"I was laying in bed and when he took my blanket off I hit him with a log from the fire place. I had me bag packed and I grabbed it and ran. I stayed in back packers for a while, then got me job at the music store. They let me stay there at night. So I'd stay awake for hours teaching meself how to play. Lisa came in one day and boy did I fall hard. She was the world for me. She took me in, and we fell in luv. At least I fell. She gave me a job in the band, and all the drugs a bird could want. I always suspected she was cheating, come to find out, she did on me with Pammy. Lisa would get angry and take it out on me. I don't know why I didn't leave sooner."

"Maybe you were waiting for me?" Sonata smiled.

"I think me mum sent you to save me. I'm just glad you came here." Eddie looked up and kissed Sonata. "I'm falling fer you Sonata Williams." Eddie smiled.

"I already have." Sonata kissed Eddie.

They laid in each other's arms and fell asleep, both dreaming of the life they would soon share together.

❧   ❧   ❧

The ringing phone startled Sonata. She slid out of Eddie's embrace and went to answer the phone.

"Hello." she said sleepily.

"Sonata Williams please." The deep voice said on the other end.

"Speaking."

"This is Lee Reynolds."

"Oh Mr. Reynolds, I didn't recognize your voice sir."

"Well, I hope I'm ok with the time difference."

Sonata looked at the desk clock. It was 3:00a.m. "Yes sir, it's fine."

"Well, I didn't think you would mind me calling, especially when it's with such good news."

Sonata smiled. "Sir?"

"Bring them to the States."

"Mr. Reynolds, are you kidding?"

"We are very impressed with them. We want to get them here to cut a full length and get them out on tour as soon as possible."

"Thank you, sir. You won't be disappointed!" Sonata beamed.

"And the gal who sang that ballad…I am very impressed with her voice."

"Yes, that's Eddie Sutcliffe, the drummer."

"Well, I can hardly wait to meet her. The airline tickets are on their way for you. The day after tomorrow you will be on your way back to the States. Good work, Sonata."

"Thank you, sir."

"Call me Lee."

"Well thank you…. Lee. See you in a few days."

Sonata hung up the phone and screamed.

Eddie jumped up. "What the bloody hell? Are you ok?" She rubbed her eyes.

Sonata jumped onto the bed and into Eddie's arms. "Baby I am better than ok."

"What?" Eddie asked.

"Eddie, we got the call. You are going to the States!"

"No bloody way." Eddie grinned.

"This is going to be great!" Sonata said.

"It will, you'll see. Every song I sing is for you Sonata."

"Oh, Eddie."

Eddie kissed Sonata.

"We need to call the others." Sonata said.

"It can wait a bit. We got our own celebratin' to do first."

She moved Sonata to the bed and started to kiss her.

❦   ❦   ❦

Eddie jumped in the shower while Sonata phoned the others. It was 7:00a.m. but she figured that the good news she was calling with was well worth the early morning jolt.

For the last three hours, Sonata and Eddie made plans. They decided not to announce their romance until things settled down, and they were safely in the States.

Lisa yelling on the phone interrupted sonata's thoughts.

"Who the fuck is this?" Lisa yelled again.

"It's Sonata."

"Well why don't ya talk then?" Lisa said.

"I just wanted to tell you that we are leaving for America the day after tomorrow." Sonata smiled.

"Are you on the level?" Lisa asked.

"Yes! Yes! Mr. Reynolds just phoned. He wants a full length CD. They want you in the studio as soon as possible."

"This is bloody incredible!" Lisa yelled. "I gotta give you your dues Sonata. You did it."

Sonata couldn't believe it. Lisa O'Brien was being nice? "Can you pass along the news to Annie?"

"Oh yeah, you can bet I will." Lisa snickered.

Sonata frowned. What a slime.

"Ok, I'll see you at the show tonight. We'll talk more." Sonata hung up the phone.

Eddie came up behind her and wrapped her arms around Sonata's waist.

"You're wet." Sonata giggled.

"You could say that, luv." Eddie laughed. "Sonata, I can hardly wait until we get to the States and get our life started."

Sonata turned around and hugged Eddie. "It will be the romance of a lifetime, won't it Eddie?"

"Luv, no one will ever see a luv like ours." Eddie kissed Sonata. "No fears, beautiful."

"We should call Linda and Pamela." Sonata said as Eddie placed small kisses all around her neck.

"It can wait." Eddie looked deep into Sonata's eyes. She led her back to the bed.

Sonata happily followed. She had no cares in the world right now. It was all about the love of Eddie Sutcliffe.

The Candy Bar was packed. Reynolds Records leaked out the news about signing the Travelers. Sonata had to agree to call a make shift press conference before they left for the States. Anyone and everyone suddenly wanted a piece of rock and roll's newest sensations.

The girls were huddled in the small dressing room that they were accustomed to. Sonata was on the phone trying to set things up as the Travelers got dressed.

"Can you believe the lot of folks out there?" Pamela said.

"It is filled to the brim. Not even standing room." Linda added.

"It's fuckin' fantastic!" Lisa said.

"It's incredible. We have been at it fer years and almost overnight we are sensations."

Eddie sat at the mirror brushing her hair. Hearing what the others were saying made her nervous. She was used to the small gigs at the local gay bars. They had also played a pride festival. But that was local. It all got put on a huge scale now. Eddie's stomach started to turn.

Sonata hung up the phone. "Listen up ladies. It is imperative that we be at the airport by 1:00 p.m. tomorrow. We will be holding a news conference there, before we leave. I will meet you all in front of the Virgin Airway terminal at Heathrow Airport."

There was a knock at the door. Linda answered it.

Leo, the bouncer stood there. "Sorry to bother you. There is a girl at the door, says she is a guest of yer's. Shall I let her pass?"

"Did she give her name?" Sonata asked.

"No ma'am. She does have a card from Sonata Williams. Said ya passed it along through her brother at the police station."

"It's the guard's sister." Eddie said. "Please bring her back."

"Right away." The guard hurried off.

"We promised her." Eddie looked at Sonata for approval.

"Absolutely." Sonata smiled back.

"Ya see there." Lisa stood up. "Now we're all gonna go soft and let any bird with a wet dream of ya in here. We are rock and rollers. We are the unattainable. We need to bloody well act like it."

"Funny, Lisa, seems like there are lots of birds that find you very attainable." Linda looked at her.

"Are you picking a row with me Linny? Cause, if that's what yer after, I will gladly accommodate ya." Lisa said.

"Stop it, now!" Eddie looked at the girls. "These are our fans. If it ain't fer them, then they don't buy our music. We just stay the nobody's we were. I don't care what the lot of you think, we need the fans, and I will be there fer them like they are fer us."

Eddie stood up and stormed off.

Lisa looked at Sonata then at the others. "You go on and watch the little birds drool all over ya. Yer blind if ya don't know they want a little blow and a quick bang."

"Is that all it is to ya, Lisa? Sex?" Pamela stood up.

"I heard no complaints from you, Pammy." Lisa winked at her.

"Maybe that's cause you had the fear of God put in me head."

Lisa walked up to Pamela and looked her in the eye.

They stared in silence as the other's watched. Linda wanted to hit Lisa, but she held herself back. She knew that Pamela was capable of handling herself.

"I know ya miss it." Lisa whispered. "You know where I am if ya need a reminder." She slowly licked her lips. She grabbed her leather jacket and walked to the door. "Showtime ladies." She smirked and walked out.

"I swear, Annie, do yourself a favor and get out while you can." Pamela said as she walked into the bathroom.

Annie looked at Linda. She knew that Lisa could have a temper. But then again everyone could have a bad day. Annie kept telling herself that. The sex was incredible and the drugs were free. She could put up with Lisa's little outbursts every once in a while.

Heathrow Airport was bustling with commotion at the soon to be press conference for the Travelers. Sonata had all her and Eddie's things packed and sent ahead to the airport. Linda and Pamela said their goodbyes to Oliver and their families. The limo took them over to Annie's where she and Lisa were waiting.

Sonata came out of the bathroom and looked around. "I think that's everything. Eddie, sweetheart, are you ready?"

There was no answer. "Eddie?" Sonata called out again as she walked into the living room. It was empty. She spotted a note sitting by the phone. "What are you doing now?" Sonata said out loud as she shook her head. She picked up the note and read. *"No worries luv, I will meet you at the airport. Our new journey in life and love starts at 1:00! Love Eddie."* Sonata smiled. She wasn't too thrilled that Eddie had wandered off, but somehow knew it was something Eddie had to do. She grabbed her bag and headed for the airport.

Eddie slowly walked in through the gate. She had only been here twice before the last time almost fifteen years ago. It was cold and damp and a sharp wind pierced through Eddie's skin. She continued through the wet grass looking for the final resting place of her mother. Though, only having been there twice, she knew exactly where she was going. She stopped at her destination and knelt down. She laid some flowers she had brought, by the headstone.

"Hey mum, it's me, Eddie…I know I haven't been here much…but I do think about you often. I just miss you not being here in me life. There are a bunch of things I needed to tell you. I am a musician now. I play the drums in a group called the Travelers…Ryan said I got that from you. Oh, I talked to Ryan and Denny a couple of times. We ain't as close as we should be, but then after ya passed, Stuart kicked them out. I don't know why you stayed with that old daft prick. He was a mean and hurtful bastard to all of us…but at least you are rid of the pain he caused ya…I'm doing ok. I met a lady…an American. She is beautiful. Fiery red hair. She has some meat on her bones too. Not those skinny arse model types. Her ways remind me of you. Or of what I remember. Her name is Sonata. I know you know her. I think you sent her to me. She came here and is now taking us to the States. We are gonna cut a CD…I just wish ya could meet her mum…Maybe one day…

Eddie reached for her neck and fingered the ring on a chain around her neck. Tears started to come to Eddie. She was happy to be leaving. She felt that she finally had the blessing from her mother.

"Who you talking to?" A deep voice said.

Eddie jumped to her feet. She looked around. She didn't need any kind of trouble right now.

"Who's there?" She said.

A man appeared from the shadows and approached Eddie.

"Ryan? Is that you?" Eddie smiled.

"Yep sis, it is." He embraced his sister.

"How did ya know where to find me?"

"I didn't. I come visit mum everyday. Just got lucky I guess." Ryan smiled.

"How have ya been?" Eddie asked.

"Good. Just busy working. I see that you are heading fer the States."

"Yeah, hard to believe, ey?" Eddie winked.

"Does Stuart know?"

"Stuart can sod off an go to hell for all I care. He was no father to me." Eddie's eyes narrowed.

"He wasn't yer father, Eddie. Mum was married before she met Stuart." Ryan said.

"What?"

"Yeah, yer real pop died in a car crash just after you were born."

Eddie started to cry. Tears of relief streamed down her face. "Ryan, you don't know what that means to me."

"Eddie you thought all this time he was yer pop?"

"Yeah."

Ryan wiped a tear from his sister's cheek. "I'm sorry luv. I thought you knew."

Eddie looked at her watch. "Buggart! I gotta scoot. I have to be at the airport in twenty minutes."

"I have me car let me drive ya and that way I can see ya off"

"I'd like that Ryan." Eddie smiled.

He watched as his sister kissed the headstone.

"I luv ya mum." She said.

She took her brother's hand and headed to the airport where her destiny awaited.

The airport was packed with press as well as onlookers and fans. The Travelers were all the rage. There was a table set up in the corner of the main lobby. There were two microphones and a PA system. The ladies were in the VIP lounge of the Virgin Airways terminal.

Sonata looked at her watch.

"Where the hell is Eddie?" Lisa looked at Sonata.

"She'll be here." Sonata said, not too convincing.

"How will she know where we are?" Pamela said.

"You all stay put, I'll go down and look for her. I'll be right back." Sonata took off to the front of the terminal. She hoped that Eddie would show up.

"Looking fer me, beautiful?" the familiar voice said.

Sonata beamed. She turned around and jumped into Eddie's open arms. "You had me worried for awhile."

"Didn't mean to. Just had to tie up a few loose ends. Hey, I want you to meet someone." She took Sonata by the hand and led her over to the tall thin gentleman standing by the escalator.

"Sonata, this here's me brother Ryan. He came to see me off." Eddie smiled.

"Ryan, nice to meet you." Sonata offered her hand.

"Pleasure, Sonata. I have heard a lot about ya." Ryan smiled.

Sonata could see the resemblance limitedly. "Uh oh." She looked at Eddie.

"It was all good." he chuckled.

"I'm sorry to cut this short, but I have to get Eddie to the press conference."

"Not a problem. I should be getting along myself."

"Do ya have to?" Eddie looked disappointed.

"Please, Ryan. You are more than welcome to join us."

"I don't want to be in the way."

"You won't be." Sonata assured him. "Besides you're family."

Eddie beamed. She loved the fact that her two favorite people were standing beside her.

"Lead the way." Ryan smiled.

CHAPTER 6

Eddie smiled as she sat on the plane. She was nervous and excited. It was her first time ever on a plane. She was amazed at how spacious it was up in first class. Sonata had her sit next to the window, so she was sure not to miss a thing. Pamela and Linda sat in front of them with Lisa and Annie to their side. They were all a buzz as the cute auburn haired flight attendant acted out the plane's safety features.

Lisa quickly made eye contact with her and winked. She had heard about sex in the bathrooms of airplanes. She was always willing to try something new.

"Ya nervous, luv?" Annie looked at Lisa.

"Nervous, no." She grinned at Annie.

Annie smiled back. Lisa had a voracious sexual appetite. She looked around.

"Fancy a fuck in the loo?" Lisa whispered into Annie's ear.

Annie giggled. "What if we get caught?"

"Well now, I guess we would ave to invite 'em in."

Lisa leaned in and kissed Annie on her neck. "Damn, you taste sweet."

Sonata leaned over and took Eddie's hand. "Are you ok?"

Eddie turned around and smiled. "I'm sitting next to the most beautiful woman in the world, on a plane headed to the states, getting ready to record a CD. Naww, I'm not good at all." She grinned at Sonata. "I don't think happiness could get any better."

"It will, Eddie." Sonata whispered. "You'll see."

Eddie smiled.

Linda handed Pamela another tissue. "What's wrong Pammy?"

"I miss Oliver. Did you see his little face as we pulled off? Nearly broke me heart in half."

"There now." Linda put her arm around Pamela. "We'll send fer him just as soon as we're settled."

"I hope we're doing the right thing Lin. I don't like being apart from him."

"Pammy, look what we'll be able to do fer Ollie. He will have the best from now on. We can help out yer folks too. I bet we can get him a tutor when he comes to the States, that way he can do his studies and be with us at the same time."

"Oh Lin, do you think that's possible?"

"We'll talk to Sonata. I promise you my luv, we will work things out."

"Do you know how much I love you?" Pamela smiled.

Linda smiled. "I love you too, bird."

Hours had passed as the plane continued its flight to California.

Linda and Pam were fast asleep.

Sonata drifted in and out of restless napping. She hated long flights. She could never sleep on them. She looked over at Eddie who finally fell asleep. Sonata reached under the blanket and took Eddie's hand.

Eddie looked up. "Can't sleep?" She said half awake.

"No."

Eddie sat up and moved the armrest up, and put her arm around Sonata bringing her close. "How is that?"

"Better." Sonata sighed. She leaned into Eddie's chest so she could hear her heart beat. It didn't take long for her to drift off.

Lisa looked around. Most were sound asleep. She nudged Annie. "Meet me in the loo in about two minutes."

"Lisa, I'm trying to sleep." Annie said.

"C'mon. I'm getting an urge."

"You always have an urge. Go an ask that airline whore. I saw ya flirting with her."

Lisa shrugged her shoulders. She stood up and headed toward the front of the plane. The flight attendant was finishing cleaning up her workstation. Lisa stopped and watched.

"Can I get you something?" She smiled.

"Well…You certainly got what I want, I just don't know how ya feel about giving it to me." Lisa winked. "What's yer name, luv?"

The flight attendant looked down at her name badge. "Becky."

"Well then." Lisa said as she slowly traced the name badge with her finger. "Becky."

Becky giggled.

"I'm Lisa."

"I know who you are."

"You do?" Lisa grinned.

"Yeah, I've seen you perform."

"I don't think ya have, luv. At least not the good way."

Becky had been a fan of the Travelers for some time now. What a grand story she would have to tell her friends.

Becky licked her lips. She felt the stir of excitement start to rumble from within.

Lisa took her hand and led her to the lavatory.

"You know, I could lose my job if I get caught." She said as she stepped in the restroom followed by Lisa.

"Well, I won't make ya scream too loud then." She grinned as she locked the door.

The space was tight. Lisa managed to get her flight attendant up on the sink. She slid her hand between her legs. She could feel her wetness starting to grow. She kissed the flight attendant hard. Lisa was amazed how she kissed back. Lisa looked into Becky's deep blue eyes. They looked like Eddie's. She laughed to herself as she felt Becky's hand fondle her nipple.

Lisa bent down and quickly slid off Becky's hose. She ran her hand up and down Becky's wetness. She quickly slid her finger inside Becky.

Lisa's aggressiveness sent Becky quickly over the top, coming quickly with force.

Becky looked at Lisa. She took her in her arms and sucked her gently on the neck. The rhythm of her sucking on Lisa's neck sent her into a haze. She never felt Becky unzip her jeans and start to grope her.

"Damn!" Lisa said under her breath.

Becky expertly started to rub her finger over Lisa's swollen clit.

Lisa leaned up against the wall, loving every second of it.

Suddenly there was a knock at the door.

"C'mon, I need to get in there." The deep voice bellowed.

Becky quickly stopped and tried to gather herself.

"Sod a dog. Who the fuck is that?" Lisa said as she pulled her pants up.

"Shhh." Becky said. "Just be quiet and they will go away."

Lisa looked at Becky. "No sense in wasting time."

She took Becky in her arms and kissed her.

Becky gladly let her explore with her tongue.

The knock grew louder.

"Sod off! Can't you see there is someone in here?"

They laughed as they heard the sound of angry feet stomping away.

"I need to go." Becky looked at herself in the mirror.

Lisa came up behind her and started kneading her breasts. "Can I see you again, luv? I hate to leave business unfinished."

Becky turned around and kissed Lisa. "I'm sure you'll be seeing more of me."

Lisa grinned. "I wanna see a lot more of ya." She kissed Becky.

"Stay in here and count to ten before you leave." Becky said. She carefully unlocked the door and peeked out. The coast was clear and she exited.

Lisa waited for the ten count by snorting some coke she had snuck on board. She made her way back to her seat. She was wired. She couldn't sleep now. She needed a drink. She stopped and looked at Annie sleeping soundly. She wondered why she couldn't stay with just one woman. Annie was more than willing to comply with anything Lisa wanted to do. All she wanted was a commitment. A commitment Lisa wasn't willing to make. She had to keep her options open. If Annie ever became boring to her, she would have thousands of women waiting to serve her every need. She was a big star, and would be treated like it. She looked over and saw Eddie and Sonata sleeping. She could easily have Eddie back if she wanted to. *Hmmm,* she thought. That would show that Sonata bitch who was boss here. Lisa grinned as she thought about the perfect way to get Eddie Sutcliffe back in her bed.

The landing was textbook perfect.

Eddie couldn't believe how beautiful California was. She wanted to see it all. The beach, Hollywood, the mountains, anything and everything she had ever read about, was now on her list to see.

As the girls made their way off the plane, Becky slipped a piece of paper into Lisa's hand. "I have lay overs in L.A. once a month," she whispered. "Call me on my cell."

Lisa quickly grinned at her flight attendant. "Oh I intend to, luv."

Annie frowned as they walked off the plane. "You're such a pig sometimes." She said.

"Sod a dog! Here we go again. You ain't never had a problem with it before."
She looked at Annie.

"Well, maybe I do now!" Annie raised her voice enough to warrant the
looks of the other passengers.

"I'm not gonna row with ya now."

"We'll talk about it later." They said in unison.

"We know, Lisa. You can't face anything."

Lisa took Annie by the arm and pulled her to the side.

The rest of the group stopped and looked back.

"Looks like trouble in paradise." Sonata said.

"I say we leave 'em." Linda chimed in.

Eddie watched as Lisa gave Annie a piece of her mind. She felt sorry for
Annie. She knew if they had been anywhere else, that Annie would be at the
end of one of Lisa's nasty blows. She only hoped that Annie would take the hint
of both her and Pamela and get away from Lisa. She leaned over to Sonata. "Do
somethin' fer her, luv." She whispered. "Please."

Sonata looked up at Eddie's rich blue eyes. She saw the sadness and the pain
she was feeling for Annie. She smiled and squeezed Eddie's arm then walked
back over to Lisa and Annie.

"Leave us be, we're talking." Lisa snarled.

"Yes, so I heard. In fact, the entire airport can hear you."

"So fucking what?" Lisa said.

"Look Lisa, there is an entire brigade of reporters and photographers waiting just outside for us. You have no clue how big this is. We are talking Beatles.
It wouldn't serve any purpose, to have your first press release to be about you
throwing a temper tantrum in the airport! I suggest you get your attitude in
check and emerge from this tunnel all smiles and happiness. This is real now. A
lot of people are now depending on you. If they see this temper, they will drop
you so fast you won't have time to unpack before you are shipped back to the
UK. Shall we?" She held her hand out.

Annie grabbed her bag and joined the other ladies. Sonata started to turn
away, Lisa grabbed her arm.

"I don't know if you realize who you're talkin' to, but just a little warnin' to
ya. Watch yer self, Sonata."

"Is that a threat?"

"No luv, its just things that come yer way sometimes have a tendency to go
back to where they came from." She puckered and made a kissing sound to
Sonata. She put on a smile and joined the others.

What was she up to? Sonata thought to herself as she walked back up to the group.

The second the Travelers emerged from the gates the flashes of the cameras were non-stop. There were also a handful of fans that knew about the Travelers.

Sonata had to admit when Lee Reynolds wanted it done big, he would pull out all the punches.

Eddie immediately walked up to the screaming fans. She signed autographs and posed for pictures. Some of the local news crews interviewed the girls as well. Sonata looked around and noticed that the crowds of onlookers started to grow. She looked around and spotted their chauffer holding a sign. There was no way they would be able to get to the limo with out a security escort. She quickly headed for a security guard.

In an instant, security guards came in to help. Sonata recognized the publicity crew from the record label. They waved at her and walked up.

"Pretty great isn't it? Austin said.

"It's insane, Austin. Where is all their security?"

"Lee felt it was better this way."

"Better what way? Sheer lunacy? How are we going to get them to the limo?"

"Stop worrying, Sonata. Let them sign a few autographs and talk to the reporters. "Lee has them on such a tight schedule, this will be as much fun as they'll see for awhile."

"Austin, they just got off a plane from England. They need to rest."

"They can rest in about two years. It's magic time now."

Sonata didn't want to hear it. She wanted to start a life with Eddie. But now it looked like Eddie was going to share her life with the world first. Sonata knew the routine. A weekend here, a stop over there. It was going to be hard to keep the relationship going. Sonata knew what she wanted, and she was ready to do whatever it would take to make it happen.

"Ladies this is Austin Reed. He is in charge of all your publicity."

"It's an honor to be a part of the Travelers. Welcome to America."

"Thanks, Austin." Eddie smiled.

"Where are we off to now?" Lisa demanded to know.

"Lee Reynolds has requested your presence at a little reception he is throwing for you at the House of Blues on the strip. You all have suites at the Saint James across the street. You have one hour to freshen up."

"Only an hour?" Pamela asked.

"Ladies let me be honest with you. Mr. Reynolds's knows that you will be the biggest female group ever. You don't have time to be nervous. Just be yourselves. We want the Travelers that we heard on the CD. Have fun, but remember this is a business. Our business is selling you."

"Are we singing tonight?" Annie asked.

"Don't be ridiculous. We just flew in." Lisa looked at Annie.

"You will be expected to sing a few tunes." Austin said.

Eddie looked at Sonata. She was starting to get a little nervous. It was all happening so fast. She was thrilled to be in America, but all she wanted to do was to walk along the beach, holding Sonata's hand.

Sonata gave Eddie a reassuring smile.

"Here we are. Sonata will take you to register and I'll make sure your bags are taken straight to your rooms. Remember, one hour and I'll meet you here."

The ladies registered and were taken to their rooms. Sonata's was next door to Eddie's, which made it nice. As soon as they got to the room, Eddie closed the door and took Sonata in her arms. She kissed her.

"It's been too long since we kissed." Eddie smiled.

"I know, I've missed those sweet lips." Sonata giggled.

"Well miss them no more, luv." She kissed her again.

"Eddie, I was thinking…" Sonata said.

"Oh no. Anytime someone starts out with I've been thinkin' its always bad news."

"I just don't want you to ever think that I am holding you down. You are going to be famous Eddie. A superstar. There is going to be thousands of women throwing themselves at you."

"Yeah, there will be luv, and not bloody one of 'em will be Sonata Williams. Sonata, this is all because of you. I want to share it with you. You and me together all the way."

"Eddie, you are so special." Sonata kissed Eddie lightly on the lips. "I have to tell you something."

"What?" Eddie looked concerned.

"Well…Sweetie, I'm not sure that I will be part of your future professionally."

"Meaning?"

"My job is to scout out talent and bring them to our label."

"No Sonata, I want you with me. I need you by my side…No, I won't go on if you're not there…you are a part of the Travelers…Linny and Pam would think so too. I'll tell Mr. Reynolds meself."

Sonata laughed. "Oh yeah? What are you going to tell him? No one is supposed to know about us."

"It doesn't matter, Sonata, if you're not with us, then I ain't gonna sing. It's that simple."

Sonata kissed Eddie. It was a long, lingering, passionate kiss. Sonata knew in an instant that Eddie's heart belonged to her. She had to make Lee see that she in fact needed to be with the Travelers every step of the way. Then, there was Lisa. She would do anything to make sure that Lee saw how Sonata really didn't need to fit into the picture.

Lisa was flying, as she got dressed. She was so glad that the stash she brought over went unnoticed through customs. She definitely needed to find who she could hook up with now that she was in L.A. It couldn't be that hard, she thought. Half the town were crack heads, the rest were silicone.

"You ready, luv?" Annie said as she put on her earring.

"Flying high babe. Care to join me?"

"Thought you'd never ask." Annie chuckled.

Lisa quickly pulled out the small vile she had in her pocket. She poured out the powder and quickly divided it into four lines. She handed Annie her straw. "Ladies first." She winked at Annie.

Annie smiled as she took the straw from Lisa. She quickly snorted the two lines and passed the straw back to Lisa.

Lisa snorted her lines quickly. She grabbed Annie. "I say we go in the bedroom and take care of a few things." She squeezed Annie's ass.

"Baby, we can't be late to our first meeting. We ave all night to play."

"They get one hour of our time, then we come back here and celebrate." Lisa kissed Annie. She took her hand and led her to the door.

"Sonata and Eddie will meet us at the elevator in five minutes Pammy, move yer bum, luv!" Linda called out.

"I'm ready. I'm getting a bit dizzy Lin. All this madness in such a short time. All I want to do is curl up in your arms and sleep fer a week."

"Later, luv. Now we have to prove to this lot that we are the best bloody band the world has ever seen."

"That shouldn't be too hard. We are the best."

"Yeah, I just hope they get to hear Eddie sing tonight. No telling what Lisa might do."

"I'm tired of her freakin' mind games. I'm thankful fer what she's done fer the band, but there are times I wish she wasn't around."

"Well, she's quite the lucky bird. But lucky only goes so far. She has hers coming soon, and Eddie will shine."

❧   ❧   ❧

The limo pulled up to the House of Blues. There were cars and limos everywhere. The limo slowly made it's way to the entrance.

"This is all fer us?" Eddie asked.

"Yep. It's only the beginning ladies." Austin smiled.

"Look at all the cameras." Pamela said.

"Those are the same blokes from the airport." Linda said.

"First lesson. Paparazzi will follow you anywhere and everywhere. If you try to have a secret, then good luck to you. They will hunt you down like dogs and sell the worst possible picture of you."

Eddie looked at Sonata. She was staring out the window, her thoughts a million miles away. She missed being home. But look what she brought home. She had her soul mate sitting next to her. She only hoped she wasn't making a tragic mistake.

The limo door opened to the roar of the crowd of onlookers. Lisa got out first and started to work the crowd.

Eddie stopped Sonata. "You ok, luv?"

Sonata smiled back. "C'mon it's magic time for you Eddie Sutcliffe."

Sonata stepped out of the limo. She stood there watching the band as they mingled with the press.

"I'm impressed, Sonata." Lee Reynolds said from behind her.

"Oh thank you, Lee."

"I appreciate all you've done. We will talk later."

Sonata watched as Lee walked over and shook Austin's hand. Her heart sank. She felt like Eddie was going to be torn away from her.

"Ladies' and gentleman," Lee said as he took the microphone. "I want to thank each and every one of you for joining me tonight here at the House of Blues…I am thrilled to be introducing you to one of Reynolds's Record's greatest finds, and sure to be one of the world's greatest female rock and roll bands of all time!"

"Did you hear what he called us?" Eddie yelled backstage.

"At least the man is telling the truth." Lisa said un-amused.

"This is your time to shine ladies. Have fun and be yourself." Sonata smiled.

"Thanks to you." Linda hugged Sonata.

"I second that." Pamela hugged Sonata.

"Thanks, Sonata." Annie joined in.

"C'mon birds, he just called us." Lisa said.

The ladies took to the stage, except for Eddie. "Thank you, luv." She smiled.

"Go on." Sonata said choking back her tears.

Eddie leaned over and softly kissed Sonata. "We'll continue this later." She winked, and ran to the stage just as Lee introduced her.

The girls beamed as the crowd stood before them screaming and applauding. Some were taking notes.

Sonata walked around from backstage and merged into the crowd. Eddie looked so happy up there on the stage.

"Where did you find the UK trash?" A voice Sonata hated whispered in her ear.

Kenny Clark. The jerk of life and Lee Reynolds's assistant. He was known around Hollywood as a crack head, and a big kiss ass. The water cooler talk was that he had his head so far up Lee's ass; his voice came out of Lee's mouth.

Sonata looked at Kenny. "What do you want, Kenny?"

"I want to know why you kept the dykes under wraps?"

"Shut up and go away." Sonata tried to move away but Kenny grabbed her arm.

Eddie looked down and saw Sonata trying to get away.

"Listen to me, Sonata. If you think you are gonna get to the top of Reynolds's by bringing the Travelers in, you have another thing coming to you. Just remember, I call most of Lee's shots. If I hate it, Lee will too." He stroked Sonata's cheek and calmly walked away.

Eddie frowned. She didn't want anyone touching Sonata. She wondered who he was. Just a friend? An ex? Whoever he was, Eddie didn't like him.

"How about a song ladies?" Lee said.

The curtain went up to reveal a drum set, keyboards, a bass, and two guitars.

The girls quickly took their places.

"We'd like to sing an original tune fer ya." Lisa said into the mike. "It's a song I wrote called "Time Will Tell." Enjoy."

Eddie pounded out a three count and the band took off. Their excitement and raw energy poured off the stage and through the audience.

Lee beamed as he made his way over to Sonata. "Damn, Sonata, we got ourselves a goldmine here."

"They are pretty terrific." she smiled.

"I want them in a recoding studio tomorrow." he looked at Sonata.

"Yes sir."

Eddie watched as Lee and Sonata talked. She wondered what she was telling him.

The band finished their song to a thunderous ovation. It seemed like forever.

"Thanks." Lisa said.

Lee walked up to the stage and took the mike. "What do you think about our gals?"

The applause was deafening, and the girls were all smiles.

"Time Will Tell" is going to be the launch single."

Lisa beamed. She knew that she would get paid for writing the songs as well as singing. She also was the publisher. The dollars kept adding up. She thought.

"Now, if you would appease an old man, I'd like to hear another song."

The crowd went wild.

"Eddie. Come out here please." Lee called her.

Eddie looked at Sonata. She climbed out from behind her set and walked over to Lee.

"Eddie, would you do the honor of the next song?" He asked.

Lisa was pissed.

Linda laughed as she could tell at once that Lisa was about ready to come unglued.

Eddie smiled shyly as she sat at the piano. She looked out and found Sonata smiling.

Their eyes locked.

"Ah…ya kind of took me off guard there, Mr. R. I don't know quite what to sing fer ya all. So, I'll just play an old favorite."

Eddie started to play Elton John's "Don't Let The Sun Go Down on me." Eddie's sultry voice took over. The entire crowd was silent as Eddie sang. Sonata looked around. They were all hanging on every word Eddie sang. She smiled. Even Lee Reynolds himself was mesmerized by Eddie's incredible vocals.

When Eddie finished, most of the crowd was in tears. The applause and whistles were non-stop.

Lee came out and gave Eddie a hug. He thanked her for playing one of his favorite songs. He thanked everyone for coming and called a meeting first thing in the morning of his top team. There was no time to waste. They had to strike while the iron was hot, and right now it was smoking!

The girls mingled for a bit. Eddie stayed close to Sonata. Lee would bring people up to meet her.

"I don't think this is what Lee had in mind when he said to mingle." Sonata giggled.

"I just want to spend some time alone with ya. Ya think we could sneak out soon?" Eddie smiled.

"There's my girl!" Lee yelled as he put his arm around Eddie.

Lisa was well aware how Lee felt about Eddie. She had to do something to take his focus off of Eddie and put it on her.

"How does it feel, Eddie?" Lee smiled.

"Oh great, sir. Me head is spinning. It's all happening so fast."

"Well my dear, it's just the beginning."

"Ya know Mr. R, if it weren't fer Sonata here, none of this would be happening."

Lee smiled. "Sonata will be handsomely rewarded."

"Thank you, Lee." Sonata said.

"Mr. R? I wanted to make sure that Sonata is here to see this through with us." Eddie said, much to Sonata's surprise.

"I'm not sure I follow you, Eddie." Lee said.

"I want to make sure Sonata stays with the Travelers. She is one of us now."

"Oh, I see. And that would make a difference to you?"

"Fer me, Mr. R, it's the deciding factor."

Sonata couldn't believe Eddie's honesty. She smiled at Lee.

"Lee, I think there is something you should know." Sonata said slowly.

"I'm sure there are a lot of things I should know. Sonata, we will talk tomorrow. Eddie, I think we will be able to accommodate your request. We will talk more later. See you all in my office at ten a.m. sharp."

"Yes sir." Sonata said, as they watched Lee find Kenny, and disappear.

"You are too much." Sonata smiled.

"It was all that cheering. It really got me going."

"Oh, really?" Sonata said licking her lips seductively.

Eddie grinned. "And one beautiful redhead."

Sonata found Linda and Pamela who were ready to leave as well. They were exhausted.

Sonata knew that when Lee said ten, he meant ten.

They spotted Annie, but Lisa was nowhere to be found.

"Do you want to get going with us?" Linda asked Annie.

"I'd better wait fer Lisa. She went off with Mr. Reynolds and Kenny."

Sonata frowned. She knew all the rumors of Kenny and Lee's huge appetite for women and drugs. She knew Lisa was going to get herself in a whole bunch of trouble.

"Suit yourself" Sonata said. "Be in the lobby by nine a.m. tomorrow. We have a meeting with Lee and we can't be late."

"Will do." Annie smiled.

Sonata followed Eddie as they left the House of Blues and headed back to the hotel.

The limo driver opened the door for them, but Eddie stopped.

"Did you forget something?" Sonata asked.

"Yeah…give me a sec, luv." Eddie smiled and ran back in.

She spotted Annie still standing near the door. She ran up to her. "Hey ya got a sec, Annie?"

"Sure, Eddie, what's up?"

"Ah…I…Look, Annie, I know that you've been seeing Lisa fer awhile and all…I just wanted to tell ya…"

"Tell me what, Eddie?"

"Just watch yerself, Annie…Lisa can be…She gets…." Eddie tried to say.

Lisa came up. "Well now, what's going on here?"

"Couldn't tell ya. Can we go home now, Lisa? I'm pooped." Annie took Lisa's hand.

"Yeah, we're going back, but I ain't got sleeping on me mind." She started to laugh and looked at Eddie. "Care ta join us, Eddie? The three of us could definitely give it a go."

Eddie looked at Lisa. She felt sorry for Annie. Lisa was using more each day.

"Ah the limo is just about to leave fer the hotel." She offered.

"Good. C'mon Lisa." Annie tugged her.

Lisa looked at Eddie. She winked at her, and grinned.

Eddie rolled her eyes and headed for the limo.

Sonata unlocked her room. Eddie came up behind her.

"Where do ya think yer goin to, eh?" She softly kissed the back of her neck.

Sonata turned around and kissed Eddie. "I was so proud of you tonight." She smiled.

"Yeah?" Eddie kissed her. "You liked the song?"

"Yes, silly, I always love your songs. You could sing the names out of a phone book and it would sound like poetry, Eddie."

Eddie chuckled.

"But you stood up to Lee Reynolds tonight, and for us. He respected you for doing it."

"Baby, I told the truth. I won't sing another note, if you ain't by my side. I know I can get Pamela and Linny on board too."

"I couldn't let you do that, Eddie. You all have come so far."

Eddie took Sonata's face in her hands. She looked deep into her eyes. "You don't get it, Sonata Williams. I have hopelessly fallen in love with you. I wouldn't sing another note if you asked me not to."

"Oh, Eddie." Sonata said as tears came to her eyes. "No one has ever made me feel like you do."

"Good. That makes me the lucky one then." She kissed Sonata deeply.

They were unaware that a couple that had been watching them from down the hall until Sonata looked over.

"Maybe we should take this inside."

"Why? I want the world to know I love you." She looked over at the couple.

"Evening folks. Just wanted to let ya know that I am madly in love with this beautiful redhead."

Sonata giggled.

The couple shook their heads.

"We're gonna go in now and make love and we'll try ta keep it down."

"Eddie!" Sonata whispered and laughed. She pulled Eddie in the room and closed the door.

"You're gonna get us kicked out of here."

"Why cause I love a woman? You American's are so stodgy when it comes to sex. You wouldn't have half the trouble you do if you all would just let folks love who they love."

Sonata kissed Eddie. "You are so smart."

"Naw, not me. Just trying to keep it real."

Sonata smiled. "Eddie, how would you like to go somewhere?"

"Now?"

"Yes."

"It's late me luv, and I thought…"

"Please say yes." Sonata looked into her eyes.

"Of course, for you, Sonata, yes." Eddie smiled.

Sonata grinned as she picked up the house phone. "Yes this is suite 200. I need a taxi please…Right now, if possible. Yes…Great, thanks, we'll be right down." She hung up the phone. "You ready?"

"Just what are ya up to, Sonata?"

"You'll see." She took Eddie's hand and headed for the elevator.

❦   ❦   ❦

Sonata gave the taxi driver the address and snuggled into Eddie's warm embrace.

"You gonna give me a hint ta where we are going?"

"Crazy, Eddie Sutcliffe. Crazy."

"Eddie Sutcliffe?" the Taxi driver said.

"Yeah, that's me." Eddie looked at Sonata.

"From the Travelers?"

"You know of the Travelers?" Sonata asked.

"Are you kidding? They rock. My friend from England sends me their bootlegs all the time…oops."

Eddie smiled. "What is yer name?"

"Karli." She said.

"It's a pleasure Karli."

"Shit, no one is going to believe this!" She said. "Why are you here?"

"Were making a CD, Karli. We got us a record deal." She winked at Sonata.

"Bitchen!" She said. "Is there gonna be a tour too?"

"Yes, just after the CD release." Sonata said.

"Awesome!" Karli yelled.

Sonata and Eddie laughed.

"I'll be there, you can count on it." Karli pulled over to the address Sonata had requested. "Here you are. Would you mind if I asked you for an autograph?"

"I'd mind if ya didn't ask." Eddie smiled.

Karli handed her a piece of paper.

"How old are ya, Karli?"

"Twenty one. My uncle owns the cab company. He lets me work at night so I can practice during the day."

"What are you practicing?" Sonata asked.

"The drums of course! I want to be like the great Eddie Sutcliffe. I have a band and everything. We're called The Hollywood Hussle."

"Karli, I'll tell ya what. I'll do ya one better. You write down yer name and number, and I'll make sure you have tickets for our first gig here." Eddie signed the paper.

"Oh my God, are you kidding?"

"She never kids about things like that." Sonata said.

"This is outrageous!" Karli beamed.

"Sonata, you have a card luv?"

Sonata handed Eddie her business card.

"Here you keep in touch with us and let me know how yer drumming is going."

"You want me to call you?" Karli looked stunned.

"Yeah, we want to be invited to yer first gig too."

Sonata reached into her pocket and pulled out some money. Eddie took out a hundred dollar bill.

"This is fer the cabby. This is fer the drummer." She handed Karli the hundred."

"Oh no I…I…couldn't."

"Yes, you can. Trust me, I know what drummer's can make startin' out."

Sonata opened the door to get out. "Good luck to you, Karli, keep in touch."

"Man, can I give you a hug?" Karli said as she turned the cab off and got out.

Eddie hugged her long and hard. Karli was just like her when she was eighteen.

"I'll never forget this night." Karli said as she clung to Eddie.

"You listen to me, Karli." Eddie looked into her eyes. "You keep yer nose straight. None of that drug crap. You don't need it. Stay away from it. You hear me?"

"Yes." Karli looked wide-eyed at her idol.

"If you need anything you call me, ok?" Eddie grinned.

"Thank you so much. You too." She hugged Sonata.

"You're welcome, Karli." Sonata smiled.

Karli quickly wiped a tear from her eye. She jumped in the cab and drove off.

Sonata hugged Eddie. "You are so special." She kissed her drummer.

"I was just like that at that age." Eddie smiled.

"You know, you can't do that for every kid you meet."

"Why not?" Eddie looked puzzled. "Why not help em out?"

"Eddie, trust me, when you hit it big, everybody and their brother will want a piece of you. You can't throw it all away. Fame is fleeting. You need to manage your money right. Bank it away. Let it work for you."

"Let it work fer us." Eddie kissed Sonata. "I guess I still have a lot to learn about the business part."

"We'll get a business manager. I'll teach you all I know."

"We're gonna be so good together." Eddie yawned. "Oh sorry luv. I think the time difference is starting to get to me. Where are we anyhow?"

"C'mon, I want you to see this."

Sonata took Eddie's hand and walked up some stairs.

Eddie could smell the salty sea air. The light sea breeze blew against her tired face. She felt like she was in heaven.

Sonata unlocked the door and turned on the light.

Eddie stepped in and looked around. It was beautiful. There were photos of sea animals all around. There was a huge shelf with CD's on them, and a guitar sitting on a stand.

"Sod a dog, will you look at that? I've never seen so many CD's. Ya got a record store right here in yer room."

Sonata laughed, "The perks of working at a record company. Eddie, I know it's small, but I want you to make this your home too. I mean if you want to?"

"If I want to? Luv, I'd stay in a shoe box if you were in there with me."

She pulled Sonata to her and kissed her. She was falling deeper in love by the second with this magical woman she held in her arms.

"C'mon, I think we need to get to bed."

"I feel a second wind coming about." Eddie scooped up Sonata in her arms.

"You're crazy, Eddie."

"Fer you, my luv, yes I am!"

Eddie made her way to the back of the house.

Sonata reached for the light.

"No don't." Eddie whispered. She moved to the bed and lay Sonata down.

She felt like she was finally home. She was safe and she was free. Sleep was the furthest thing from her mind.

Sonata woke up to the screeching alarm. She had made love to Eddie all night. She looked at the clock. It was 6:30am. She went to sleep only two hours ago, and didn't much care. Eddie put a lot of her fears to rest. They talked about what their plans would be. Eddie was dead set on Sonata being with her, even if it meant quitting her job. Eddie assured her that she would take care of Sonata, and Sonata loved what she had heard.

She rolled over to give Eddie a good morning kiss, only to find her side of the bed empty. She rolled out of bed and grabbed a robe, then walked out of the bedroom and looked around. Eddie was sitting on the deck. She had CD's spread out everywhere and a Walkman hooked to her ears. Sonata walked out onto the deck, and tapped Eddie on the shoulder.

"Oh, hey. Ya startled me, luv." Eddie stood up and took Sonata in her arms.

"I feel like a drowned rat. I am so tired." Sonata said, as she laid her head on Eddie's chest.

"I'm on a rush. I don't want to stop now. I have a blooming record career and the most beautiful woman in the world who is in love with me."

Sonata sighed.

"I love the view from the deck here too. It's a good thinkin' spot."

"Well, my dear, it is here anytime you need to do some thinkin'"

"Sonata, I love these Cd's! You have everyone. I love this one."

"Wynonna. She is incredible. One of my favorites." Sonata smiled.

"I love her voice. So much soul. So pure. And that red hair. You know I am practical to that" Eddie smiled.

"Really? I hadn't noticed." Sonata giggled. She leaned over and kissed Eddie.

"Ya mind if I bring some of these with us?"

"Eddie, I want you to make this your home…our home. Anything within these walls is yours."

"I also found this." She handed a case to Sonata.

"Oh, "If You Only Knew." Sonata smiled. "What did you think?"

"It's beautiful. I luv the words."

"Yeah, it came to me one night. I sat right there and wrote it."

"You wrote this? Do ya have the charts?"

"Eddie, it's not that good."

"No, it is luv."

"The music is all off, and I was so depressed when I wrote it."

"She must ave been a special one."

"I thought so, now I know she wasn't." Sonata looked at Eddie.

"And I luv the title. "If You Only Knew."

"Just throw it out. I have the one I want right here, now. That was just a phase." She kissed Eddie.

"Please, I'd like to take a crack at it if it's ok with ya?"

"If you really want to. It's in the wooden box next to my guitar, but I wouldn't waste much time on it."

Eddie beamed. She jumped up and ran to the box.

Sonata shook her head, and went back inside.

"We need to get going soon."

"I know, I just want to ave a look at these."

Sonata laughed. "If it becomes a big hit for you let me know, I could use the royalties…I'm going to take a shower."

Eddie picked up Sonata's guitar and started to play. She dove deep into the song quickly picking it apart and rearranging it. It sounded good, really good. Good enough to be cut for the CD. She quickly scribbled some notes. A grin came over her face.

❦   ❦   ❦

The girls were all a chatter as they waited in the conference room at Reynolds Records.

Eddie was telling Linda and Pamela about Karli, and Sonata's home, while Annie and Lisa were huddled in a corner talking about last night and the things they had planned for later.

The door opened and Sonata walked in followed by Lee Reynolds, Austin, Kenny and few others.

"Ladies, please have a seat." Lee said.

They all took seats at the large cherry wood table. Eddie sat across from Sonata. They stared at each other.

Eddie winked.

Sonata blushed. She cleared her throat and raised an eyebrow at Eddie.

Eddie smiled.

Linda and Pamela watched as the two kept exchanging glances. They smiled and exchanged a look.

Lisa also caught their look. She frowned. "So, are we gonna sit here making goo goo eyes at each other all day or what?"

Sonata shot a look at Lisa.

Lisa grinned.

What a bitch! Sonata thought.

"Yes, let's start shall we? Ladies, on behalf of myself and Reynolds Records, we would like to welcome the Travelers to our home."

The others applauded.

"We hope you find what you are looking for here with us."

Eddie grinned at Sonata. She slowly started to sink a bit into her chair.

As Lee talked about what to expect, Eddie was playing footsies with Sonata. Sonata tried not to giggle. She casually took a sip out of her water bottle.

Eddie slowly started to ease her foot out of her boot. She ran her foot across Sonata's foot.

Sonata looked wide-eyed at Eddie.

Eddie grinned and started to slowly extend her foot up Sonata's pant leg.

Sonata started to choke on her water. She sprayed it across the table hitting Eddie.

"Sonata, are you alright?" Lee asked.

"Yes sir, went down the wrong pipe. Excuse me." She looked at Eddie.

"Well then, are there any questions?" Lee asked.

"Yes sir, I have one." Linda said. "I know you are aware of the lifestyles we lead, but Pamela and I have a son, and we want him here with us."

"Yes, I am aware of this. When you feel the time is right, I have no problem with your son joining you here."

"Thank you, sir." Pamela smiled.

"I also wanted to make it known that we have a new director of A and R. Sonata Williams."

Lee started to applaud. The others started to follow. Eddie smiled.

"Thank you Lee." Sonata smiled.

"As head of A and R, Sonata will be in charge of making sure you are up to Reynolds Records standards."

"Meaning, she's our bloody baby sitter now?" Lisa frowned.

"Well, I wouldn't say that. Sonata is a smart woman. You will be glad she is on your team."

"A lot of no good is gonna come from this. She is doing Eddie, We know where the favors will lie."

Eddie blushed. Part embarrassed, part anger. *How dare she.* Eddie thought. She looked at Sonata.

Sonata was livid. She was so close to just calling it quits. She wanted no part of Lisa. She was about to say something, but stopped when she saw Eddie's eyes.

"I am well aware of the relationship between Sonata and Eddie. Sonata and I talked about it earlier this morning, and I was assured that it would not conflict in any way, shape or form, the judgment of Sonata's duties."

"We have no problems with it." Pamela said.

Sonata looked at Lisa and smiled. *Take that you bitch!* Sonata said to herself.

Lisa frowned. *Don't think for one moment this is settled*, she thought.

"So Ladies here is your contract. Simply put, we are signing you to a one record deal. Upon the success of the single and the full length, a tour will ensue for six months. At which time we will option to sign you for another full length. We will release the single in one week. The full CD in less than two months. I want you in the studio by tomorrow, I have Lan Rivers signed on to produce, and Amy Wilde will produce and direct your video."

"Lan Rivers…he produced the Stone's." Eddie said.

"Yes Eddie, he did. He feels that you all can work very well together."

"What about song choice? We ain't singing no crap." Lisa said.

"Lan will meet with us after lunch. He has brought some songs for you to listen to. We also want to record a few of the Travelers original songs." Sonata said.

"Time Will Tell will be the first single" Lee smiled.

"What if some of us have some songs to contribute?" Eddie asked.

Lisa laughed. "And what song ave you written?"

"Ladies please feel free to bring any original material to the table. If it's good, we will use it."

Eddie smiled. She had big plans for Sonata's song. She just needed to step carefully around Lisa.

❦   ❦   ❦

The girls loved Lan Rivers. He was an on the edge producer. He had big plans for the Travelers.

Lisa made it clear that she would in no way compromise her original tunes.

Lan assured her that he was in no way out to compromise her music. He had listened to their demo, and a live bootleg. He knew exactly where he wanted to go.

Sonata made arrangements to meet with Lan at the recording studio first thing in the morning. She wanted to give the girls, as well as herself, some much needed rest.

It was 3:00pm when the limo dropped Eddie and Sonata off at the beach house.

"So what do you want to do now, luv?" Eddie said as she took Sonata in her arms.

"Hmm. I can think of a couple things." Sonata giggled.

Eddie looked into Sonata's eyes. She started to trace the outline of her face with her fingers.

"You are more beautiful each time I look at ya." Eddie smiled. She leaned over and kissed Sonata. "Ya make my knees go weak. You know that don't ya?"

Sonata smiled. She had never thought it possible to make anyone go weak-kneed, or feel the feelings that Eddie said she felt. It amazed her.

"I got an idea." Eddie said.

"Well, if it's anything like this morning's, I like it." Sonata said as she kissed Eddie.

"Can we go to the market?" Eddie asked.

"The market?" Sonata looked confused.

"Yeah, I think it would be great to have the gang over fer supper. We can fire up the grill; maybe hang out on the beach. I know Linny and Pam would go mad."

"Sure, if you want."

"And you don't I take it?"

"No, it's not that I don't want to, It's just…I kind of wanted to have you all to myself."

"We have all nigh, luv." Eddie winked. "I just want to share the beauty of the ocean with me friends."

"I understand…does that include Lisa and Annie too?"

"Oh, I guess we kind of hav ta." Eddie frowned.

"Listen, Eddie. The Travelers are going to be huge. There is an entire campaign to push you into America. You are going to be everywhere. Unfortunately, Lisa is gonna be there too. She is a part of the team."

"I don't care about Lisa no more. I am grateful to her fer making me a part of the band, and that's only cause I met you."

Sonata kissed Eddie. "I some how think our hearts would have found one another some how."

"Absolutely." Eddie agreed. "So whatta' ya say?"

"We'll phone the other's on the way to the market. C'mon."

A grin came over Eddie's face. "I luv ya, Sonata."

"Just remember that when you are rich and famous."

They laughed as they headed for the door.

🍁   🍁   🍁

Linda and Pamela arrived about 6:00p.m., just in time to watch the sunset from the deck.

Sonata and Eddie went all out, steak, corn on the cob, baked potatoes, wine, beer, chips and dips, and a big cheesecake. They finished dinner and went down to the beach, where Eddie and Linda built a huge bonfire.

"This is insane I tell ya." Linda said. "I want a house on the beach Pammy. I think Ollie would love it."

"Easy there, big spender, yer already blowing a wad ya don't even have yet."

"We'll have enough fer a house won't we?" Linda looked at Sonata.

"Well, if Lee's instincts are right, you'll have enough for quite a few houses on the beach."

Linda smiled. "We only need one, luv."

"So where are Lisa and Annie? I was sure they would be here fer steak. It's Lisa's favorite." Eddie said.

"They had other plans." Pamela said.

"Yeah a couple of lines, a couple of girls. You know Lisa, why wait." Linda frowned.

"I feel kind of sorry fer Annie." Eddie looked at Sonata.

"You do?"

"She has no clue that Lisa's takin' her down. All she wants is to be loved. I mean, don't we all?" She grabbed Sonata's hand. "But ya don't need all the crap that's gonna go down, just to say yer luved."

"That isn't love, Eddie." Sonata said. "It's just someone to occupy your down time. And in the end, all the shit Lisa's into…It's gonna catch up to her, and she'll take Annie down too…and sadly, it won't be pretty."

"I can't believe how brilliant Lisa is. Sonata, her music is incredible. Some of the shit she comes up with blows me away, but she's also the most daft bird I know." Linda said.

"Well, personally, I don't see Lisa with the group that long, Annie either if she stays with her. Their drug problem will become such a liability to the company, they will end up dropping them." Sonata said blankly.

"You think that will happen?" Eddie said.

"Can we stop talkin' about Lisa for the rest of the evening?" Pamela looked around.

"I'll second that." Sonata said.

Lisa not in the Travelers? Eddie thought. It was too strange. Lisa was the Travelers. Besides, Lisa was a sly one, and ahead of the game. That's why Eddie learned to keep her guard up around her. Only now, she had another reason. Sonata was her world, and she would lay her life on the line to protect her.

"Isn't it beautiful out here?" Linda said, looking up at the sky.

"Yep. Beautiful night, beautiful meal, and a beautiful woman to share it with." Eddie winked at Sonata.

"You are so cute." Sonata bent over and kissed Eddie.

"So, what happens tomorrow?" Pamela asked.

"Lan will meet with us. We will go over the single, maybe record it. He will have a bunch of demo tapes to listen to. Since we will use a couple of original tunes, and maybe a cover, we will narrow down the choices to about twenty songs. He will put you in a recoding studio and the top twelve or thirteen will make it on the CD." Sonata explained.

"How long will it take?" Eddie asked. Can we have a couple days at least?"

Sonata chuckled. "Baby, try more like a couple of weeks. Although, Lee has made you top priority, so you are looking at a little less time."

"We don't need that much time, luv." Eddie said, "We can ave it done in a few days."

"This is the big time, ya knuckle head." Linda said. "We get to lay tracks down, and mix. This is gonna be fantastic!"

"Yep, and I am gonna have you by my side the whole way Sonata." Eddie grinned.

Sonata kissed Eddie again. "How about a walk?" She asked.

"Yeah, sure." Eddie stood up and held her hand out for Sonata.

"You want to join us?" Sonata asked Linda and Pamela.

"No thanks luv, we'll just cozy on up to the fire fer a bit." Linda said.

"Ok, see you in awhile."

"Ave fun you two." Pamela yelled after them.

"They are sure great together, huh?" Linda took Pamela in her arms.

"Yep just like us." Pamela giggled. She kissed Linda.

"Here's to the start of our new life, baby. We did it together." Linda smiled.

"I luv you so much Linny." Pamela kissed Linda passionately.

"I luv you too."

✦   ✦   ✦

Eddie and Sonata walked along the soft moonlit beach, hand in hand, with Eddie closer to the waves, as if to protect Sonata from the approaching sea.

"I really luv it here." Eddie said as she looked out at the ocean.

"I'm glad you're here to enjoy it."

Eddie pulled Sonata to her and kissed her. "I am so excited. This is all happening so fast, me heads gonna explode, I think."

"You ain't seen nothing yet, sweetie." Sonata said. "Wait till the world gets a load of the Travelers, you won't have a moments peace."

"It scares you doesn't it?" Eddie asked.

"No, don't be silly."

"I think I'm getting the jest of it now. Yer thinkin' that once we get famous, I'm gonna toss you out like yesterday's rubbish."

Sonata moved closer into Eddie's embrace. She buried her head in her shoulder.

"I'm just not like the others that are going to be chasing after you. Your fans will be cuter and skinnier than me…"

"Stop it will ya? That has never mattered to me." She took Sonata's face in her hands. "I'm only saying this one time, I have done the sleepin' around bit, I'm over that. You, my luv, Sonata, are the most beautiful being that the heaven's put on this earth. I may not be the smartest of the lot, but I promise you, if I never sing another note, and this madness all disappears, I will do whatever it takes to make sure you and I are always together. In case you hadn't noticed, I am in luv with you."

"There are going to be thousands of others that will throw themselves at you. I just don't want you to think that I am holding you back."

"I ain't answering that, Sonata. That is utter nonsense. Do you luv me?"

"Yes."

"Do you trust me?"

Sonata looked at Eddie in the moonlight. She hadn't known Eddie long at all, but she was in love. She wanted her in her life, forever.

"I trust you with my life."

"Then, trust me when I tell you that I luv you and I will forever." She reached in her shirt and pulled out the gold ring she was wearing on a chain. She fumbled for the clasp, and took the ring off. "I've been saving this fer the right woman in me life. Sonata Williams, you are that woman. This here's me mum's wedding band. It's the only thing I have of her's…Would you accept this with me luv?"

Tears came quickly to Sonata, as Eddie lifted her hand and placed the ring on her finger.

"Eddie…I love you so much." Was all she could get out before she started crying. She hugged Eddie hard. "I would be honored to wear your mother's ring."

"She'd luv you too, you know." Eddie wiped tears from her eyes as well. "Maybe when we get back to England, you could meet her. I've told her all about you."

"There's nothing I would like to do more. She had to have been special, to have such a wonderful daughter. I am sure she is proud of you Eddie."

A grin came across Eddie's face. "Thank you, luv."

Sonata leaned in and kissed Eddie.

"We should get back." Eddie said.

"I know, but I could just stand here on this deserted beach, in your arms, forever."

"Me too. This can be our getaway place. We won't tell no one we are here."

"If it were only that easy Eddie. This is probably the first and last time we'll get to do this."

"You mark me words, we will my luv, we will."

CHAPTER 7

Eddie and Sonata were the first to arrive. The recording studio was amazing. The halls were all decorated with gold and platinum record awards. Eddie grinned as she recognized some of her favorites who had great successes with their careers.

"I was thinkin' what if we do a country song?" Eddie said out loud.

Sonata looked at Eddie. "Honey, I don't think that the Travelers fan base is country."

"Well, how can it be if we never sing it? I just like the words to the songs. They are real life."

"I know. I love it too, but right now, you are all about rock and roll. Besides, Lisa would pitch a fit about it. She already does when you sing your ballads."

Eddie frowned. "Why is it always about Lisa? She doesn't own us now that we're here."

"It's not only Lisa, baby, Reynolds Records are selling a product. The product is rock and roll."

"Fer now." Eddie grinned at Sonata.

The door opened to Lisa, Annie, Linda and Pamela.

"Hey there." Linda smiled.

"You are the early birds." Pamela joined in.

"Eddie hasn't slept since we landed." Sonata giggled.

"So, where is Mr. Hot Shot producer?" Lisa frowned as she plopped down on the couch.

She was coming down after a night of partying with some women she picked up in the hotel bar.

The door opened on cue and Lan Rivers entered followed by an entourage of three. His dashing good looks were only hindered by his arrogance. He was good and he knew it. He had a slew of Grammy's and a waiting list of the who's who in music begging him to produce them to prove it.

Lee came in followed by Kenny, Austin, and a photographer.

"Ladies it's magic time." Lee announced. "Lan they are all yours."

"Very well. I've gone over the single, and I want to do it on the first take. I want it raw, with an edge. Just get in there and play your asses off." Lan said.

Lisa stood up and moved to Lee. "Yer payin' this prick fer a one shot take?" She said quietly.

Lee looked at Lisa. She was right. But he had to have a huge name behind these girls.

"Have you come up with a song for the B side?" Kenny asked.

"First things first." Lan shot Kenny a look.

"Let's get you in there and take a shot at this."

The girls got up and started to wander into the studio.

"Excuse us a second." Eddie said as she dragged Sonata into the hall.

"What are you doing?" Sonata asked.

Eddie kissed Sonata. "Needed one fer luck."

Sonata giggled. "You don't need any luck. You're incredible Eddie."

Eddie looked at Sonata. "You ain't seen nothing yet. C'mon."

Eddie walked back in.

Sonata wondered what Eddie meant by that.

Lan had the Travelers in the studio singing an hour later. It only took them two takes to get it. Lee had a huge grin on his face. He knew that the Travelers were a positive cash flow for his company. He didn't care about what they did in their bedrooms, as long as they sold records.

"Lee, I think we have us a goldmine here." Lan smiled.

"I think you are right, Rivers." Lee leaned over to the PA mic. "Brilliant ladies." He turned to Sonata, "I gotta say this again Sonata, you were right on the money with them."

Sonata smiled. "I'm glad you approve."

"I want the video shot by the end of the week and on MTV by Monday."

"Lee, that's only four days." Sonata said.

Lee headed for the door then stopped and turned, "Amy will be here in thirty minutes."

He left followed by Kenny who had a smirk on his face.

"Four days…Wow, not a lot of time." Austin said.

"Yeah, but we can pull it off."

"Do you have the idea storyboarded?"

"Austin, we don't even have a video camera." Sonata stopped. That was it. She had all the footage she took of the Travelers in England, the photo shoot, and the concert. This might just work.

Everyone sat around as Lan played back the recording.

"Damn close to perfection I'd say. That hook on the chorus, is a killer." He grinned.

The girls all cheered. They too knew they had something special happening.

"Okay ladies, listen up. I don't want to put a damper on your day. This is an amazing cut, but Lee Reynolds wants a video in the can and on MTV by Monday. Amy Wilde who will be directing will be here any minute."

"In the can?" Eddie looked at Sonata.

"Completed, it means completed, you daft moron." Lisa snarled.

Eddie slid down in her chair.

"Look, we are all gonna be under a lot of pressure this week. I think it best for all of us to put our egos aside and try to get along. We don't need your attitude, to bring the rest of us down." Sonata looked at Lisa.

Lisa was about to say something when the vision walked into the room.

Amy Wilde. Tan, tall, boobs and bleached teeth. She was at the top of her game in video directing. She had won numerous Grammy's and video awards.

Lisa was smitten at once. She wanted her. She knew she had to have her and would do what ever it took to get her.

Sonata got up and hugged Amy.

"Sorry, I'm late, sweetie." Amy said as she hugged her friend.

"No problem. Amy Wilde I'd like you to meet the Travelers. This is Linda, Pamela, Annie, Lisa, and Eddie."

The ladies smiled and said their hellos as Amy shook their hands. Lisa held her hand and squeezed it tight.

"It's a pleasure to make yer acquaintance." Lisa said awkwardly.

Eddie rolled her eyes as she saw Annie frown.

"Well ladies, please go on with what you were doing. I just want to observe for a bit." Amy said as she sat down.

"You missed it Amy, two takes and out." Lan grinned.

"You still have it Lan." Amy winked.

Or so he thinks. Amy thought. *What a loser.* Amy remembered her brief affair with Lan Rivers. He was the "ME" king. Only cared what he looked liked, how he was in bed. Amy went off men for a year after Lan. She found that women were more about pleasing one another. Although, Amy didn't give up a good man when one came her way.

"So what do you think?"

Sonata's question brought Amy back from her thoughts.

"Come again?"

"Well, I thought if you didn't have an idea for the video, I have some stuff I shot of them in England."

"Great, I'll take a look at it. Did we get any film of them recording?"

"Yes." Austin said. "Lee brought in a camera man."

"Super. Sonata, did you bring yours?"

"Yeah." Sonata reached for her camera.

"Can we put them back in I want to get close-ups and such."

"Sure." Sonata said.

"Lan can you run a playback?"

"You got it sweet thing." Lan winked.

The girls got up and started to walk back into the studio.

"So, which one are you doing?" Amy looked at Sonata.

"What?" Sonata giggled, She could never keep a secret from Amy. "Not doing." She held up her ring. "Eddie and I are very much in love."

"Ah, you always have had a weakness for the drummers." Amy laughed.

"She's incredible, Amy. I am so lucky." She smiled at Eddie who was peeking out from behind the drums.

Amy smiled. She could tell her friend was in love. It was nice to see.

Lisa also saw the ring that Sonata had held up. She knew it had to be Eddie's mother's ring. She walked up to Eddie.

"You gave her yer mum's ring?"

"What's it to you, Lisa?" Eddie said sharply.

"Just don't want to see ya go down like a lead balloon."

"Lisa, yer just stewing in yer own juice aren't ya? Angry cause I never gave it to you?"

"Shut yer yap, Eddie." Lisa looked at her.

"You don't own me Lisa, so sod off." Eddie said.

Linda looked over and saw the two starting to get into it. She walked over, with Pamela and Annie, closely following behind her.

"Will you two stop! Yer gonna ruin this fer all of us."

"Piss off, Linny, this doesn't concern you." Lisa turned around.

"If it affects this group then it does concern me. Just leave Eddie alone, Lisa. You ave the one you wanted. Let her be happy fer once."

Lisa started to laugh. "Can't you see she's got a foot in both camps? She wants a part of the Travelers. Were just big dollar signs to her. Eddie's just her meal ticket, and she's too daft to see it." Lisa walked over to her keyboards.

The others walked back to their instruments.

"What was that about?" Amy asked Sonata.

"I have a feeling that Lisa O'Brien was up to her usual tricks again."

"She's a player?" Amy smiled.

"It's a long story, I'll tell you sometime, right now we have a video to shoot."

After three hours the girls finally had a lunch break. Lee had Wolfgang Puck cater a five-course lunch, with all the works. Lisa downed three beers and went off with Annie to do some lines. The others sat around and got to know Amy and Lan better.

"Lies all lies." Sonata laughed.

Eddie watched as Sonata smiled. She was so beautiful.

"This food is wonderful." Pamela said.

"I know I stuffed me self." Linda said.

"Ah, Lan, can I ask you a question?" Eddie said.

"Anything." He said as he ate the last bite of his smoked salmon pizza.

"Are you lookin' to fill the flip side of this single?"

"Well, we were thinking of adding two other versions, why you got something?"

"As a matter of fact, yeah."

"Lay it on me."

Eddie jumped up and looked at Sonata, she grinned. She walked in and picked up a guitar. She motioned to Linda and Pamela to come join her. She pulled out two pieces of paper and handed it to them. Pamela got behind the keyboards, and Linda grabbed her bass. Eddie gave them a four count.

Sonata's mouth dropped as Eddie started to sing her song.

Amy grabbed the camera and started to film.

"Holy shit, this is incredible." Lan said.

Lisa and Annie walked in as Eddie finished the song.

Sonata had tears in her eyes. It was incredible. Eddie took her song and turned it into a work of art.

"What the fuck is this?" Lisa growled.

"It's a hit! A certified grade A number one with a bullet flippin hit." Lan said.

"Where did that come from?" Linda asked.

"Sonata wrote it. I just kind of rearranged it."

"It's awesome Eddie." Pamela added.

Eddie smiled and looked at Sonata.

"I gotta call Lee!" Austin said.

Sonata came into the studio and hugged Eddie.

"Yer not angry?" Eddie looked into Sonata's eyes.

"Angry, oh sweetie it was beautiful." She kissed Eddie.

"Well, you wrote it, luv."

"No Eddie, this was all you. I had an emotional mess on paper, you turned it into something wonderful."

"Get a jist of Lisa, I think her head is gonna explode." Linda laughed.

"Yer not gonna release that piece of fluffy crap." Lisa looked at Lan.

"You should be proud, this song is gonna make you guys super stars!" Lan said.

"This is bullshit!" Lisa said as she walked into the studio.

"What the fuck do you think yer doing Eddie?" Lisa demanded.

"We needed another song, I had one…We had one." She smiled and took Sonata's hand.

"We'll just see about this." Lisa said. "C'mon Annie." Lisa stormed off.

Annie looked at the others. "She's just tired. It was nice Eddie." She said, then turned and left.

"Well, that went over well." Linda smiled.

"Lee's on his way back" Austin's voice said over the intercom.

"Great." Sonata frowned. This was not what she wanted to happen. Lisa would some how poison Lee's mind and she would be sidelined from the Travelers for good.

"Did I do something wrong?" Eddie asked as she pulled Sonata over to the corner.

"No…It's just…."

"Don't worry about Lisa, luv, I will tell Lee the truth. I found yer song. You didn't pawn it off on me."

Sonata smiled. "I know. I just don't want to blow this for you. The last thing you all need is tension from Lisa and me."

"She'll get over it. She always does. Just throw her a party and invite a few cute birds, she'll be back to herself in no time." Eddie tried to make light of the situation.

Sonata didn't know what to think. She was close to just stepping out. She loved her job. She worked so hard to get where she was. She was also madly in love with the tall, strong drummer who stood in front of her. She just didn't know how long she could stand it until she was ripped apart at the seams.

❈   ❈   ❈

After careful consideration, Lee chose to release "Time Will Tell". He felt that it was best to keep his new wonder group happy, and Lisa wasn't happy. He put "If You Only Knew" as the B-side. He figured whichever song the public embraced, would be a major hit, which meant major money. Lee loved money. Money bought Lee the kind of happiness he had always wanted. Women and drugs. Lots of both. He knew he was old, and the young wannabe starlets who threw themselves at him were only there for the money. But Lee didn't seem to care. That was Hollywood. Everyone was out to use everyone else. Lee was just one of the many who liked to play the game.

"Time Will Tell" took off like a rocket. It soared up the charts and became the number one single on all the major charts. MTV and VH1 had the video on heavy rotation, and was on at least every half hour on the biggest radio stations.

The girls were in high demand. They quickly made their way to the radio stations, and were featured on Entertainment Today, and Back Stage Pass. Sonata couldn't get them booked fast enough. There was no time to rest, and before anyone knew it, three months had passed. The girls were in New York to do their first live performance. A spot on the Grammy Awards, broadcast live from Radio City Music Hall. It was also the first time an artist was invited to play that wasn't nominated.

They were sent first class and had suites at the Waldorf. It was all too much for the girls to handle.

"This is sheer madness." Linda said as their limo pulled up at the hotel.

"We are supposed to go in around the back, please." Sonata told the driver.

"Why?" Eddie asked. "There is a lot waitin' for us out front."

"Eddie, they will mob you and the hotel just doesn't have the security to ensure your safety."

"That doesn't seem fair." Eddie said.

"Welcome to yer new life, Eddie." Lisa laughed. "There ain't nothing fair in this business. Get that through yer daft head. You keep them at bay, you be elusive and they'll want more. Ya give them what they want the drop yer arse the next day."

"They just want to wish us well, where's the harm in that?" Pamela asked.

"There's nothing wrong with it." Sonata said. "But, if they can't protect you, then we can't take that chance. Lee has arranged for bodyguards for you. They will meet us in the hotel, and stay with us until we leave the day after tomorrow."

"Body guards? That's wild." Annie chuckled.

"I ave dibs on the cute bird." Lisa said.

"Body guards ain't cute." Linda said.

"Sod off." Lisa shot Linda a look.

"Ok, before this goes any further, let me give you your itinerary." Sonata passed out a single sheet of paper to each. We have three hours to settle in and then we will be taken to the hall for rehearsal. There is a banquet tonight that you have been invited to. No matter what anyone asks, the Travelers are not allowed to perform at this banquet. Our premiere is on the awards show. If we sing before, we are in violation of our contract. Tomorrow you will have a rehearsal at noon, make up and hair is at three at the hotel. You will be driven to the red carpet. You are the last act to play after Jennifer Lopez."

"Jennifer Lopez?" Lisa smiled. "Now there is a nice piece of ass."

"If you want to do anything or go anywhere, please call me so we can arrange the limo and your body guard. But from the looks of things, you will only have about two hours of down time."

"Only two?" Annie asked.

"They have us doing interviews at three radio stations, MTV and the local news." Sonata said. "Welcome to show biz."

The girl's barely had time to change before they were whisked off to rehearsals. Everyone was making a big fuss over the girls, and Lisa loved every second of it. Being catered to quickly became Lisa's number one priority. What a stroke of luck for her to be standing next to Lee Reynolds when he told Sonata to *"See that these girls get anything their hearts desired."*

Radio City was huge. It was the biggest venue the Travelers had ever played, let alone had ever seen.

"This place is enormous." Eddie said as she looked around. "It makes me head spin."

"Kind of gives me the willies that we're gonna play here." Pamela said.

"C'mon guys, this is what you worked for. After tomorrow the world will know about you, not that they don't already, but you will have arrived." Sonata said. "Just be yourself and enjoy the ride."

"Is that an invitation, luv?" Lisa said softly as she started to walk by. "Cause if it is, I may just take you up on it." She traced Sonata's arm with her finger.

Sonata's skin crawled. The thought of Lisa touching her made her sick to her stomach.

Eddie caught her uneasiness. "You ok, luv?" She asked.

"Ladies! Ladies! Ladies!" A feminine male voice shouted. "Welcome, Travelers. I'm your director, Kendall Raines. We don't have much time. Dressing room six is yours. You are the last performers of the evening, following Ms. Jennifer Lopez. You will sit there." He pointed to the second row of empty chairs that had a cardboard sign with their name on it. "Once you walk up the Red, you are to come backstage. Brandy will pick you up...Where is that girl?" He said looking around.

Eddie chuckled at the director's feminine actions.

"Brandy! Brandy!

A young slender blonde came out from backstage. She was carrying a clipboard. Her hair was neatly pulled into a ponytail. She had on a headset, hooked up to a walkie-talkie, and was talking on the cell phone.

"Yes, Kendall." Brandy said as she continued to talk on the phone.

"This is Brandy. She will meet you at the entrance...Not talking on the phone I hope."

Brandy said goodbye and hung up. "Sorry...Hi." She smiled, as she held out her hand to the girls. She shook each one's hand.

"Sonata Williams. I believe we spoke on the phone?"

"Oh yes, of course. It's a pleasure to meet you all. Shall we get started? Brandy smiled and winked at Linda. Pamela caught it.

"Now, if you'll follow me..." She walked off followed by Sonata, Lisa, and Annie.

"What the bloody hell was that about?" Pamela asked.

"Here in the States, I think they call it putting the make on ya." Eddie teased.

"Yeah, well, I call it putting my boot in yer arse, if ya don't leave me woman be!" Pamela looked at Linda.

"I didn't say a word. It's probably just a twitch or something." Linda said as they started to catch up with the others.

"I'll twitch that head right off her body."

Linda and Eddie laughed.

"No worries, luv...She's much too young fer me...besides, she's not you." Linda winked at Pamela, and kissed her on the cheek.

Pamela smiled. She was so lucky to have Linda in her life.

Brandy was opening the dressing room when the others walked up.

"If you have a copy of your rider, I'll see to it that everything you want is in order for tomorrow."

"Anything we want?" Lisa winked at Brandy.

Brandy blushed. She had been thrilled since she heard the Travelers would be performing on the show. She became an instant fan from the moment she heard them on the radio. "Ah, within reason." she said to Lisa, flirting back.

Annie walked up and took Lisa's hand. She had had just about enough of all these women throwing themselves at Lisa. Great sex or not, Annie wanted what Pamela and Linda, and now what Eddie and Sonata had.

"Ok then…if you'll follow me I will show you where you can rehearse."

Annie pulled Lisa back, as the others followed Brandy.

"What now?" Lisa growled.

"Lisa, I'm tired of the bullshit."

"What bullshit?"

"All this flirting an crap. I want us to be together."

"We are, ya silly goose." Lisa chuckled.

"No Lisa, I want it to be like them. No one else, just us two." Annie looked into Lisa's eyes.

"Annie you knew goin' in that I ave to have me women." She took Annie in her arms. "Yer still me number one." She kissed Annie.

"Am I? I don't see no ring on me finger."

"That's just material crap. If you want a ring Annie, we'll go an get ya one."

"Don't you get it?" Annie's voice cracked.

Lisa got it loud and clear. She knew she couldn't buy much more time.

"C'mon Annie, we'll talk about this later. You're bringin me down."

Lisa walked out.

Tears started to roll down Annie's eyes.

There was a knock at the door. She quickly tried to dry her tears.

"Yes." she said.

Eddie opened the door and slowly walked in.

"They sent me to fetch ya. You ok?"

"Eddie, can I ask ya something?"

"Sure." Eddie smiled and handed her a tissue.

"How did you and Lisa…. make it happen?"

"I'm not sure I know what yer getting at."

"You were with Lisa fer a long time. How did you make it work with her?"

"Annie, I didn't make anything work. I almost died trying. Lisa is selfish."

"I know she luvs me. She says she does."

Eddie rolled up her sleeve and showed Annie the scar on her arm. "Lisa told me she luvd me too. Then she cut me with a knife. That ain't luv. Look, I like ya, Annie, but you need to get away from her. She will bring you down."

Annie looked at Eddie. Why couldn't she have found her? She was so kind and so special. She slowly walked over to Eddie and hugged her "Thanks, Eddie." She smiled. "I can get her to change, you'll see. I'd bet my life on it."

Eddie tried to smile. She only hoped that Annie would come to her senses before that bet was cashed in.

"Hey, where are you two?" Sonata's voice came from the hallway.

Eddie reached for Annie's cheek and whipped away a tear.

Annie closed her eyes. Why couldn't Lisa be more like Eddie?

Sonata walked in. "There you are. They're waiting for you to rehearse."

"We're on our way." Eddie smiled at Annie.

"Yeah, we are." Annie smiled and walked out the door.

"Is she ok?" Sonata asked.

"Fer now. C'mon luv, I don't want me A and R gal getting upset with me, cause I'm late fer rehearsal."

Sonata laughed. She kissed Eddie.

"Yer tryin' to make me late huh?" Eddie took Sonata in her arms.

"I miss those lips…among other things." She giggled.

"I know we're together everyday, but I feel like I still don't get see ya."

"I told you things would be different. That's why-."

"Sssh…not another word. Just enjoy the moment."

She kissed Sonata deeply and hugged her tight. She agreed that things were different. They were so busy during the day, and too exhausted at night. They hadn't had a moment to themselves since their moonlit walk on the beach.

"Whatta' you say, we take a little holiday after this?" Eddie said.

"You wish, sweetie. After the world sees you tomorrow, you'll be lucky to have time to go to the bathroom." She kissed Eddie again. "C'mon, we better get going."

Eddie frowned. This was after all, exactly what she wanted.

Sonata was right, Eddie thought as the huge crowd of industry members and peers stood before them in a thunderous ovation.

The Travelers were a smash!

Lisa was mesmerized. She held them in the palm of her hand.

When the applause started to die down the girls ran from the stage and into their dressing room.

"Did you see em?" Pamela asked.

"What a rush." Annie added.

"Think we're a hit." Linda kissed Pamela.

"Did you see who was out there?" Lisa said.

"I saw Aerosmith." Linda smiled.

"Elton and Aretha in the front row! I nearly pissed meself!" Pamela laughed.

"Did you see Melissa? What a hot little number she is." Lisa smiled. "I'd like to ave a go at that."

"You and every other lesbian in the free world." Linda shot back.

"Hey Eddie? Wasn't that your country singer gal you like out there? You know the redhead Judd bird." Annie said.

"Was she? I didn't notice." Eddie half smiled.

She did in fact notice Wynonna Judd sitting there, rocking out to their song, and some of her other favorite singers too. She also noticed that Sonata wasn't sitting out in the crowd. She had suddenly disappeared.

There was a knock at the door. Linda opened it.

"There are my girls!" Lee Reynolds's booming voice came through the door. "You were brilliant ladies, simply brilliant. I expect you all to be back here next year receiving an award your self!"

"Thank you sir." Pamela said.

"No, thank *you*." Lee smiled.

"What brings the likes of you to New York, Lee?" Lisa asked.

"Well ladies I am here to escort my favorite group to a wonderful party. A party Reynolds's records is holding in your honor.

"A party fer us?" Annie asked.

"Awesome!" Lisa grinned.

"Get used to it ladies, this is one of many." Lee walked to the door. I'll let you change and I'll be right outside."

"Ah Mr. R? Ave ya seen Sonata?" Eddie asked.

"I sent her ahead Eddie. This party is going to be huge. She was needed there…Oh, she did ask me to give you this." He pulled out an envelope from his jacket and handed it to Eddie. "Don't be long." He smiled and closed the door behind him.

The girls started to change; Eddie sat down and opened the note.

❧

My dear sweetheart Eddie. I am so sorry that I am not there to celebrate your shining moment. Though you didn't see me out in the audience I did see you from the side of the stage. As always, my love, you were incredible. If we don't get a chance to spend time together at the party, let's save a little time afterwards, for us! (Grin)

I love you, Eddie.... Always yours. Sonata.

Eddie smiled as she fingered the letter. Here she slept next to the woman every night and she felt so distant.

"Move yer bum Eddie." Linda said. "Lee doesn't want us to dottle."

"Ok, I just need to change me shirt." Eddie jumped up and went to change.

The party was lavish, to say the least. There were posters of all the Reynolds's Records artists including a huge banner of the Travelers. The movers and shakers were roaming about, making deals, as well as the not so moving crashers who were stunned at all of music's elite, gathered in the ballroom at the Waldorf.

Eddie was stunned as she walked in and saw the huge banner that bared her resemblance. She peered over her sunglasses, and grinned. She looked around the room for Sonata. How could anyone find anything in this mass of bodies. As soon as the huge crowd realized who had walked in, they erupted into applause.

The Travelers waved and smiled. Lee was grinning ear to ear.

Sonata heard the applause and knew who it was for. She wanted so badly to go over and just hug Eddie.

"Ladies, enjoy this night." Lee said. "Tonight belongs to you!"

Eddie carefully sifted through the partygoers and well wishers. She signed autographs, and posed for photos. Three women stuffed their phone numbers in her hand.

"Ms. Sutcliffe? May I have your autograph?" The sultry voice said behind Eddie.

Eddie turned around with her pen in hand. She smiled as she saw Sonata standing in front of her. "There you are!" Eddie grabbed the woman and held her tight.

"Sorry, Eddie, but Lee sent me on a wild goose chase." Sonata said.

"Is there somewhere we can go and have a moment fer ourselves?" Eddie looked at Sonata.

"I'll see what I can do, hun."

"Don't see, just do! Meet me in the loo in ten minutes." Eddie grinned.

"You're crazy." Sonata giggled.

"You keep saying that. I'm starting to believe it." She laughed.

"Well, well, well." Kenny came up behind Sonata. "I got to give you credit Williams, for no notice, you pulled this off rather nicely."

"Thanks." Sonata said smugly.

"Nice job you did tonight, Eddie. You gals should be proud."

"Thank you."

"Don't thank me. We have plans to keep you in the public eye for at least the next year. Like Lee said, enjoy tonight." He winked at Sonata.

"What does he mean?" Eddie looked at Sonata.

"It means that what happened to us tonight, is going to be the norm." She hugged Eddie. "I'll see you in ten." She kissed Eddie on the cheek and walked away.

Linda and Pamela walked up. "This is grand isn't it?" Pamela asked.

"Yeah, grand." Eddie said.

"What's eaten you?" Linda said.

"I don't quite know, I just know I don't like it."

"What the devil are you talking about Sutcliffe?"

"Well sense that day at the recording studio, it just seems…I dunno."

"Yer not making since Eddie." Pamela giggled.

"Haven't you noticed it? Lee is always around Lisa."

"Naw, more like Lisa always has her lips on Lee's arse!" Linda laughed.

Eddie saw Sonata as she walked into the ladies room. "Excuse me, I need to use the loo."

She walked over to the restroom, stopping along the way to sign more autographs. She looked around and walked in.

"Did you see the keyboard player?" A girl asked her friend as she re-applied her lip-gloss.

"She so wants you! But the drummer…She is hot!" She giggled.

Eddie came around the corner, scaring the two girls when they realized who was standing before them.

"Evenin'." Eddie smiled.

The girls giggled with delight.

Eddie signed some things for them and waved as they left the restroom. She looked around to see if there was anyone else. "Sonata?" She whispered.

"In here." Sonata called to her.

The stall door opened. Eddie slipped in and locked the door.

"Oh my God, that drummer!" Sonata giggled, like the fan.

Eddie grabbed Sonata and kissed her hard. "God, I've missed you." She said as she came up for a breath, and then went on to kiss Sonata's neck.

"I missed you too. I hate this Eddie." Sonata brought Eddie's face back to her so she could kiss her again. "I feel like I am sneaking around to see my own partner."

"I know luv. We will work it out." Eddie started to knead Sonata's breast.

The door opened as more guests started to use the bathroom.

Sonata put her finger to her lips.

Eddie kissed her again.

"I need to go." She whispered in Eddie's ear.

"No more work. This is yer party too. You need to enjoy it." Eddie whispered back."

Sonata smiled. It sure didn't seem like it.

Lisa took the intoxicating white powder quickly into her nose. "Good shit, Lee," she laughed.

"Only the best for my gals." Lee winked.

Lisa looked around. She was sitting in the middle of the penthouse suite at the Waldorf, doing a line with her boss and now in the company of five beautiful women.

"Lisa, I want to thank you for making me an extremely wealthy man." He chuckled.

"Yer welcome. Here's ta more…much more." She picked up her gin and tonic and toasted Lee.

"I'd like to show my appreciation to you and the girls."

"Oh yeah?" Lisa grinned.

"Yes, when we get home, there will be a brand new Porsche waiting for each and every one of you."

"Sod a dog!" Lisa shouted. "That's fuckin' great, Lee."

"Well, you scratch my back and I'll scratch yours." He grinned.

"Now, what could I possibly do fer ya?"

Lee moved to the couch and sat next to Lisa. "What if I told you that through that door, there were four beautiful women all waiting to fuck your brains out?"

Lisa grinned. "Now yer talkin'…But what's in it fer ya?"

"Annie." Lee grinned.

"Annie?" Lisa laughed. "What could you possibly want with her?"

Lee raised his eyebrows and winked.

What a sick pervert. Lisa thought. Annie wouldn't touch him with a ten-foot pole. Still she didn't want to disappoint her boss. "We'll see what we can do, Lee."

CHAPTER 8

The next six months were hectic.

The new Travelers' CD debuted at number one. Their second single "If You Only Knew," was a major hit. The song went gold in three days time. It crossed over to the adult contemporary market and was having air play on country radio.

Sonata enjoyed her minor moment in the spotlight. She had always dreamed of writing a number one hit, and now it had come true.

Eddie had claimed Sonata's box of songs and promised her there were more hits to come.

The girls quickly started spending some of their newfound wealth.

Lisa and Annie bought a sprawling mansion in Beverly Hills. Lisa loved the fact that her neighbor was none other than Mr. Playboy himself, Hugh Hefner. She bought herself a Hummer and a diamond ring for Annie. She had to keep her in tow and the ring was the easiest way she knew how.

Annie was thrilled. She finally got the commitment from Lisa. She also happily agreed to merge their bank accounts.

Linda and Pamela bought a nice home over looking the ocean in Malibu. They flew Oliver out, and found a wonderful tutor and nanny. He would study at home and out on the road.

In four weeks, the Travelers were going to embark on a four and a half month major world tour. Amy Wilde was brought back on board to film the documentary for a DVD release, just after the tour was completed.

Lisa was thrilled at the news. She didn't have any time to try to get to know Amy, the way she wanted to. This time she would be with them on the road, and Lisa vowed to also have her in her bed.

After Sonata's endless badgering, Lee agreed to give the girls a week off to do absolutely nothing. It was a great release to get ready for their opening night at the spot that brought them to the world, the Radio City Music Hall.

Sonata and Eddie decided to keep the beach house in Venice and keep things simple. To them it was about love, not the material things that destroyed so many of the great entertainers before them.

"Here's to me favorite songwriter." Eddie smiled as she held up her glass.

"And here's to my favorite singer and drummer."

"And lover?" Eddie grinned.

"My only lover." Sonata smiled. "Because, after having been loved by Eddie Sutcliffe, there could be no other."

They clinked their glasses.

"I like that." Eddie said.

"Oh, do you?" Sonata said teasingly.

Eddie was about to say something when the waiter came up.

"How are you ladies doing?"

Better if you would get lost! Sonata thought.

"Did we save room for dessert?"

Sonata looked at Eddie and licked her lips.

"Ah, I always 'ave room for dessert, but I think I'd better wait till I get home, before I partake in it." Eddie didn't take her eyes off Sonata.

"That will be all, thanks." Sonata said.

The waiter could feel the electricity that the two women were creating.

"Here's your bill. I'll take it up when you're ready." He offered.

"We're ready now." Eddie winked at Sonata.

Not even bothering to look at the check, Eddie pulled out two one hundred dollar bills. She handed it to the waiter. "That should cover it."

The waiter beamed. "Thanks, Ms. Sutcliffe."

The recognition of her name being said brought her back from her thoughts.

"You know who I am, eh?"

"Who doesn't? The Travelers are my favorite. I could get in a lot of trouble for asking, but can I get an autograph?" The waiter asked as he held out a cocktail napkin.

"Absolutely." Eddie smiled, as she looked up at the waiter's name badge. "Here you go, Mark."

"Thank you so much I love your new single." He added.

"Oh yeah? Well there's the beautiful lady who wrote it." She winked at Sonata.

"Really? Oh man you are awesome. Would you sign it too?"

Sonata laughed. "Sure." Sonata signed the napkin.

"Thank you." Mark smiled.

"It's a pleasure." Eddie smiled. She took Sonata's hand and started to walk away.

The valet quickly brought their car around, as Eddie continued to sign autographs.

Eddie walked to the driver's side and opened the door for Sonata. Then ran around and got in.

"Thank you for dinner." Sonata said.

"Thank you for dessert." Eddie chuckled. She slowly moved her hand to Sonata's thigh.

"Your gonna make me crash." Sonata giggled.

"I plan on making you do more than that." Eddie said as she unbuckled her seatbelt. She leaned across the car to steal a kiss from Sonata.

"I'm glad we have some alone time, finally." Sonata said.

"Hmmm…" Was all Eddie said as she slowly started to kiss Sonata's neck, and nibbled on her ear.

Sonata could feel herself aching. She missed not having Eddie with her.

Eddie slowly started to slide her hand under Sonata's skirt.

"Hey now." Sonata swerved the car.

"That ain't hay." Eddie smiled as she could feel her wetness. "I think you need to hurry home though." She whispered into Sonata's ear.

Sonata completely agreed.

They pulled up to the house ten minutes later. Sonata turned the car off and kissed Eddie long and passionately.

"We need to get inside." Eddie said.

Sonata laughed as she opened the car door.

They quickly made it to the front door, where Eddie took Sonata in her arms and kissed her.

Sonata fogged over and dropped the keys.

Eddie chuckled as she picked them up and quickly opened the door.

Sonata reached for the light, but Eddie stopped her.

Eddie brought Sonata close to her and held her tight. No words were exchanged, but a lot was being said to Sonata. She felt the need in Eddie's embrace.

"Oh, how I want you." Eddie's raspy voice echoed into Sonata. She kissed her.

Eddie led Sonata into the bedroom. They carefully started to undress each other, stopping here and there to kiss one another.

"I love you." Sonata said.

Eddie pulled Sonata down on the bed, then on top of her. "Promise you'll never leave me, Sonata" Eddie said as the touch of their bodies together started to make Eddie's temperature rise.

"I promise, I'm not going anywhere." Sonata said as she kissed Eddie.

Sonata started to caress the length of Eddie's side.

Eddie moaned as goose bumps took over the top layer of her skin.

Sonata started to make her way down in between Eddie's thighs.

Eddie trembled with delight. She reveled in the love she made with Sonata. It was so special and so personal, unlike anything Eddie had ever known.

Just as Sonata slid her finger deep into her lover, there was a knock at the door.

"Sod it!" Eddie said as they both came to reality.

"Who could that be?" Sonata asked.

"Just lie still luv, they'll leave.

The knocking turned to pounding.

"I don't think so." Sonata got up and put on a robe. She leaned over and kissed Eddie. "Hold that thought," she said.

Sonata turned on the light at the entry hall, and looked through the peephole. "Oh my God, Eddie!" she hollered.

Eddie jumped out of bed and found her sweats and a t-shirt. She quickly threw them on.

Sonata opened the door. There stood Karli, bloody and cut up, her clothes torn.

"Help me." She mumbled and fell into the house.

Eddie came from the bedroom "What the…?"

"It's the cab driver, Karli. She's hurt. Help me get her inside."

They worked together slowly, bringing Karli to the sofa.

Eddie reached for the phone.

"What are you doing?" Sonata looked at her.

"Calling 911. She needs help."

"You can't. It will be all over the news."

"We can't just leave her be."

After an hour, Karli came to. She looked around.

"Karli…it's Sonata and Eddie…you're safe. Eddie said.

Karli tried to smile.

"Do you need to see a doctor?" Sonata asked.

Karli mumbled again then drifted off.

"She'll be ok." Eddie said.

"No Eddie, she needs medical attention. She keeps falling in and out of consciousness."

"Then we'll take her." Eddie stood up.

Sonata stopped. "Once the press gets a hold of this…"

"Sod them, she needs our help luv, and we're the only ones she has."

Sonata smiled. "I'll call ahead." She reached for the phone.

Eddie looked out the window, a crowd had gathered outside of the hospital. Lee had called three times over different reports of Eddie being stabbed, shot, and hit by car. It took Eddie herself ten minutes to convince Lee that she was fine.

Sonata called Linda and Pamela, to assure them that everything was ok. Linda said she would pass the news on to the others.

She came back into the waiting room and saw Eddie looking out the window. She came up behind her and softly put her hands on Eddie's shoulders.

"You were right on the money Sonata." Eddie said.

"It's like a bunch of sharks swimming around its prey. They wait for them to be hurt, then go in for the kill…Linda said it's on every channel."

Eddie took Sonata's hand and gently kissed it. "I'm so glad you are on this journey with me. I wouldn't be able to make it without you."

"Eddie…I wanted to talk to you about something." Sonata said.

Eddie turned around. Just as Sonata was about to say something, a handsome, rugged doctor entered.

"Excuse me." he smiled, as he realized who he was standing in front of. "I have some news on your friend."

"Is she ok?" Eddie stood up.

The doctor sighed. "Why don't we sit down." He looked at both of the ladies.

Sonata and Eddie took a seat.

"Karli was assaulted. She also has a concussion, a broken ankle, and some severe lacerations on her back."

"Was she…raped?" Sonata choked out.

"From the looks of it, I'd say attempted. We used the rape kit and found some samples on her thigh and stomach. We are waiting for the results, to confirm penetration." He looked at the ladies. "She's a tuff little cookie though." he smiled.

"Is she awake? Can we see her?" Eddie asked.

"She is in and out still, and the fact that you are not family, I shouldn't. But she does keep asking for you...so follow me."

Eddie and Sonata followed the doctor across the hall and into Karli's room.

"Karli?" The doctor's soothing low voice filled the room. "You have company."

Karli opened her eyes and struggled to focus. She smiled. "Eddie, Sonata...you're here."

"Where else would we be?" Eddie moved to her side.

The head nurse came into the room and pulled the doctor to the side. She started whispering. Sonata looked as the doctor motioned to her.

"You two visit. I'll be right back." Sonata excused herself and followed the doctor and the nurse into the hall.

"Is there a problem?" she asked.

"Yes, a big one." The head nurse said. "Your friend has no insurance, therefore your friend has to go."

"What?" Sonata looked at the nurse.

"We need the bed for paying customers."

"You can't just toss her out...My God, where is your compassion?"

Eddie walked out. "Problem here luv?"

"Karli doesn't have insurance, therefore the warden here says she has to go." Sonata said mimicking the nurse.

"Is that all?" Eddie looked at the nurse. "I'll take care of all the bills, problem solved." She took Sonata's hand and led her back into the room.

It was around one in the afternoon when the crowd outside reached a feverish pitch. The hospital administrator asked Eddie if she would please make a statement so the crowds would disperse.

Eddie happily agreed to.

Sonata told Eddie what she needed to do and how to handle everything.

"I'll follow yer lead me lady." She smiled at Sonata.

Security had all the media gather around the back of the hospital, where a podium was set up. Every news reporter fought for the perfect microphone position.

Sonata and Eddie walked out.

Eddie stood just behind Sonata, her sunglasses on.

"Hi. First of all we want to thank you all, and especially the fans of the Travelers for their concerns over Eddie Sutcliffe. As you are aware, there were some rather disturbing reports of the possibility of Eddie's demise. As you can see she is standing right behind me, in one piece and perfect condition. She would now like to make a brief statement…Thank you."

Eddie grinned at Sonata as she moved to the podium.

"Thanks, Sonata…Ah, I just want to let all the fans know that I am ok. I as well as all of the Travelers appreciate your loyalty and concern. A friend of ours was in an accident last night, and she was apparently mistaken fer me. Sorry about the frenzy it caused you, and fer all of you who waited all night out here, I thank you. 'Ave a good day, and thanks." Eddie smiled as the camera's flashes went off from every direction.

"Well, that should do the trick" Eddie said as they walked back inside.

Sonata was about to say something when her phone rang. "Hi, Lee…what…ok, ok…will do." She turned her phone off. "Lee said he loves you, you are awesome, and you are incredible."

"That's only because of you, luv." Eddie said.

"Well, Lee doesn't see it that way…Can we go somewhere and talk?"

"Sure."

"Excuse me, Miss Sutcliffe?" A woman's voice came up to her.

Eddie turned around. A stunning black woman about forty years old smiled at her.

"Yes?" Eddie smiled back.

"Hi, I am Monica St. Regis. I am head of the children's cancer center."

"It's a pleasure." Eddie shook her hand.

"Don't say that until you have heard what I am about to ask. I am sorry to inconvenience you, with your friend in the hospital, but I wondered if you may have a few spare moments and maybe visit the children?"

Eddie looked at Sonata, who smiled at her.

"We'd love to." Eddie said. "I just need to spend some time with me friend first."

"Absolutely." Monica smiled "Thank you so much. Both of you. We're on the fifth floor, all the way to the back.

"We'll be there." Eddie smiled, as she watched the beautiful woman walk away. "Ok, me luv, what did you want to tell me?" She said through a yawn.

Sonata looked at Eddie. She hadn't had a decent night's sleep since she came to America. It was all go go go. "It can wait," she said.

"You sure?"

"Yes."

"You know, I was thinkin' that we should get the rest of the band here. It would be nice fer the kids an all."

"Yeah, Lee would love the publicity. Hey, I bet I can get Austin to run over some CD's, posters and photos."

"Perfect." Eddie smiled.

Sonata called Lee with their idea. Lee thought it was a stroke of genius.

Eddie had no problem convincing the girls to come down, all were game except Lisa. Like always, she would be the hard sell. She bitched and moaned about it, but finally agreed to come down too.

Eddie sat next to Karli, she reminded her so much of herself. She remembered the first time that Stuart hurt her. The memory made her skin crawl.

Karli opened her eyes and groggily looked around. "Eddie, you're still here." she smiled.

"How ya feeling?"

"I'll be ok...I fought him off this time Eddie...I really did." She started to cry.

"Who did this to you Karli?" Eddie asked as she handed her a tissue.

Karli was about to say, as there was a knock at the door.

A mousy looking man limped in. He was wearing sunglasses, and sweating.

"Can I help ya?" Eddie asked, a bit on guard.

"Who are you?" he looked at Eddie.

"I think it's the likes of you that should be answering that question."

"I'm her uncle."

It hit Eddie over the head like a brick. She re-processed what Karli had just said. *I fought him off this time....* She looked over at Karli, who was shaking. Tears streaming from her eyes. She turned and looked at the sweaty man. He had scratches on his hands and neck. "You bastard! You did this to her!" Eddie said, trying to hold herself back.

"I don't know who you are, or what you think you know, but if you don't leave, I'm going to call the police."

"Let's just ave you do that, and ya can tell em what ya been doing to Karli!"

The man lunged forward, taking a swing at Eddie.

Eddie was much too fast for him and stepped out of the way.

He tried to regain his balance.

Eddie kneed him in the crotch, sending him straight to the floor, wracked in pain.

Karli franticly pushed the nurse's call button.

"Want some more you pathetic excuse for a man."

She kicked him in the stomach just as Sonata walked in the room followed by the nurse.

"Oh my God, Eddie! What are you doing?" Sonata hollered.

"It's this piece of shit, who did this to Karli."

"I'll get security." The nurse said and ran out.

Sonata saw the rage in Eddie's eyes.

"C'mon ya big hot shot, get up so I can kick yer arse some more!"

"Get away from me!" The man yelled.

Eddie got down on the floor and grabbed the man by his hair. "You listen good you piece of shit. You ever come near Karli again; I'll come find ya. If it turns out ya did what we think ya did, you're gonna wish ta hell you never had when I get done with ya." She shoved the man's head back down on to the floor.

A security guard came running in, followed by Karli's doctor and the nurse.

"Here's the man I think you'll be wantin' to talk to." Eddie looked at the doctor.

The security guard grabbed the man and took him out.

"I think we may need to have a security guard posted outside until Karli is released."

"Not a problem, but I can assure you he won't be around." The doctor checked Karli. He wrote some notes in her chart then walked out followed by the nurse.

Karli smiled as Eddie took her hand.

"He won't be back, Karli. And I promise you, no one will ever hurt you again."

Tears of relief started to pour from Karli's eyes. "Thank you…Thank you both."

"Yer welcome, kiddo." Eddie said. She looked at Sonata. "Can I talk to you fer a moment, luv?"

"Sure." Sonata said, still stunned over what just happened.

"You rest, we'll be back in a bit." Eddie took Sonata's hand and led her out of the room. They walked down to the lounge. Eddie was happy it was empty. She closed the door behind them.

"I need to ask you something." Eddie said seriously.

Sonata took a seat, not sure what to expect.

"Ok…Please don't go sayin' no until ya hear me out."

"Alright." Sonata agreed.

Eddie sat next to Sonata and took her hand. "Ya know how much I luv ya…and everything you've done fer us. You have the biggest heart of anyone I know…I just wondered if maybe you have room in yer heart fer one more?"

Sonata looked at Eddie.

"It's Karli…I want her to come live with us."

"What?" Sonata said surprised.

"I thought about it all night, Sonata. It's the only thing that makes sense."

"It does?"

"Yeah, you've been on me case about getting an assistant, and Karli could be her. I also need a drum tech fer me set ups, this way I get a two fer one."

"Eddie…I don't know. That's a lot of responsibility."

"She's young, but not that young."

"And you want her to live with us?" Sonata looked at Eddie.

"Yes."

"Sweetie, our house isn't that big to begin with. We would be all on top of one another. Plus, I am sure she has her own life, friends, a boyfriend, her band. They would be over all the time."

"Look, we'll buy a bigger home. We'll live on one side, Karli can have the other. She's a good kid Sonata, and if that asshole was all she had, then she has nothing. I can't live with me self knowin' we turned her away."

Sonata stood up. "I don't know about this, Eddie."

"Please luv. Think about it before ya say no…. Please."

Sonata looked into Eddie's eyes. She could tell she had her heart set on this. It was indeed her idea for Eddie to get an assistant. She couldn't be out on the road with her all of the time. And she did need a drum tech. But to have her move in?

"Eddie, I need to tell you something too." She sat back down next to Eddie.

"Uh oh, this doesn't sound good." Eddie said.

"No, it's good…or it could be…if you like it too."

"Well, I can't tell ya now, if ya don't tell me."

"I want to leave Reynolds's Records she said.

Eddie looked stunned. "That's madness!" Eddie said. "Why do you want to leave us?"

"Eddie, I don't want to leave you. It's just I am so tired of having my ideas shot down, only to see them being implemented by someone else. I am tired of having to take orders from Lee's little lackey, and watch as he takes all the credit. His head is so far up Lee's ass, he is just Kenny's little puppet. Sweetie, I am good at what I do.

"You are brilliant at what you do, Sonata. Not to mention beautiful too."

Sonata smiled. "Eddie, I want to open a management company…I know I can do this."

Eddie stood up and took Sonata in her arms. "I know you can do this. You can do anything, Sonata. You are an incredible woman, but I want you with me."

"Eddie, I will be with you. It will take some time to get things going. Once I get some clients and a few agents, things will settle down, and I will come out with you."

Eddie wasn't thrilled, but she could see the passion, and could tell that she had been wanting this for some time now. She was in no position to keep Sonata from chasing her dream. "Can the Travelers be yer first client?"

Sonata giggled. "I love you." She kissed Eddie.

"I luv ya too, but I am serious here. The Travelers could bring in some big names fer ya."

"Plus, if I was your manager, I could get you more money on the next contract, which by the way, they are going to offer you before you leave on tour." Sonata said.

"It sounds great to me, luv, and I know the others will hop on board.

"Even Lisa?"

"We're talking bout more money, that's Lisa's luv…. She'll be in."

Sonata kissed Eddie. "Are you sure you're ok with this?"

"Well, yeah, if it makes you happy." Eddie said. "But ya know you don't have to work Sonata I can take care of ya. I want to take care of ya."

"Yes I know Eddie and I love you and thank you for that, but this is something I have to do. For me."

"I understand luv. Like I said, if it makes ya happy."

"Oh it does. I'll show you just how much a little later." Sonata smiled. "Should we go and welcome Karli to the family?"

Eddie looked at Sonata. "Are you yanking me chain?"

"I would love to yank your chain, but I think we'd get into trouble if I did it here."

Eddie laughed. She looked at Sonata.

"What?" Sonata asked.

"Just." Eddie continued to stare.

"Just what?" Sonata raised her eyebrow.

Eddie kissed Sonata. "Just wondered why the man upstairs put me with ya. I am the lucky one."

Sonata kissed her lover. She too felt blessed to have fallen for such a wonderful woman.

Karli was flabbergasted by the invitation from Eddie and Sonata. It was truly a divine blessing that she was their cab driver that night.

The rest of the Travelers joined Eddie at the hospital. The kids loved it and so did the band. Even Lisa was taken by the courage of some of the kids.

They signed autographs and took photos with the kids. Lisa brought a guitar and they sang a few songs with a small group of the kids that were able to get out of bed.

Lisa walked into a dimly lit room. A young boy sat in his bed, hooked to all kinds of machines and monitors.

"Hi." he said softly.

"Hey there."

"You can come in, though most folks don't want to."

Lisa moved closer to the bed, and set her guitar down. "I can assure ya, I'm not like most folks."

"You talk funny. Where are you from?"

"England. So do you, where are you from?"

The little boy laughed. "I'm from here...but I always wanted to go to England."

"So, why don't ya?" Lisa asked.

"I'm too sick."

"Right now maybe, but yer gonna get better."

"No, I won't. The doctor said so." He put his hand on Lisa. His little test to see who would pull away from him.

Lisa didn't. He smiled as she took his hand.

"What do them bloody doctors know? What's wrong with ya anyhow?"

"If I tell you, you'll run. They all do." The little boy said.

"What's yer name?"

"Scott."

Lisa swallowed hard as a flood of memories over took her. "Well Scotty, why don't ya give me a go, ey? I'll bet you'll be surprised."

She knew what was wrong with Scott. She had lost her own brother Scotty to it years ago. They were as close as could be. She never got over the loss.

Sonata slowly opened the door. She couldn't believe her eyes. Was Lisa O'Brien suddenly being human?

"Sorry to interrupt, but when you have a moment Lisa, we need you in the hall."

"Who is she?" Scotty asked Lisa.

"One of the birds from our record label." She motioned for Sonata to come in.

"This here's Scotty."

"Hi Scotty, it's a pleasure. I'm Sonata." She held out her hand.

Scott smiled as he took her hand and held it tight.

"The little bloke was just about to tell me why he can't go to England."

"Oh yeah? Why is that?" Sonata asked.

"I have HIV." He said.

"That don't mean nothin' You'll be up and about in no time." Lisa's voice cracked. Tears starting to form in her eyes.

"The doctors say it's too far along." Scott said.

"What's yer mom and dad say?" Lisa asked.

"I don't have a dad, and my mom works a bunch to pay for my treatments, so I don't see her much. I'm usually asleep when she's here."

Lisa let out a sigh, and looked at Sonata.

"How old are you, Scotty?" Sonata asked.

"Eight."

"Well Scotty, I think you're very brave for an eight year old." Sonata started to choke on her words.

"I'll tell ya what, Scotty, let me go fer a moment and take care of some things, then if yer up fer it, I'll bring the rest of me mates back to meet ya."

"That would be cool, but I don't expect you to come back." Scott said.

"Now what kind of bloody rubbish talk is that?" She looked around and picked up her guitar. "Here ya go, me guarantee I'll be back." She handed it to Scott."

Scott smiled. "Will you come back too, Sonata?" He smiled at her.

"I'd love to." she smiled. "We'll be right back." She smiled and followed Lisa out of his room.

Lisa pulled her to the side. "Look Sonata, I know we don't see eye to eye on some things…"

"I won't say a word."

"Thanks."

"Who was he?"

"Who?"

"The one you lost that reminded you so much of Scott?"

"Me brother Scotty." Lisa said and looked into Sonata's eyes. She saw the warmth and understanding. She knew why Eddie was so drawn to her. "He had HIV himself. He was me best friend. Loved me unconditional…" She cleared her throat. "I guess we best move our bums, ey?" She turned and started to walk down the hall.

Sonata wiped a tear from her eye, and followed Lisa.

Sonata was now juggling two jobs. She was setting up her new talent agency while still working with Reynolds Records. Like she had explained to Eddie, Lee would only want her to be out on the road for a bout a week. What she didn't tell Eddie was that Lee also had other plans for her. She needed to break away. She would push herself hard and have things set up. If the Traveler's signed tonight she would tell Lee she was finished. She knew that it wouldn't be an amicable split. Kenny would be sure to put thoughts into Lee's head. But, her Ace was she had the Travelers. Lee couldn't balk that they were his top-selling act in the history of his label, and he wasn't about to let them go.

She put her plan into motion. She was having the band over for dinner. They had to sign tonight.

"So, what are you calling it?" Karli asked as she chopped vegetables.

Her words startled Sonata. "Hunh?"

"The agency, what are you gonna call it?"

"I don't know. It has to stand out, has to be classy."

"Just like you." Eddie kissed Sonata's neck as she came up from behind her."

Sonata giggled. "Eddie, stop it."

"Why? Karli knows we are two women who are very much in luv."

"Still…" Sonata said.

"Does it bug ya, Karli?"

Karli laughed. "No, it's nice to see two people who care so much about one another."

"Smart kid." Eddie winked.

"So, what was your first date like? Was it all fireworks and stuff?"

Eddie laughed. "Well, the second I laid me eyes on her." Eddie recalled fondly. "We went to a pub with Lisa, to discuss her bringing us to America."

"Cool" Karli said.

"Well, it was fun, once Lisa left." Sonata said. "We played darts, remember?"

Eddie laughed. "Yeah, ya swept the floor with me."

"Mmm, then that long walk back to the Savoy. I love that hotel, great memories." Sonata smiled at Eddie.

"Oh my God, that's it!" Karli yelled.

"What?" Eddie looked puzzled.

"The name for Sonata's company. The Savoy Talent Agency of Beverly Hills."

"Hey now that's snappy." Eddie said.

"I love it!" Sonata smiled.

Eddie quickly poured some ice teas all around. "Here's to the Savoy Talent Agency."

"Of Beverly Hills." Sonata added.

"Cheers." Karli said, as she raised her glass.

Sonata beamed. Everything was now falling into place.

Dinner was an event. Sonata made steaks, mashed potatoes, a huge salad and garlic bread. For dessert she offered cheesecake and coffee.

After dinner, the girls sat out on the deck and talked, while Karli kept Oliver busy playing video games.

"You out did yerself tonight, luv." Eddie said, kissing Sonata on the cheek.

"I'll say, I'm stuffed." Linda said.

"Me too, I feel like a pig." Annie added.

"Not to worry, we'll work it off later." Lisa grinned.

"Thank you. And thank you all for coming. I have to admit, that I have some other motives for having you all here."

"I knew something was up." Lisa smirked.

"Yes, something is up. I wanted you all to know, that tomorrow I am giving notice to Reynolds's Records that I am stepping down from my position, effective immediately." She took Eddie's hand for comfort.

"Are you mad?" Pamela asked.

"Sonata, we need you." Linda said.

"Eddie, you have to stop her." Annie looked at her.

"Sorry birds, her mind is well made up." Eddie winked at Sonata.

Even Lisa was shocked at Sonata's announcement. Even though there was no love lost between them, Lisa did have to admit that the American kept her word, from day one.

"Getting' too hard fer ya there?" Lisa asked.

"Yes, Lisa, in a way. Hard because the music business is a man's world, and women get no credit. The fact is, besides being on the plane with you all, I haven't gotten credit for anything."

"You all might not realize this, but all the things we get...It's because of Sonata. She fights for us." Eddie looked at her friends.

"And, I want to fight more." she looked around. "I am opening up my own talent management company, and I would like the Travelers to be my first client. All of you have trusted me before, and I hope you will now. There is so much that will be coming your way. You are the ones that worked so hard to get where you are, and you deserve the rewards, not the shaft."

"I already signed this afternoon." Eddie smiled.

"Yer a stooge, Eddie." Lisa said sharply. "There's got to be something in it fer ya, Sonata."

"Yes, there is. Fifteen percent from the group, and ten percent from anything solo. Ladies, I don't know if you are aware, but the contracts you signed with Reynolds were a one way deal, theirs. They stand to make an extra two to five hundred thousand dollars in merchandise sales from this tour. After it's divided up between the five of you, do you know how much each of you will make?" Sonata looked at Lisa.

"Nothing ladies. You signed a waver for merchandise. Tomorrow morning, Lee will be offering the Travelers an extension for a new two CD contract. If you sign the contract you will stand to lose hundreds of thousands of dollars."

"Sod. Are you sure?" Pamela asked.

"She had a meeting with Lee and Kenny this morning." Eddie said.

"So, if we signed with you?" Annie looked at Sonata.

"You would retain all the rights to any and all merchandise plus sixty percent of the sales. I promise you ladies that if you give me a chance, I will work for you. Not just to land the record deal but afterwards as well."

"What does that mean?" Lisa asked.

"It means that tomorrow afternoon I have a meeting with one of the top show business accountants. I want all of you to live your dreams, but I want you to enjoy the rewards of your dreams, after the spotlight fades."

"I like what I hear Sonata. Count me in." Linda smiled.

"Where do I sign?" Pamela smiled at Eddie.

Sonata beamed.

"We trusted you before and you haven't lied to us." Annie looked at Lisa, then at Sonata. "I'm in."

"Great." Sonata looked at Lisa. She knew that this would be a hard sell.

"C'mon Lisa, what about ya?" Eddie said.

"I don't know. Lee has been pretty damn good to us. I don't know if we should be betraying him like this."

"Lee is a nice man, Lisa, but he's also a business man. Don't think for one second he wouldn't step on anyone to get what he wants. And what he always wants is money." Sonata looked Lisa in the eye. "It's your choice."

Linda, Pamela, and Annie were all inside signing the contracts. Lisa stayed out side. Sonata started to walk out side, but Eddie stopped her.

"Let me." She kissed Sonata's cheek. She stepped out onto the deck, closing the door behind her. "You ok?" she asked.

"Yep." Lisa said, as she took a long drag from her cigarette. "Ciggy?" She held out her pack to Eddie.

"No thanks, I gave em up."

"Seems like ya gave a lot of things up Eddie."

"What's that mean?"

"Ya lost yer edge, Eddie. Not that ya had much of one in the first place. But yer like a little puppy following Sonata around…just dangling from er leash."

Eddie frowned. Lisa knew exactly what buttons to push.

"Don't go being jealous, Lisa. It's not becoming."

"Jealous…Me?" Lisa laughed. "Yer Mad! What do I 'ave to be jealous about?"

"Cause we are equals, she respects me for who I am, that eats you up."

Lisa laughed. She looked into Eddie's eyes. She still saw a weak spot. Fear. She moved closer to Eddie. "Don't forget, Eddie, I've kissed yer lips, touched your skin, been inside you, you'll never let me go."

"Lisa stop!" Eddie turned around and looked out at the ocean.

"Ya know I'm right, Eddie." She moved up close behind Eddie and slid her arm around her waist. She pulled her in close. "Anytime you wanna come back, luv. Ya know where I am." She moved Eddie's hair with her free hand and slowly kissed her neck. She turned and walked away.

Eddie shivered. Why did she let that woman get to her?

"Where is it, Sonata?…Sonata?" Linda said in a raised voice.

Sonata jumped as she heard her name being called. She couldn't take her eyes off of what was happening on the deck. "Wha?"

"The sugar fer the coffee? Where was yer head?" Linda laughed.

"Oh nowhere, here I'll get it." She got up and went into the kitchen.

"Look, Lisa, I am very happy and very much in luv with Sonata, and not you or any bloody-one else is gonna ruin this fer me. I only came out here to see if ya were gonna sign the contract."

Lisa laughed. "Really now? Eddie yer a daft bird if ya think Sonata is in it fer luv? You just signed a contract, she owns you now."

"No one owns me, Lisa. Get that through yer brain. Not Sonata and espe-cially not you…You don't want to sign, it is fine by us, but don't be beggin' when yer money runs out. And in yer case Lisa, it always runs out. Eddie left Lisa standing on the deck, and walked inside.

Linda was trying hard to stuff money into Karli's hand.

"Linda don't. Oliver wasn't any trouble." Karli said, handing back the money.

"Yeah, and yer being nice. Ollie is a handful."

"No, he was cool."

"Please take it, Karli." Pamela said. "Otherwise I'll ave ta hear about this on the drive home."

Eddie walked up to Sonata and put her arm around her.

Sonata looked at Eddie, who just smiled.

Eddie pulled her close to her side and held her tight.

"Ok, ok." Karli said. "I'll take your money she laughed, as she held out her hand.

"So, is she gonna sign?" Annie asked.

"Dunno." Eddie said. "She's a stubborn one."

Lisa walked in.

"We were just talking about you." Annie said, as she walked over to Lisa.

"Are ya gonna sign?" Pamela asked.

"Gonna sleep on that one."

"The meeting is tomorrow." Linda said.

"Well then, I still ave till tomorrow, don't I? C'mon Annie." She took Annie's hand and walked out the door.

The phone rang for the fifth time before Sonata picked it up. "Yeah?" she said groggily into the phone.

"Do you know what just happened?" The male voice on the other end asked.

"You woke me up?" Sonata tried to focus on the clock.

"Well, how does eight Grammy nominations sound to you?"

What? Sonata yelled waking Eddie up. "Are you sure?"

"It's on every news channel. See you here in a few hours." The phone went dead.

Sonata found the remote and turned on the T.V. "Eddie! Eddie! Wake up." She pushed her.

"What? Sonata it's too early fer me, luv…"

"No, Eddie." She took her pillow and hit her with it. "Look!"

Eddie sat up as the T.V reporter started his report. "An astonishing eight Grammy nominations for the Travelers. They are the best bet to sweep their categories this year...."

"Bloody hell, did you hear that?" Eddie yelled.

They screamed.

Karli came running in "What's wrong??"

"We got eight Grammy nominations." Eddie yelled. She grabbed the phone and called Linda.

"No way." Karli's mouth dropped. That's insane.

"This is the best thing that could have happened. Do you realize what a bargaining tool this is? We have Reynolds Records by the balls now!" Sonata beamed.

"Wait a sec shhhhh." Karli said. "Listen."

"...And in the song of the year category, Eddie Sutcliffe and her partner, Sonata Williams, got a nod for their hit "If You Only Knew..."

Sonata looked at Eddie who hung up the phone.

"Did you hear that?"

"Lisa's gonna shit a brick!" Karli laughed.

"This will be a tough category for song of the year, since both number one hits of the Travelers are nominated..." The report on the TV continued, "Guess we'll have to wait until the awards ceremony to find out..."

"Wow." Eddie said, as she ran her hands through her hair.

"This is perfect." Sonata said as she kissed Eddie. "I'm gonna hop in the shower."

She jumped out of bed and headed for the bathroom.

Eddie looked at Karli and smiled. Karli smiled back. Eddie motioned to the bathroom, then smiled at Karli.

"Oh! Oh...Got ya." Karli giggled. She left the room.

Eddie laughed out loud and headed to join Sonata in a celebration shower.

"Oh baby, I'm so happy." Annie said.

"Yeah pretty great fer us." Lisa kissed Annie. "Eight nominations, I think this calls fer a celebration."

"And you and Eddie up for song of the year against one another..."

Lisa jumped up and got her travel bag. She jumped back into bed. "How bout a shot befer breakfast?"

"Hmm, I think it can wait." Annie reached for Lisa and slid her hand between her legs.

Lisa looked at Annie and grinned. "Oh yeah. It can." She put her bag on the nightstand and rolled onto Annie. She kissed her hard.

"Lisa, I love you." Annie said breathlessly.

Lisa didn't answer. She kneaded Annie's breast, Annie arched at the pleasure. Lisa slid her hand between Annie's legs and spread them apart. She slid her leg in-between and pushed her knee up to Annie. In slow deliberate rhythms, she caressed Annie's clit with her knee. Annie was glued to the sensation as she matched Lisa's rhythm. Lisa sucked on Annie's hard erect nipple, as she continued to rub up and down on Annie.

Lisa slowly entered Annie with three fingers, sending Annie into a furious orgasm. Lisa kept the pressure on Annie until she came again.

Annie was panting, trying to catch her breath. "Lisa…. Look at the time…Son…Sonata…"

"What about er?" Lisa said lighting up a cigarette.

"Her meeting…. You didn't sign…" Annie said.

"Oh shit!" Lisa said. She handed her cigarette to Annie and jumped up. "Don't leave, I'll be back in a bit." She laughed as she ran into the bathroom.

❧   ❧   ❧

Sonata grabbed her things as she and Eddie sat in the parking garage of Reynolds Records. "Are you sure I'm ready for this?"

"C'mon now, luv, stop getting the cold feet. Yer awesome. Everything's gonna go one way…yers." Eddie leaned over and kissed Sonata.

"You always make everything seem ok." Sonata smiled.

"It is ok. You'll see." Eddie smiled, "Whatta ya gonna do about Lisa?"

"There's nothing I can do, sweetie. I just hope she realizes how tough things are going to be for her, 'cause she wanted to be the hot shot and not sign."

Eddie looked at her watch. "You best be getting in there…But, one more fer luck." She kissed Sonata again. "Wish I could be there with ya."

Sonata grinned. "Eddie you can. Come with me and be by my side."

"Ya sure, luv?"

"Yes, you could be the spokesperson for the band."

"If it'll help ya, I'd luv ta." Eddie smiled.

"I feel lucky already."

They got out of the car and started to walk toward the elevators.

"Hey, wait a sec!" A voice from behind them called out."

Sonata and Eddie turned around. They were surprised to see Lisa running toward them.

"Is it too late?" she asked.

"For…?" Sonata played it cool.

"To sign up. Look Sonata, yer not me idea of a good time, but I ave ta do what's best fer me, and go along with the others."

Sonata smiled, she won this round. She pulled out the contracts and a pen, and handed them to Lisa. "Welcome aboard."

Lisa signed them and handed them back. "There now, that's all settled."

"You wanna go in with us?" Eddie asked.

Sonata shot Eddie a look.

"Two band members ave ta be betta than one. Lisa is the founder of the Travelers. If she's on yer side, old man Reynolds can't do a thing!"

Sonata thought about it. Eddie was right. "That is a great idea, Eddie. Lisa would you care to join us?"

"Err, yeah, sure." Lisa said.

"Great. Ladies, let's go kick some butt." Sonata smiled.

❦   ❦   ❦

"Is this some kind of a joke?" Lee asked, not laughing at all.

"No, Lee, it's no joke." Sonata kept her cool.

"It won't work, you'll be out of business in a month!" Kenny added.

"Well, anything is possible, but I do have five clients already." She stood and walked to the door. "Two of them are here." She opened the door and motioned to Eddie and Lisa to come in.

Lee's jaw dropped as he saw two of the Travelers walk in.

"Savoy Talent Agency is happy to announce the recent signing of the Travelers." Sonata grinned. "I believe you were ready to offer the ladies a new contract."

"Well, you got it wrong." Kenny tried to bluff.

Eddie and Lisa looked at one another, then to Sonata.

"Ok, fine, Virgin Records offered us a dream package anyway. The girls wanted to stay loyal to Reynolds but you really couldn't match what they were going offer. Gentleman…" She picked up her briefcase and grinned at Eddie. "Ladies shall we"

"Yep." Lisa said.

"Wait a sec, hold it." Lee said. "How do I know you are not bluffing?

"You don't. But, don't think for one second that there isn't any label that wouldn't give their eyeteeth to have the Travelers. Let me lay it on the line for you. If you keep the Travelers you stand to lose, oh about ten million, per year give or take. With the projected record sales, as well as the Eight Grammy nominations. Oh lets not forget a nationwide sold out tour, tickets sold out in Thirteen minutes…and you didn't sign them…you would stand to lose over a hundred million dollars."

A grin came over Eddie's face. She loved to watch Sonata work.

"This is the contract we expect from you. If you agree, have your people redo it and send them over to me. My clients will be happy to sign. Good day."

Sonata walked out followed by Lisa and Eddie.

She walked over to the elevator and pushed the button.

"What in bloody hell are ya doing? Are ya daft or something'?" Lisa whispered loudly.

"Just get in and trust me." Sonata looked Lisa in the eye.

"Trust her Lisa, she knows what she's doing."

The elevator door opened and they stepped in.

"We are walking away?" Lisa asked after the door closed.

"They won't let us leave. I saw it in their eyes."

Eddie smiled.

The door opened and they stepped off.

"Ok, just go to the door." Sonata said softly.

Just before they reached the door a familiar voice called to her.

"Hey Sonata, wait a sec." The receptionist yelled.

Sonata smiled and turned around.

"Phone for you. Mr. Reynolds."

Sonata walked over to the phone. "Yes?"

"You have got to be out of your mind." Lee bellowed on the other end.

"Take it or leave it, Lee, it's that simple."

"I won't." He tried to show a bluff.

"Not a problem, we'll go elsewhere…try to have a nice day."

"Wait! Wait a second he said.

"Yes?" Sonata grinned. She had him, and it felt great!

"Ok, you win, I'll send the contracts over this afternoon."

The phone went dead.

Sonata composed herself, as she hung up the phone. "Ladies, shall we?"

Eddie opened the door and they walked to the parking structure.

"Well?" Lisa asked.

"We did it. We got what we asked for. The Travelers will be very, very wealthy.

Lisa grinned. She liked what she heard.

CHAPTER 9

"Dammit! Dammit to hell!" Eddie yelled as she slammed down the phone.

Karli came in from the other room. "Hey, are you ok?" She looked at Eddie knowing full out that she wasn't.

"No, Karli, no I'm not." Eddie looked up at her.

"She's not coming, hunh?"

"Nope, has a meeting with a new client…like always."

Karli watched as the last three months started taking a toll on Eddie.

Sonata's new agency took off like a wildfire. In the short time she had opened her business, she had to take on three more agents to handle all the clients, while she booked The Travelers. She would fly out on Friday afternoon and meet up with Eddie. Stay until Sunday afternoon, and fly back home.

Eddie hated it. It was never enough time. She wanted Sonata with her, by her side. She needed Sonata there to keep her head level. Now she was lucky to have five minutes with her on the phone each day.

"Eddie, why don't you hit the hay? We travel tomorrow."

"I don't care no more, Karli. This isn't worth it." She threw her pillow across the room, knocking over a vase.

"It's after midnight, you need to rest." Karli tried again.

"I'm not in the mood fer sleepin'" Eddie stood up. "I'll be back in a bit."

"I'll go with you." Karli looked at her friend.

"No worries little one. I just need me some air." She walked over and hugged Karli. "I'm glad yer on this journey with me, kiddo." She smiled and walked out the door.

The bar was quiet. Just a few couples and an empty piano bar. Eddie walked up to the bar and sat down.

"What's your pleasure miss?" The bartender asked.

"A g and t please."

"Make that two." A voiced came from behind her. "Can't let ya drink alone." Lisa said.

"Can't sleep either?" Eddie asked.

"Sleep is overrated. Besides you know me, Eddie, the nightlife is me life." The bartender sat the drinks down.

"My treat." Lisa looked at Eddie, as she threw some money down.

"We stop serving at 2:00am ladies." The bartender said.

"Well then we 'ave a lot of drinkin' ta do in an hour don't we?" Lisa grinned.

"Here's to ya." Eddie held up her glass.

Lisa raised her's. "Bottom's up."

Eddie downed her drink. She held it up to the bartender. "I'll ave another go she said.

"Why such a long face, Eddie Sutcliffe?" Lisa asked.

"Just missin' me lady."

"Buck up there, she'll be in tomorrow."

"No, she won't. She has a meeting." Eddie took a swig of her refreshed drink.

A grin came over Lisa's face. "Two more here."

After three drinks, Eddie was feeling light headed. She hadn't drank that much since she and Sonata got together. But it did feel nice sitting around and shooting the bull with Lisa.

"I told ya, Eddie, women like her are nothin' but trouble. They think they are high and mighty n' shit."

Eddie didn't need to hear it again from Lisa. She looked at her watch; it was almost 3 a.m. "Sod it! We best be getting upstairs." She stood up and helped a now drunk Lisa to her feet.

"I knew you'd come around, Sutcliffe." Lisa smiled.

Eddie tipped the bartender, and lead Lisa into the elevator.

Lisa looked at Eddie. She moved closer. Inching her way into Eddie's personal space. Eddie was backed into the corner of the elevator.

"Let me show you what you've been missing." She softly touched Eddie's cheek.

Eddie swallowed hard, she looked at Lisa.

Lisa slowly unbuttoned Eddie's top two buttons on her shirt. She buried her face in the tall drummer's cleavage, licking her breastbone, and nibbling at her breasts.

Eddie froze. This was how Lisa used to be. Soft and gentle, she missed this side of her.

Lisa had unbuttoned three more buttons when the elevator stopped. Lisa stopped her pursuit.

"Ah…here we are." Eddie said, flustered, as she tried to button her shirt.

Lisa smiled as she saw that Eddie was flushed. They stopped at Eddie's suite.

"Maybe we can finish this later, Lisa winked, it was nice Eddie."

Eddie just stared at Lisa. She unlocked the door and went inside.

Lisa laughed and staggered down the hall to her suite.

"Karli, are ya here?" Eddie called as she looked around. The silence was deafening.

Eddie walked over to the huge balcony and opened the double doors. The cold breeze rushed at her. She walked to the iron fence and looked over. *Thirty stories up. Could do some damage if one fell off. Or jumped.* She thought. *One quick jump and no more worries. For anyone.*

Tears started to fall from her eyes. She walked back in and plopped down on the couch. She grabbed a pillow and buried her face in it. "Why me?" She yelled into it, stifling the pain and cries of her loneliness. A pain she was becoming all too familiar with.

Sonata looked at her watch. She had to hurry. She had decided to fly to Detroit and surprise Eddie. Things had become stressful since Savoy went into action. Her attention was needed at the office. But Eddie also needed her. She was being pulled at both ends, and something had to give.

There was a knock at the door.

"Come in." Sonata said, as she put some things in her brief case.

"Your cab is here." Gary said as he walked in.

"Oh great." Sonata smiled. "Are you sure you guys will be alright? I left where I'll be staying with Sue, and you have my cell number."

"Yes, and I am sure you will have it off all weekend. Sonata, we will be fine, go and have your little tryst with the Rockstar."

Sonata looked at Gary. "A tryst would have been a heck of a lot easier. Silly me, I had to go and fall in love with her."

"That's the price you pay my dear…however, if you want to live the way of the straight, let me know…I'd love to tryst with you." He grinned.

"Gary, you're every lesbian's dream."

"Hey, don't knock it until you try it."

"Been there, tried it, hated it." She smiled. "I'm off, see you Monday." She grabbed her briefcase and her carry on. She couldn't wait to see Eddie.

❦   ❦   ❦

The Travelers and their crew checked into their hotel in Detroit. Eddie hadn't slept in a few days and it showed.

The limo waited to take the girls to sound check. Linda sent Pamela to check in while she went back to the limo to talk to Eddie. She got in and sat next to Eddie. Eddie smiled at her friend.

"You know you're lookin' like shit, Eddie."

"Sod off Linny…I'm fine." Eddie snapped. She leaned back in her seat.

"Well, I'm beggin' to differ with ya…. C'mon' Eddie…it's me. Yer pal Linda…What's eating ya?"

"It's…It's this bloody tour! It's too damn long." Eddie said.

"We're hot, Eddie. We are the biggest thing that has happened in the U.S. since the Beatles. Enjoy the ride while it lasts, bird."

"Enjoy what? All of these women throwing themselves at me, or watching you and Pammy going into your room at night while I go into mine alone? Sorry, not my cup a tea."

"Ah, I thought it had to do with Sonata." Linda felt sorry for her friend. She couldn't imagine being without Pamela for a day let alone weeks at a time. "Why don't you give her a shout? Use some of that Sutcliffe charm. I bet ya can get her to fly on out."

"Ya think so?" Eddie looked hopeful at her friend.

"Sure. Ring er up, Eddie."

Eddie took out her cell phone and dialed. She frowned as she heard Sonata's voice mail pick up. She hung up and dialed Savoy.

"Savoy Talent Agency, how may I direct your call?"

"Hey Sue, how are ya, luv?"

"Why, Eddie Sutcliffe as I live and breathe, how are you girl?"

"Hangin' in there." Eddie smiled. She loved Sue. She was so funny and always up. What an asset to Savoy. "Any good looking redheads wandering around there?"

"I was a redhead last week. Where were you?" Sue teased.

Eddie laughed. "Now ya got me thinking, luv."

"Well, it's about time you saw the light." Sue laughed. If you're looking for your woman, try her cell, she ran off to a meeting, we're trying to snag Will Smith."

"I tried that, but got her voice mail. Perhaps, I should ave another go at it."

"Yes do, and if she calls in the meantime, I will have her call you A.S.A.P."

"Yer a livin' doll, Sue." Eddie smiled.

"Talk is cheap girl, I want action. Oops, gotta go, the other line is ringing, take care, baby."

Eddie listened as the phone went dead.

"Any luck?" Linda tried to stay positive.

"Sue said she's off to a meeting with Will Smith."

Linda could see the disappointment on Eddie's face. She looked at her watch. "Damn these women, can't they ever be on time?"

Eddie laughed.

A few fans had now gathered by the limo and the entrance to the hotel. They were holding CD's and photos, waiting for autographs.

"Well they are right on time." Linda chuckled.

"Not too many though. Geese, give a look at the redhead. She looks like…"

"No Eddie she doesn't." Linda said.

Eddie happily rolled her window down.

"Oh my God, it's Eddie!" The cute redhead screamed.

Eddie smiled. The fan looked a lot like Sonata. She was very pretty.

"Do you know how much I love you guys?" She said, as she held up a photo for Eddie to sign.

"Well, thank you, we luv ya too…What's yer name luv?"

"Sara." she barely got out.

Eddie looked at the photo of her playing the drums, it was quite impressive. "Did you snap this?"

"Yes, it was opening night in New York." She smiled at Eddie.

"Really? And now yer in Detroit."

"I've also seen you in Ohio, Atlanta, Chicago, and Tennessee."

"Yer a crazy lot aren't ya?" Eddie smiled.

"You're so worth it Eddie." Sara said as tears welled up in her eyes.

"Well, thank ya, luv, whatta ya say we snap a shot to remember the day by?"

"Are you serious?"

"Sure, Eddie laughed as she opened the door of the limo and climbed out. "How old are ya Sara?"

"Twenty five. Well, twenty-four, tomorrow's my birthday. My friends brought me here for a present. I hoped I would get the chance to meet you."

"Well, I am glad we got the chance, Sara." Eddie took Sara into her arms. She felt like Sonata too. Eddie closed her eyes as she gently started to rock her in her arms. "Happy Birthday, Sara." Eddie said, as she leaned over and kissed her gently on the cheek.

"I think I'm gonna die." Sara said, as she melted into Eddie's embrace. She held onto Eddie's leather jacket.

Eddie laughed. She posed with Sara as her friends came and took pictures. Eddie was happy to meet the rest of Sara's friends. It was nice to meet the future. Especially the good clean kids. It was a good pick me up for Eddie, a nice diversion.

She found out that Sara and her friends were staying at the hotel, and had bought front row seats. Eddie wrote down their names and invited them to come backstage after the show and meet the others. "I'd better get going. Nice ta meet all of ya. Sara, see ya after the show, luv." she smiled. She stopped for a second. She took her leather jacket off and handed it to Sara. "Happy Birthday." she said again, and jumped back into the limo.

"Feel better now?"

"A bit."

"That one there, she did look a bit like Sonata." Linda pointed out.

"Did she now? I hadn't really noticed." Eddie tried to play it down.

"Don't go getting yerself into trouble, Eddie. She's yer fan, not yer lover."

"Sod off, Linda, I was just being nice."

"Excuse me." The limo driver said. "The others hopped into the bus with the crew and said that they would meet you at the venue."

"Ok thanks." Linda smiled. "Looks like it's just you and me kid."

Eddie smiled. She liked Linda a lot. She always tried to make her feel better when Sonata was a no show. She kept thinking of Sara and how much she looked and acted like Sonata. Maybe tonight, things would be different.

Detroit was great. Both nights were sold out, and the girls loved it. They honed their craft in the U.K. and really knew how to work a crowd. They had men as well as women all hot and bothered for two solid hours. Lisa and Eddie were definite crowd favorites, especially when Eddie would climb down off her drum perch and play the piano or the guitar.

Karli watched wide-eyed from the side of the stage, each night the ladies would bring something new to the show. She was in awe of the way they would arrange their set lists, as well as the drumming skills of Eddie. She had picked up so much wisdom out on the road, as well as some new best friends. She and Eddie had become close. At first she dreamt about Eddie as her lover, but after seeing the bond that she and Sonata shared, she quickly let that fantasy fade away.

"Where is your head?" Sonata asked as she came up behind Karli.

Karli turned around. "Sonata." She hugged her. "Thank God you're here."

"You missed me that much?' Sonata giggled.

"No. I mean of course I missed you, but Eddie…"

"Is she ok?"

"She's been having trouble sleeping. Eddie misses you something terrible."

"I know, sweetie. Look, I want to surprise her, I'm gonna go back to the hotel, can you get her back there after the show?"

"Are you kidding? She only leaves her room to do the show. She'll be back." Karli reached into her fanny pack. "Here suite 817." She handed Sonata the room key.

"Great, don't tell her I'm here." Sonata said as she left.

"I won't." she yelled after her.

Sonata didn't like what Karli said. Maybe it was a mistake opening up Savoy so soon.

After the show, Eddie had Sara and her friends join them backstage. She gave a lot of thought to what Linda had said, and decided it was best just to keep Sara as her fan. She was just missing Sonata. She would go back to the hotel, shower and spend the rest of the night on the phone falling asleep with Sonata's breathing on the other line.

"Did you see those girls outside?" Karli laughed.

"The loosey goosey ones?" Pamela asked.

"Those birds? Custom made fer Lisa don't ya think?"

"Sod off, Linny." Lisa said, even though she was right. She would send Annie to bed and head back down. Couldn't disappoint the fans.

"That crowd tonight was mad. I liked that hall. Good acoustics." Eddie said, trying to change the subject for Annie's sake.

"Yes, they were." Annie agreed, smiling at Eddie.

"If that stupid arse bloke keeps messing with me ear monitors I'll ave his head on a platter."

"Tell me, I couldn't hear me own bass fer the first seven songs." Linda added.

"I think he needs to be cut." Lisa said.

The elevator stopped and Linda and Pamela stepped off.

"Sleep well ladies." Pamela said.

"Sleep, Eddie, sleep!" Linda pointed at her friend.

"Yeah, Sure." Eddie said as the door closed and they continued upward.

She hated this part. Every night, the same thing. Pamela and Linda, Lisa and Annie would go to their rooms, talk about the night's show, make love, and just hold one another all night long. She would go back to her room and play gin with Karli, or watch old movies all night long. There she was, Eddie Sutcliffe…famous, rich, she could have anything she wanted, and at the same time she had nothing at all, when Sonata wasn't around.

The elevator opened and the rest of the group got out.

"Goodnight, Eddie." Annie smiled.

"It will be fer ya after I get done with ya." Lisa took Annie in her arms and kissed her.

"Nite you two." Eddie frowned.

She and Karli walked silently to the door of her suite.

"Whatta ya say to a couple of burgers and a game of rummy?" Eddie looked at Karli.

"I'm gonna pass. I am pooped. Think, I'll take a bath and call it a night. Besides, you need to rest, Eddie."

"I will, I promise." She hugged Karli. She held her and took a deep breath.

"What?" Karli stepped away.

"Nothing, you just smell like…never mind." I think I do need to rest. Sleep tight, kiddo." Eddie said. She watched Karli walk to her room and open the door. When she heard the door close, she opened her door and stepped inside. She turned on the TV and plopped on the couch. She picked up the phone and dialed. "Room service please." She started to change the channels. "Yeah, this is suite 817, I'd like to place an order…what do you mean another one?…I just got here…Look, I just want a burger well done and some fri…"

Eddie looked at the bar and saw a glass of champagne and a note. "Never mind." She hung up the phone. She walked over to the bar and picked up the note. Rose petals fell from it, onto the floor. Eddie looked down and saw the trail of petals that led to the bedroom. The double doors were closed.

Great, a groupie Eddie thought. They were always trying to sneak, or buy their way into their suites, Lisa loved when they succeeded.

Eddie took a sip of the bubbly liquid. It was nice. She stopped for a moment. Could it be Sara?

Eddie decided she would get rid of her guest, shower, and finish off the bottle of champagne. Maybe she would pass out and finally get some sleep. She quickly downed the rest of the glass and walked to the doors. She took a deep breath and opened them. "Look birdie, you are gonna' ave ta go, or I'll ave ta call…" She froze.

"Call who?" Sonata said. She was in the hot tub filled with bubbles, sipping on her champagne.

"Sonata." was all Eddie could say.

"Surprise, sweetie."

"Oh my…is it really you?" Eddie moved closer.

"Yes, silly, it's me. All naked and in your hot tub. Care to join me?"

Eddie walked to the tub and jumped in clothes and all. She grabbed Sonata and kissed her.

"Baby, your clothes." Sonata got out before Eddie kissed her again.

Eddie looked at Sonata as tears welled up in her eyes. She touched her hair, her cheek. "I…can't believe yer here with me."

"I missed you so much, Eddie." Sonata kissed her, and started to unbutton Eddie's wet blouse.

Eddie quickly took the rest of her clothes off and tossed them out of the hot tub. She took Sonata and held her in her arms. "This has to be a bloody dream." Eddie whispered as she kissed the back of Sonata's neck. Her hands rubbed expertly over the familiar territory she loved. She stopped at Sonata's already erect nipples.

Sonata groaned as her body ached for Eddies touch. She leaned back, sitting on Eddie's lap, leaning her head back against Eddie's shoulder.

Eddie slowly started to slide her hand between Sonata's legs. She nibbled on Sonata's ear as she slowly pressed her finger against Sonata, rubbing over her.

Sonata gasped as she felt the swell of her wave quickly reaching its crashing point. She arched back to press harder against Eddie's fingers which were now moving in and out of her.

Eddie could tell Sonata was almost there. She pulled her hand away. "Not yet me luv. I want you to remember this night fer the rest of yer life." She stepped out of the hot tub and grabbed a towel. She held her hand out for Sonata.

Sonata took Eddie's hand. Weak-kneed she stepped out of the tub. She stood in front of her lover, watching her every move.

Eddie took the towel, she started to wipe off Sonata's shoulder, then kiss it. She repeated her action wiping, and kissing, starting at Sonata's shoulders and working her way down.

Sonata shivered. She knew she couldn't take much more of this.

Eddie knelt in front of her. She dried off her leg; she looked up at the beautiful woman who stood before her. She dried off the second one. Eddie carefully and methodically started to lick and nibble the inside of Sonata's thighs.

Sonata was ready to crumble as Eddie's tongue swept over Sonata's eager swollen clit. She stepped back. Breathless she pulled Eddie to her feet and kissed her. They stared at one another as Sonata led Eddie to the bed.

Eddie grinned as she watched Sonata lay on the bed. She slowly came up between Sonata's legs and continued where she left off.

Sonata's build was fast, as Eddie moved in and out of Sonata with her tongue.

Sonata arched one more time as she exploded.

Eddie continued sucking, and licking, She moved her fingers back in and out, pumping hard. She didn't intend to stop.

"Wai...wait..." Sonata gasped for air. She pulled Eddie to her. She was still shivering. Every nerve in her body was standing on end.

Eddie reached for the covers and pulled them over Sonata. "Welcome home me luv." Eddie laid down and wrapped herself around Sonata.

"Don't...think that...this...is...over." Sonata panted.

Eddie laughed. "It will never be over, luv."

After hours of making love, talking, eating and making love some more, Eddie lay in Sonata's arms, lost in deep sleep and safe from anything or any one.

Eddie stretched, as the light coming from the bright Detroit morning bounced off the stark white walls. Her body was aching from last night. She smiled as she recalled their lovemaking. She rolled over to find Sonata's side of the bed empty. She got out of bed and stumbled to the bathroom. Retrieving her flannel pants and t-shirt she quickly threw them on and brushed her teeth. She felt like she had a huge hangover. She walked out of the bedroom and kicked an empty bottle. "Sod it!" Eddie yelled as she hopped around on one foot. She looked down and saw two other empty bottles laying by the bed. She smiled and walked to the door. She looked back at the bed and smiled again, and opened the bedroom door.

Sonata and Karli were sitting in the living room, Sonata on the couch, talking on the phone, Karli in the chair eating an apple.

Eddie smiled at Karli as she climbed over the back of the couch and straddled Sonata. She wrapped her arms around her waist, and kissed the back of her neck.

Sonata tried to wiggle away while she was talking. "Yes that sounds great. I will ask them and get back to you…Well thank you too…Bye."

Eddie buried her head in Sonata's back. She let out a big sigh.

"Happy?" Karli asked.

"Elated." Eddie looked up and smiled. "I got me baby back."

Sonata giggled.

"Morning, luv." Eddie kissed Sonata.

"Good afternoon, sleepy head."

"Afternoon?"

"Yep it's 4:00 pm, and you have sound check in one hour." Karli said looking at her watch.

"I'm not going anywhere, cept maybe back to bed with a certain redhead." she kissed Sonata.

"Hon, you have a show tonight." Sonata said.

"Show shmo, I want to be with you."

"I'm here." Sonata said.

"Fer now." Eddie frowned. "In the morning you'll be back on a plane, and then you'll be gone fer who knows how long this time!" Eddie got up and went back to the bedroom, slamming the door behind her.

Sonata looked at Karli.

"That's pretty much the norm for her these days. She's either pouting about you, or trying to drink away her loneliness." Karli said. "It's pretty sad actually…tell her I'll do sound check, that way you two can have more time together." She smiled as she walked to the door and opened it.

"Thanks, Karli." Sonata said as she watched her leave. She thought about what Karli said. She knew Eddie drank, but now she was drinking to get drunk, to kill the loneliness. She didn't want Eddie to turn out like her father, sitting on some barstool in a sleazy pub. She picked up the phone and started to dial.

Eddie sat on the overstuffed chair in front of the balcony. She had the door open. The cold wind blew over her as she watched the storm brewing in the distance, creeping closer. Eddie could hear the thunder growing stronger and see the flashes of light as the sun now darted behind the clouds.

Sonata knocked and opened the bedroom door. She walked over to Eddie. "Can we talk?"

Eddie looked up at her.

"Sweetie, I'm sorry our jobs are conflicting. I didn't know Savoy would take off like this…but it did. I thought you would be happy for us."

"Sonata, I am happy fer ya. It's just…"

"I know. We don't see enough of each other. It bothers me too, Eddie, I just think if we hang in there a bit longer, things will settle down."

"Yeah, I know they will, I've been thinkin' and at the end of this tour, I'm hanging up me drumsticks." Eddie announced.

"What?"

"Sonata, I luv ya too much to let our jobs get in our way. I know what Savoy means to ya, so it's settled."

"Sonata sat on Eddie's lap. She kissed her. "You have an enormous heart Eddie, but I know you love what you do too. We will work something out." She kissed Eddie again.

"Ya think we can just sit here all night? Maybe they won't miss me." Eddie squeezed Sonata.

"How about for the next week?" Sonata giggled.

Eddie looked at her.

"I just called Savoy and extended my stay. You're stuck with me for the next week, Eddie Sutcliffe."

"Are ya yankin me chain?" she looked at Sonata.

"Nope, I'm all yours for the next week."

"Whoo hoo!" Eddie shouted. She stood up, keeping Sonata in her arms, and plopped onto the bed.

Sonata giggled. "I'll have to buy some clothes, I only have enough for three days."

"Tomorrow." She kissed her. "I feel a surge coming on now."

They laughed. Eddie started to kiss Sonata.

❦   ❦   ❦

"Try it again!" Lisa growled.

"Sod you, Lisa, I've been trying. They have a do not disturb on the bloody phone." Linda said.

"Wait, I'll try Eddie's cell." Karli said as she pulled out her's.

"At least someone has some wit's about her." Lisa looked at Linda.

"It's ringing." Karli said.

"What?" Eddie answered the phone out of breath.

"Eddie we need to talk to Sonata."

"Karli…now? We're kind of busy."

"Please, Eddie, it's urgent." Karli said.

Eddie handed the phone to Sonata. "Karli said it's urgent."

"Karli?" Sonata said.

"Sonata it's Derrick, he's gone."

"What do you mean gone?"

Lisa took the phone from Karli. "Sonata, That rat bastard of a tour manager stole our fucking money and left."

"Ok, just stay calm, we'll be right down." She hung up the phone.

"What's wrong?"

"Derrick decided to leave the tour."

"Oh." Eddie said.

"And he took off with the money from the venue."

"Oh!"

"Come on, sweetie, we need to get down there."

Sonata and Eddie arrived twenty minutes later. The rest of the band was sitting in the dressing room.

"My, you all are a sad lot." Eddie said as she walked in.

"Eddie, Sod off. Yer so daft. Don't you know what happened?"

"Yeah, Lisa, I know what happened. I also know that our wonderful and very sexy manager has also taken out a huge insurance policy fer us. We are covered fer this." Eddie smiled.

"What a relief." Annie said.

Sonata walked in. "They found him."

"They did?" Pamela said.

"Yes, he was at the airport. He had already cashed the check. They recovered all of the money minus the cost of his flight to the Bahamas." Sonata said.

"Well done, Sonata." Linda smiled.

"Ok, so let's let this crap go, and have a great show." She kissed Eddie. "I'm gonna go tell the crew, and make a few calls. I need to get you another tour manager. I'll be back." She kissed Eddie again.

Eddie smiled as she watched her leave.

"Still all smiles are ya?" Linda winked.

"It's nice to have her back in me arms, ya know?"

"We're happy for ya, Eddie." Pamela smiled.

"I just wish I could wake up. We were uh…up late." Eddie smiled.

"Not to worry. That crowd will get ya going as soon as ya walk out on stage." Annie said.

Lisa came up to Eddie and sat next to her. "Yer looking a bit peaked there Eddie. Not used to getting it all night long are ya?" Lisa laughed. "Here, this will help ya out." She took Eddie's hand and placed a small zip-lock bag into it. "A present fer ya." She grinned.

"Lisa." Eddie whispered, "I can't."

"Sod it, Eddie, it's just like drinkin' coffee. They're just caffeine tabs, to jump start ya…Trust me Eddie, Sonata will be thankin' ya later. She laughed and walked back over to Annie.

Eddie looked down at her hand. In the bag were six blue pills. She looked up at Lisa, who caught her eye and winked. Eddie didn't know what to do. She didn't want to take them, but if they were just caffeine, then there couldn't be any harm. Besides, she didn't want to miss a moment with Sonata. She took one of the pills and popped it into her mouth. She swallowed it. She carefully sealed the bag and put it in her pocket.

Eddie flew through the concert. What a feeling. The crowd was crazy, the band was on, and Eddie shined. She had to admit that Lisa's little pick me up was indeed just that.

Sonata watched from the side stage next to Karli."

"She is so awesome." Karli yelled over the music.

"That she is, my friend, that she is." Sonata beamed.

Sonata found a new tour manager. This time she nabbed Freda Wilson. A no nonsense ball buster, from Las Vegas. She new her job, and she knew it well. She was to the point and took shit from no one.

Sonata stayed out on the road for an extra week. She wanted to get Freda used to the crew and the band. She also asked Freda to keep an eye on Eddie for her.

"She steppin' out on you?" Freda asked Sonata.

"No, nothing like that." Sonata smiled. "She just really misses me when I'm not around, and she tends to go overboard."

"Overboard?"

"Mood swings, Not sleeping."

"She using?" Freda asked.

"Eddie? Naw, a drink or two maybe."

"Well, with all the egos running around here, she seems like the least of my worries. But I'll keep an eye on her."

"Thanks." Sonata smiled.

Eddie spotted the two women talking and came up to them. "Here you are." Eddie kissed Sonata. Heya Freda."

"Eddie. Were your ears burning?" Freda joked.

"Uh oh, were ya talkin' about me again?" Eddie looked at Sonata.

"Every chance I get." Sonata giggled.

"Hey Freda, you mind if I steal me gal from ya?"

"Steal away. You two have fun. Sonata, I'll give you a call when we get to Florida.

"Thanks Freda, don't take shit from them. Especially this one."

"Funny. Very funny." Eddie said as she took Sonata's hand and walked away.

"So, what do you want to do tonight?" Sonata said.

"I don't care, I just don't want you out of me sight."

"Oh, I think that can be arranged. Sonata smiled.

❧   ❧   ❧

Sonata packed in silence.

Eddie sat and watched her.

She and Eddie spent the night making love. Eddie didn't want to talk. Sonata noticed that the past three days, Eddie had become more aggressive and forceful in bed. She knew Eddie didn't sleep much. She heard her get up at least three times in a night and usually found her sitting in the chair sleeping. She knew the stress was getting to Eddie, and to her. Now was the time she had to dig in deep and hold her ground.

"All packed...I think." Sonata said, looking around.

"Wonderful fer ya, isn't it." Eddie said flatly. She stood up.

"Eddie, please. Don't do this."

Eddie walked over to Sonata. "Do you want me to be happy that yer leavin' me?

"I'm not leaving you, Eddie. I'm going back to work. One more month and you'll be home too. Then things will be different."

"Have you forgotten? When I come home, it's fer only two weeks. We have the awards and then we leave fer Europe. What happens then, Sonata? Ya can't just hop on a plane fer the weekend now can ya?"

Eddie was right. That was a two-month tour. There was no way she could leave Savoy that long, and there was no way Eddie could make it without her there.

"We'll figure out something." she kissed Eddie. "I promise."

"Stay with me Sonata. Piss on Savoy. You don't need it. I'll take care of you. Anything you want it's yours. We 'ave enough money to last us the rest of our bloody lives."

"Oh, Eddie…it's not about the money." She took her hand and led Eddie to the bed and sat down. "I had to be an adult at a very young age. My father walked out on us, my mother is in an institution. I worked for everything I have. And I got it on my own terms. Money can buy you a lot of nice things, Eddie, but it can't buy love. Not the kind of love we share."

"I'm sorry, I'm such a needy bird, I just feel like I'm being short changed."

"I know sweetie, I feel that way too. But instead of dwelling and being angry on the time we don't get to spend together, we should relish the time we do." Sonata kissed Eddie.

"How long before ya need to leave?" Eddie asked.

"About an hour and a half."

"Just enough time to relish some more." she grinned.

Sonata giggled. "Now you're talking."

❧   ❧   ❧

Eddie watched from the balcony as Sonata blew her a kiss and waved good-bye. The cab took off and Eddie's heart went right with it. A surge of loss and rage started to build inside of her. She walked back into the room and looked around. It was empty, Sonata's side of the bed, the closet. It was all empty. She looked into the mirror. She saw a sad lonely woman. Again having been abandoned. "What the fuck are ya looking at?" She yelled at herself.

She grabbed the desk chair and threw it into the mirror shattering it. "Why? Why?" She screamed.

Anything that wasn't nailed down was thrown against the walls. She kicked the TV pulling it out of the entertainment center and breaking the screen. "You leave me just like me mum did!"

She ran into the living room and went over to the bar. She raked her hands across the shelves of glasses knocking them to the marble floor. "Big shot Rockstar I am! I have nothing! I have shit!" She yelled as she slammed her fist onto the glass shelving, slicing her hand.

Karli opened the door and stepped in. Her mouth dropped as she saw the sight before her. "Eddie, what happened?"

Eddie turned around and looked at her. "I fell in luv, that's what happened Karli. Do yer self a favor, don't ever do it."

"Eddie, your hand." Karli said pointing to the blood dripping from her wound.

Eddie took the bar towel and wrapped it around her hand. She looked at Karli and walked out the door.

Karli franticly dialed Sonata's cell phone. "Damn it!" she said. She reached for the phone and dialed Linda.

"Hello?" Linda said.

"Linda it's Karli, is Freda with you?"

"Yeah, why?"

"I think we have a problem."

"What?" Linda asked.

"Eddie." Karli said.

"We're on our way." The phone went dead.

Two minutes later Linda and Freda walked in.

"Holy shit." Freda said as she looked around.

"Where is she?" Linda asked.

"She's hurt, Linda, She cut her hand on the glass." Karli started to cry.

"The bedroom is a total loss." Freda said coming back to Karli.

"Karli, where is Eddie?" Linda asked again.

"She stormed out. She was all upset that she fell in love, and said I shouldn't. Linda, she is hurt. We need to help her."

"Ok, ok. Take it easy." Linda hugged Karli.

"I should have tried to stop her." Karli said.

"Better that you didn't." Freda said. She walked to the phone and started to dial.

"If you're calling Sonata I already tried. She doesn't have her phone on."

"Ok." Freda sat the phone down. "Linda, take Karli to your room and let her settle down. I'll go look for Eddie."

"I should be looking for her too." Karli said.

"We can cover more ground if we all look fer her." Linda said.

"I think I know where she may be." Freda walked out.

Eddie looked at her cut. It wasn't that long but it was a good slice. Luckily it was on the back and side of her hand. It wouldn't affect her drumming. She lay on her drum perch, looking into the darkness of the stage. She was glad to have the night off. Tomorrow she would be off to wherever, and the whole thing would start over again.

"How's that hand?" Freda asked as she sat down next to Eddie.

"Sore, but I'll be fine." Eddie said.

"Good, can't be losing our favorite drummer. You don't play, we don't eat." Eddie looked at her. "Can I ask you something?"

"Shoot." Freda said.

"You ever fall in luv?" Eddie looked over at her.

"Yep." Freda said.

"Woman?"

"Yep."

"Ya still with her?"

"She will always be with me, in my heart."

"She left you?"

"Yep."

"Oh."

"She died two years ago." Tears came to Freda's eyes. "She was my world. My soul mate, my best friend."

"Sorry." Eddie offered.

"Don't be. We shared fifteen wonderful years together. They found a lump. They thought they got it all…they didn't."

"You miss her?"

"Everyday."

"How did you cope?"

"I didn't at first. I got into the drug scene. It covered the pain, but it didn't take it away. I blew through my bank account, and Bev threatened to throw me out.

"Yeah, but fifteen years being together everyday, that's what luv is about." Eddie sat up.

"Girl, please. You think I just got this job? No way, I have been on the road for most of my life. I missed her like hell, but I made good use of my time away. Love is about being free, Eddie, not about being bound to someone. Plus, I made good use of my time out on the road. I bought a computer, and learned how to invest my money, next year I can retire."

"Well, I hope ya don't. Yer one hell of a road manager." Eddie smiled.

"Thanks. We will see what happens. So what do you say we get that hand cleaned and bandaged?"

"Yeah, sorry I went off the hook there Freda."

"Yeah, well it's not everyday you have a cute redhead to go off the hook for. Let's just hope the hotel see's it that way."

Eddie nodded.

"One other thing. Don't go thinking that you can do this at every hotel we go to. You can't. I don't tolerate it. Consider this your one free pass." Freda stood up. "That's only cause I like you Eddie." Freda smiled and walked away.

Lisa heard the knock at the door. She looked at the clock. 2:00am. They had arrived in New York two hours ago. They flew at night, to try to keep the level of frenzy to a minimum. The knock grew louder. *Must be another fan waiting to go down on me*, she thought. She rolled back over. The knock grew louder.

"Sod it!" Lisa said., as she drug herself out of bed. "This better be worth it." She mumbled as she reached the door.

Lisa's drug habit was starting to get the best of her. Uppers to wake up, downers to sleep, crack and heroin to get her through the day, a little heroin with Annie, and their guests. Yeah, had to be gracious to the fans. She had quite the reputation. But Lisa was an actress, a damn good one. Sure they knew she partied, but she was there for every show, and never missed a word of a song or a beat of the music.

"What?" she snarled, as the person knocked again.

"It's me, Eddie."

Lisa opened the door. "It's two in the fucking morning, if you ain't sleeping with a woman, what are ya doing up?" She started to walk to the bar. "Ya look like shit, Eddie."

"I feel like it too." She shut the door and followed Lisa to the bar.

"So, what do ya want from me?" Lisa asked, as she took a shot from a decanter sitting on the shelf.

"Ah…I wanted to know, if maybe ya had a few more of them caffeine tabs? I figure if I can't sleep, I might as well be chipper."

"Yeah, right." Lisa grinned. She had Eddie where she wanted her. "Anything to help out a mate." Lisa went into the room.

Eddie poured herself a drink. She looked at her hand shaking as she held the glass to her lips. She drank down the bitter strong liquid and poured herself another one.

"I heard ya did quite the number to yer suite." Lisa came back carrying two small pill bottles.

"Kind of lost me head for a bit."

"Well, here we are. Tabs fer wakey time, and tabs fer nappy time."

"I don't think I should take those." Eddie looked at Lisa.

"Ya said ya couldn't sleep." She moved the bottle in front of Eddie. "Now ya can."

Eddie looked at Lisa then at the bottle. She knew that she was falling in deeper, but it was the only way she knew how to cope. She missed Sonata; this would help her get over that. She took the bottle and downed the rest of her drink. She walked to the door.

"Ya can thank me later, Eddie." Lisa said as she watched her walk out. "And ya will." She smiled and walked back into the bedroom.

Eddie opened her door. To her amazement, the room was completely restored to its once pristine condition. She opened the fridge and took out a beer. She opened it and took a swig. She walked into the bedroom and saw the blinking red light on the phone. She took her two new best friends, and sat them on the nightstand. She stared at them "What am I doing?" she asked herself. She took another sip of beer. She reached for the bottle as the phone rang. It startled her.

"Yeah?"

"Shit, Eddie, where have you been?" Karli yelled on the phone.

"Karli, please, back off me."

"Sonata has been trying to reach you for hours! You didn't have your phone on."

"Ok, I'll ring her up." Eddie said.

Freda and Linda were also waiting for you. Freda said that you would be back soon, and when you didn't show…"

"Sorry, if I gave you all a fright. I am fine. If you will call Linny and Freda fer me, I'd like to call Sonata."

"Sure."

"Thanks, luv. I'll talk to ya tomorrow." She hung up the phone. She grabbed the bottle of pills. She read the label "Sleep…we'll see about that." She poured the pills out onto the nightstand and watched them dance as they rolled around. She took one and held it to her lips. The phone rang startling her again.

"What?" She snapped on the phone.

"Eddie?" Sonata said.

"Hey, luv." She quickly grabbed the pills and put them back into their bottle as if not to let Sonata see them.

"Eddie, what happened after I left? It's all over the news. The label called and they are concerned, I would expect this kind of shit from Lisa, not you."

Sonata's sharp words cut deep into Eddie. "Sorry, Sonata, I got a bit carried away."

"A bit? Eddie it was over twenty thousand dollars in damages. You call that a bit carried away. I have spent the entire day trying to do damage control."

"Then maybe ya shouldn't have left then."

"Eddie, don't start."

"Don't start what? I can't start anything, Sonata, you're never around!" Eddie snapped back.

"I was just there for three weeks." Sonata's voiced rose.

"How grand. Three weeks out of six months, Sonata!"

"Eddie, I didn't call to fight with you."

"Well, yer doin' a damn fine job of it."

"Ok, I'm done here, I can't talk to you when you're like this. I'm glad that you are ok. I love you Eddie. Sweet dreams."

Eddie listened until the phone went dead. "Yeah, real sweet." She hung up the phone. It was the first time she hadn't said I love you to Sonata. She opened the bottle of pills. She took one out and looked at it. "Sweet bloody dreams, Eddie." She said as she put the pill on her tongue and chased it with the last of her beer.

She decided to wait for the pill to kick in down at the bar. She was already packed for their travel day tomorrow. She walked to the door and opened it. As she flew out the door she walked right into a woman almost knocking her down. "Sod it! Are you ok, luv?" She said as she held the woman up.

"Yes, I'm sorry. I wasn't looking where I was going."

"Please, no. I was the daft one, zooming out of me room like that.

They stood staring at one another.

"So." She said. "You're…?"

"Oh. Eddie, Eddie Sutcliffe." She held her hand out.

"I thought so." she smiled.

"And you?" Eddie asked.

"Ruthie, Ruthie Kramer."

"I thought so." Eddie winked. "Well, Ruthie Kramer, it's a pleasure to meet ya. What brings you to the hallway at this late hour?"

"I needed to get some air. You?"

"The same thing, trying to unwind."

"Care to join me?" Ruthie asked hopefully.

"If yer game, I'd luv to."

"I am." She smiled, "Let's go."

A grin came over Eddie's face as she followed the beautiful woman down to the elevator.

"So tell me, why have I heard yer name before?" Eddie looked at her.

"Promise you won't get mad?"

"Some already think I am, luv."

"I am Ruth Kramer. Ruthie in the morning on Wuzzup."

"Ok." Eddie's guard went up. "Yer the dj who's gonna interview us?"

"Guilty." Ruth said. "I just wanted to catch a show before you came in. I wanted to have my facts in order. So I followed you in from D.C."

The elevator stopped and Eddie held the door open for Ruth. She watched as the well-built woman walked ahead of her.

"I'd say yer facts were in perfect order." she said under her breath, as she followed Ruth outside.

"So, where to?" Ruth asked.

"Ya got me, I've never been to New York before."

"Well…do you want fun, excitement, craziness, or quiet?"

Eddie thought for a moment. She started to get a bit woozy from the pill. "Quiet would be good." she said.

Ruth called for a cab. "I know the perfect spot." she said as she opened the cab door for Eddie.

"Thank you." Eddie said. She got into the cab followed by Ruth.

Ruth gave the driver the address.

"So, how do you like America?"

"Oh, it's incredible." Eddie smiled. "There are bunches of beautiful birds here."

"Birds?" Ruth looked at Eddie.

"Yeah, a bird, that's a woman. So I mean, there are bunches of beautiful women."

Ruth giggled. "I bet you say that to all the women you meet."

"Well, women are all beautiful in some way, but no, I don't say that to just anyone."

Ruth blushed. She felt an instant attraction to the tall drummer. "It's right there on the corner, driver."

The driver made a quick cut in-between two cars and pulled to the side of the street.

Ruth insisted on paying for the cab. Eddie smiled. She was a nice gal. She reminded Eddie of Sonata. Hell who was she kidding? The gum she almost stepped in, reminded her of Sonata. She needed to go back to the hotel, call Sonata and apologize for being such a pompous ass.

Ruth held the door open and Eddie stepped inside.

It was a very warm and inviting room. It looked liked a huge den. There were sofa's lining the walls, a piano sat in the middle of the room, where an older woman sat playing some jazzy version of the disco hit, "I Will Survive."

"Over there." Ruth said, as she pointed out a sofa near the fireplace. They walked over to the couch and sat down.

"What can I get you?" Ruth asked.

"Tea please. Earl Grey." Eddie smiled.

"Coming right up."

Eddie looked around. The place was incredible. She would love to bring Sonata here.

Ruth returned and sat a steaming hot cup of tea in front of Eddie.

Eddie's head started to spin; the pill was starting to bring her down. "Where's the loo?"

"The loo?"

"Oh sorry, the ladies room."

"Oh." Ruth laughed. "Down there to your left."

"Thank ya, luv, I'll be back in a flash."

Eddie stood up and steadied herself. She made her way to the bathroom, amongst the stares and murmurs. The room knew who she was.

She locked the door and ran the cold water. She splashed the coolness over her face. It felt good. She reached into her pocket and pulled out her bottle of caffeine tabs. She popped one into her mouth and took a sip from the sink.

"Kick in there mate, I gotta keep me wits tonight," she told herself as she looked into the mirror. She quickly dried her face and opened the door.

By this time the entire café was a buzz with excitement. Three people came up and asked for autographs. Eddie happily signed as the rest of the crowd gave her a thunderous applause as she walked to her seat.

"Never had an ovation for going to the loo" she laughed.

"Everyone loves you, Eddie." Ruth declared.

"Fer now anyway." Eddie took a sip of her tea.

"Hey, Eddie, how 'bout a song?" Someone yelled from across the room.

Again the café applauded.

"Your public is calling." Ruth started to applaud.

Eddie looked at Ruth. "Ya mind?"

"Not at all." Ruth grinned.

Eddie stood up and walked over to the piano. She smiled as she tried to quiet the crowd down. "Well, you are one vocal lot tonight. Can't even drink me tea." Eddie looked around. The buzz from the pill was starting to level out the downer. She was feeling good. "Ok then, how about a nice little country song? One of me favorite singers wrote a beautiful song. This is Terri Clark's, Empty."

Eddie started to play. Her voice echoed in the small café which now stood silent.

Ruth looked in awe. This woman held some kind of magical power over an audience when she sang. People, whom she had never met before, were held powerless, including herself. Ruth also found herself drawn to Eddie. She had met many singers in her time, but none held a candle to Eddie Sutcliffe.

Eddie finished her song. She signed some more autographs and talked to some of the well-wishers and she came back to the table.

"Sorry about that." she smiled.

"Sorry for what? You are incredible, Eddie, you do know that don't you?"

Eddie looked into Ruth's eyes. She was a kind, beautiful woman.

"Well I'm just me."

"Well you are incredible." Ruth smiled.

"Thanks, luv." Eddie said as she looked at her watch. "We should be heading back to the hotel soon."

"Mmm, I forgot you have a show tomorrow."

"Correction, I have a show tonight and you have one in a few hours."

Eddie said goodbye to the cafe owners as well as the patrons who stuck around to stare. They hailed a taxi and drove back to the hotel. They rode in the elevator in awkward silence. When it reached the top floor, they stepped out. Eddie walked Ruth to her door.

"Can I ask you something?" she looked at Eddie.

"Sure."

"Whoever she is, she must be something special to be loved so much by you."

"Yes, she is very special. But had I met ya first, I think you could have certainly given me a run fer me money."

Ruth beamed. "She is one lucky woman." Ruth kissed Eddie softly on the lips. "See you at the station tomorrow." She unlocked her door and stepped in.

Eddie stood there looking at the door. There were a million things going through her mind. Most were about Sonata. The elevator door opened and Annie and Lisa stepped out.

Eddie was getting concerned about Annie. She was looking horrible. She had lost a huge amount of weight, and she had dark circles under her eyes.

"Hey, Eddie, what are you doing up?" Annie said.

"Oh, I met the dj from the station, we had a spot of tea and talked a bit."

"Yeah, I bet all ya did was talk." Lisa laughed.

"Well, I guess I'll say goodnight."

"What's yer rush?" Lisa smiled. "C'mon in fer a drink."

"Yeah Eddie, come on." Annie smiled.

"Well…Ok maybe one." Eddie said.

She followed them into their suite.

Eddie walked in and looked around. They had only been in New York a few hours, and their suite already looked lived in.

"So ya bangin' the dj?" Lisa asked.

"No! Sod it, Lisa, why is it always about sex with ya? You need to focus on Annie, She a great gal."

Before Eddie could react, Lisa pulled a handgun from the waist of her pants, and held it to Eddie's head.

"Are ya after me gal, Eddie?"

Eddie swallowed hard. "No…Lisa what are you doing?"

"Don't you know, it's all about sex, drugs and rock an roll?" She slowly took the gun away. "Just showin' off me new gun, ya like it?" She laughed, as she laid the gun on the table.

Eddie wiped the beads of sweat from her upper lip. "You could kill someone with that fricken thing! Are you mad?"

Lisa laughed. "Quite mad, Eddie, and I suggest you watch yer step." She looked at Eddie.

Annie came from the room carrying a small travel bag.

"Thanks, luv." She kissed Annie. "Ya care to join us in a little snack, Eddie?"

Eddie didn't. What she really wanted was to hop on a plane home to be with Sonata. Her body had other plans. She felt herself slipping back to the past. She had battled the demons and won, now the cravings were back, and they were battling it out with Sonata, for Eddie's attention.

"It's no biggie, Eddie, yer gonna live, come party with us." Annie smiled.

Lisa walked over to Eddie and straddled her legs. She looked Eddie straight in the eye. Eddie was frozen. Lisa took her arm She slowly pushed up her sleeve, and carefully tied the rubber band around Eddie's arm.

Tears started to pour from Eddie's eyes, as she watched Lisa inject the warm liquid into her. The rush was intense, it brought Eddie back up. It was a nice feeling.

"See, now don't you feel better?" Annie asked.

"Ready to conquer the world." Eddie smiled and wiped the tears from her face.

Lisa leaned over to Eddie. "Welcome home, luv." She whispered in her ear, and kissed her cheek.

Eddie watched as Lisa shot up and then helped Annie do the same. She felt a sudden loss, she needed Sonata. She stood up. "I need to get going, I'll see you later."

Lisa and Annie watched as Eddie walked out.

"What's eating her?" Annie said.

"You'll be askin' yerself that in a few minutes." Lisa grabbed Annie and kissed her hard.

Annie giggled as she stood up and followed Lisa to the bedroom.

❦   ❦   ❦

"Still no answer." Linda said as she slammed the phone down.

"Will you stop, you'll wake Ollie. Come back to bed, luv." Pamela said.

"I can't sleep. I think there's something going on with Eddie."

"What's that?"

"I think she's using again."

Pamela chuckled. "Not Eddie. She is happy with her life. Her and Sonata have the fairytale."

"Never seen a fairytale happiness, break up a hotel room…. I'm going down there." Linda grabbed her robe.

"Linny, don't." Pamela half-heartedly said.

Linda walked over to Pamela and kissed her. "You sleep, luv, I'll be back in a bit."

Linda opened the door; She looked down the hall, not knowing what she would find. She saw Eddie sitting in front of her door, with her head between her legs.

"Hey there." Linny said, as she sat next to Eddie.

Eddie looked up and smiled. "Heya Linny, yer up late."

"So are you pally, whatta' you doing sittin' here by yerself?"

"Well I ain't got no one in me room, so what does it matter where I sit?"

Linda looked at her friend. She could tell she was on something. "What about Karli?"

"Sleepin.'"

"Seems like you should be too. And fer yer information, Eddie Sutcliffe, Sonata has been ringing you all night. Yer room and yer cell, said you didn't pick up either."

Eddie reached into her pocket and pulled out her phone. She had turned it off when she went out with Ruthie. She dropped it. "Sod it, Linny, I can't do this no more."

"What?"

"This. I want to go home and be with Sonata."

"The tour is wrapping up, then you'll see her."

"Seeing her ain't enough! I need to be with her, need to feel her next to me every night, you, if anyone should know what I mean, Lin."

"I do, my friend. I also know you ain't gonna find what yer looking fer hanging around Lisa again."

"She's just helping me out, Linny, no big deal."

"Fer yer sake, Eddie, I hope it isn't. Now why don't ya call it a night? Get off yer bum and get some sleep."

"Yeah." Eddie said as she stood up.

"But call yer woman first, ok? I'm tired of talkin' to her."

Eddie hugged her friend.

"And know that we can help ya out too, Eddie. We're yer friends and we luv and care about ya."

Eddie kissed Linda on the cheek. "I luv you guys too." she smiled as she unlocked her door and went in.

Linda waited until she heard the door lock, then went back to her room.

Sonata hung up the phone. She was relieved to have finally reached Eddie, but still felt uneasy. She didn't like what Eddie was becoming. She knew she was spending a lot of her free time with Lisa and Annie. Karli and Linda had both told her that Eddie was changing and not for the better.

Sonata decided that if their love was to last, then there had to be a big change, and it would have to be made from her end. She had one week to get it together before the Travelers finished their US leg of the tour. She grabbed the phone and started to dial.

"That was Melissa Etheridge with "Kiss Me" here on 99..5 Wazzzup. This is your morin' gal Ruthie right there with you on the drive in…In case you have been living under a rock, The Travelers are in town tonight for a sold out show, and if you can't get there, then you need to be here, cause I have not one, but all 5 of these fabulous ladies sitting in front of me…."

Eddie watched as Ruthie worked her audience. She was smooth. She knew what to say and when to say it. She was a wonderful woman, and Eddie was thrilled to have had the chance to hang out with her for the evening.

"So wow. What's it like to be the Travelers?" Ruthie smiled at Eddie.

"It's crazy." Linda offered.

"I just bet it is." Ruthie chuckled. "In case you have trouble telling them apart, we have Linda on the bass. Pamela on the rhythm guitar, Annie on lead guitar, Lisa on keyboards and vocals, and I have to say, last but not least, someone who really knocked my socks off last night. We ran into each other in the hall and ended up in a coffee shop, talking, and if you were one of the lucky ones, hearing her sing, Eddie Sutcliffe on the drums, vocals, and piano…is there anything else you play?"

"The guitar. I'll try anything once though." Eddie smiled.

Ruthie laughed. "We'll talk about that later. I want to get to some of the phone calls. Our phone lines are burning up, but I want to ask you, Lisa, it was you who started the Travelers?

"Yes it was luv." Lisa grinned.

"How did you find such an incredible group of women?"

"Well ya just kind of know, Pammy and I go way back, and we played together, then Linny joined up and I found Eddie in a record store. Annie is our newest bird." She winked at Annie.

"I just briefly want to touch on something, if I may. You five are the hottest things to come out of England since the Beatles and the Stones. You are all so open about your lifestyle, I wanted to know if you have had any repercussions, about being so public?"

"You can't let them get ta you." Linda said. "Pamela and I have a son, and we luv him the same as anyone would luv their kids. We eat, drink, sleep, just like every one else, so who cares who we sleep with?"

"We don't ask straight people who they ave slept with, so what does it matter who we sleep with?" Pamela added.

"Besides isn't about luv?" Annie said. "It's what we all want and if you are lucky enough to find it, ya hang on to it."

Ruthie smiled. "Well I say good for you, we are gonna listen to the Travelers first hit, Time Will Tell, then come back and take your calls. We have a lot to talk about…Eight Grammy nominations to boot. We got 'em, the Traveler's are here and waiting to talk to you…."

The song was cued up as Ruthie took her headphones off. "Nice job ladies." She smiled at Eddie.

Lisa saw the exchange and leaned over to Eddie. "Ya sure you ain't banging the radio bird?"

"Don't be startin' on me now Lisa." Eddie snapped back.

"What would Sonata think?" Lisa laughed as she stood up and walked over to Annie.

Eddie shook her head and looked away. Every day was getting to be harder and harder for her to be away from Sonata. Something had to give, and Eddie hoped it wouldn't be her sanity.

"Are you excited?" Sue asked, as she peeked around the corner.

"Extremely. It will be just Eddie and me for two weeks. Locked away, no fans, no music, no clients, no nothing except the two of us." Sonata smiled.

"I know it's been hard on you both, but you must really love her to give up part of your dream."

"I do, but my dream was to find true love. Eddie is true love. This business is not as important as that.

She kept controlling interest in Savoy, but sold forty percent to Gary. The agency was still growing and there was no way Sonata could handle it alone. Still, she was saddened that she had to turn away from it.

Sonata looked at her watch. "Shit, I need to get my ass to the airport." She stood up and grabbed her things.

"Remember Sue, only call if it's an extreme emergency. I'll try to check in."

"Yeah, sure you will." Sue laughed, "Like Eddie will be letting you even come up for air."

Sonata grabbed her keys and grinned as she walked out the door.

"You don't have to answer!" Sue yelled after her, "It's written all over your face!"

❦   ❦   ❦

The airport was packed. The word was out that the Travelers were coming home made it crazy!

Sonata made her way to Terminal 36. She never knew why they always put the terminals so far away, and her luck, she was always booked to fly in and out of them! She made her way back amidst the fans, paparazzi, and the people, who were in fact, trying to catch a plane. There were limo drivers holding signs that read: O'Brien, and Davis. Sonata walked over to them and said hello. She went up to the ticket counter and made sure that security was in place.

The plane slowly taxied into its dock. The crowd grew restless as they waited to catch a glimpse of their favorites.

The airline held the Travelers on the plane until the rest of the flight disembarked.

Sonata grew impatient as she waited for Eddie. It had almost been a month since she last saw her, and she was really missing her.

"Give me a hug ya wench!" Pamela yelled as she spotted Sonata and came running toward her. Linda and Ollie followed.

"Hey, how are you?" Sonata hugged Pamela.

"Doing well, luv, how about you?"

"Hanging in there." Sonata smiled.

"Well, thank God someone is here to pick up that annoying drummer." Linda joked.

Sonata laughed. "That would be me."

"You are a welcome sight." Linda hugged Sonata. Eddie will be thrilled to see you.

Sonata looked up as Eddie walked out followed by Karli. She was stunned to see the pale stick like woman stopping to sign autographs.

"It's taking a toll on her, Sonata." Linda said.

"Hanging out with Lisa don't help either." Pamela added.

Sonata moved closer until she was behind Eddie. "May I have your autograph, Ms. Sutcliffe?"

Eddie turned around to see Sonata's beautiful smiling face. Tears started to fall from behind her sunglasses. She pulled Sonata to her and held her tight.

"Welcome home, stranger." Sonata said.

Eddie remained silent.

Sonata smiled at Karli. "Welcome back, Karli."

"Thanks. Sonata, I'm gonna stay with Linda and Pam for a few days, if that's ok?"

"Thank you." Sonata mouthed. "Come on, let's go home," she said to Eddie.

Eddie released her hold on Sonata but held her hand tight. Security took them through a back route and out into the parking structure.

Sonata unlocked Eddie's side then ran around to get in. "You ok, sweetie?" Sonata asked.

Eddie took her shades off. The dark circles under her eyes told the tale. "I just missed you so much."

"I know, baby. We have a lot to talk about. Let's just go home." She leaned over and kissed Eddie softly on the lips. She seemed different. Her scent, her taste. It wasn't the same as she remembered it.

She put the car in gear and took off.

Eddie woke up and looked around. It did look like her bedroom. She looked over and saw the other side of the bed empty. She felt the soft ocean breeze coming through the open window. She grabbed her sweatshirt off the chair, and walked outside. She smiled as she saw Sonata sitting on the deck, talking on the phone. She was thrilled to be home…at last!

She felt the queasiness come to her quickly. She looked around for her jacket, and found her little bottle. Now that she was home, she would start to cut back on the pills. She didn't need them now that she was back with Sonata. She quickly popped one into her mouth and swallowed. She walked out onto the deck.

Sonata looked up and saw Eddie. "I need to go…I'll talk to you later." Sonata smiled. "Ok. Thanks…bye…Hey, sleepyhead, feel better?"

"Ok I guess." Eddie said as she climbed onto the lounge chair in between Sonata's legs.

"Well, you should be well rested, after sleeping for two days."

"Two days?" Eddie looked up, "Why did ya let me sleep so long?"

"Hunny, I tried to wake you. I just figured you were exhausted after the tour."

"But now I missed two days with ya."

"I have to tell you babe, after I saw you come off the plane looking like you did, I'm glad you did get some rest." She softly kissed the top of Eddie's head, as she ran her fingers through Eddie's hair.

"I wanted us to make love when we got home, not sleep." Eddie frowned.

What do you call the four hours of passion we shared the night you got home? Or did you forget that? I' m still sore, I used muscles I didn't even know I had."

Eddie did in fact forget. She had no memory of coming home and making love to Sonata. It scared her. She knew she was losing control.

"You must be starving, do you want something?"

"Only you." Eddie said.

"You have me, silly."

"Do I?" Eddie sat up and looked at Sonata. It doesn't feel like it sometimes…most of the time."

"I thought we agreed not to bring up work." Sonata said.

"Sonata, I think we…"

"Please, don't Eddie. Can't we just have a nice visit?"

"Oh, now it's a visit?" Eddie stood up, "What next, Sonata? Casual conversations on the phone?"

"Don't do this."

"Do what? Do what, Sonata? I am tired of this shit! I wanted a partner, a wife that wanted to stand with me, not call me on the fucking phone cause she feels like she has to. Eddie grabbed the cordless phone.

"Eddie stop!"

"Here's what I think of yer fucking phone!" Eddie yelled, as she threw the phone off the deck, toward the ocean. She started mumbling as she walked inside. She looked at her hands as they started to shake. She needed a fix.

Sonata watched. "What's wrong with you, Eddie?"

Eddie ignored Sonata as she walked to the bedroom and put on some clothes.

Sonata watched from the doorway. "Where are you going?"

"What do you care? Go on an call a client, maybe you can get off talkin' ta one of em."

"Fat chance of me calling anyone, except maybe shamu, my phone is in the Pacific Ocean!"

Eddie stopped and looked at Sonata. She could see the hurt in her eyes. She had to level off so she could enjoy this time with Sonata. She would taper off and quit by the time they leave for Europe.

She walked past Sonata and grabbed her jacket; She took the keys off the table and walked to the front door. "Sorry luv, I ave ta." She whispered as she walked out.

❧   ❧   ❧

It was after 1:00am when Sonata heard the door unlock. She had been crying since Eddie left. Her eyes were bloodshot and swollen.

Eddie slowly opened the bedroom door. She waited for a moment. Then walked further in. "Sonata? You awake?"

"Yeah." Sonata said. She reached for the lamp next to the bed.

Eddie came and sat next to her, she was carrying a gift. She could tell Sonata had been crying.

"Sorry, I lost me head earlier, I didn't mean ta go off on ya…I love ya so much, Sonata, it kills me inside when we're not together. I just get so angry, and I don't want you seeing' me temper, so it's best I leave…I'm sorry, if I upset ya."

Sonata looked at Eddie. She could see the mood change. She knew Eddie was using. "Where were you, Eddie?"

"At Lisa and Annie's. Lisa and I came up with this idea fer a new song." She lied. "Then I went to get ya this." She handed her the box.

"A new song, huh? I'd love to hear it." She called Eddie's bluff.

"You will…soon. Here, don't you want to open the present I got fer ya?" She smiled at Sonata.

Sonata slowly started to unwrap the gift. She laughed. "A phone. How did you know it was just what I needed?"

"A little birdie told me. She also told me ya might like this." She placed a velvet box on Sonata's lap.

Sonata looked at the box, then at Eddie.

"Go on open it." Eddie smiled.

Sonata slowly opened the box as two very large, bright diamond stud earrings shined like a beacon. "Oh Eddie."

"I wanted to get ya some bigger carrots, these are only two, but the lady said they would be too big. I thought you might want to wear them to the awards tonight."

"Of course I'll wear them, but Eddie, you shouldn't have."

"Yes, I should have, and I should everyday."

"I love them."

"Oh there's one more present."

"Eddie." Sonata giggled.

Eddie walked out, and came back in holding a little black and white ball of fur. "I found him on me way home."

Sonata smiled. "He's so cute."

"Yeah a little hiss and spit there, can we keep him?" Eddie looked at Sonata.

"Sure, why not. We will have to give him a name though."

"Bob. His name is Bobcat." Eddie grinned.

"I love it." Sonata laughed. "I love you too Eddie."

Eddie smiled. "I wonder why you put up with me shit sometimes."

"Well now, I have a gift for you."

"You do?" Eddie looked surprised.

"Yes, but you never gave me the chance to tell you."

"What?"

"I sold part of Savoy…to Gary. There was no way I couldn't be with you in Europe."

Eddie grinned. "Yer not yankin' me chain again, Sonata Williams, are ya?

"Come here and I'll show ya." Sonata pulled Eddie to her and kissed her.

❧   ❧   ❧

Lisa sat in her office finishing her line of coke. Her drug habit was getting enormous, and her bank account was getting smaller. She had convinced Annie to merge accounts, and now Annie was almost broke as well. She had to get more, so she could take more, so she could keep herself going.

Annie was still using, but only socially, and mostly when Eddie was around.

Lisa had become paranoid as a result of her habit. She had her house equipped with surveillance cameras. The wall in her office was all monitors, covering every inch of her estate. If she wasn't on tour, she was sitting in her office, shooting up and watching her monitors.

Annie couldn't get her to do anything. If it didn't involve drugs or sex then Lisa could care less. She started showing up ten minutes before showtime, and was now demanding cash upfront before she would step out onstage. She planned on finishing the European part of the tour and branch out on her solo career. She no longer needed to be part of the Travelers. She had hundreds of songs she had written, and knew she had a full CD of hits. She had decided to keep Annie around. She was nice enough, and a good lay. She needed the extra income to support her habit.

There was a knock at the door.

"What?" Lisa growled.

The door swung open. Annie stood in the doorway with Lisa's robe on, and only her robe. It was open, and fell in all the right places. She was holding a bottle of Champagne and two glasses.

Lisa grinned as she looked at Annie's body. She could see why she had hooked up with Annie in the first place.

"Thought we could 'ave our own celebration before the awards show." Annie smiled.

She walked around and sat on the desk in front of Lisa, grinning as she put her feet up on each arm of Lisa's chair.

Lisa looked up at Annie, then back down at the prize that awaited her.

"See anything you like?" Annie teased as she popped the cork from the bottle.

Lisa swallowed hard. "Yeah…oh yeah."

Annie poured Lisa a glass and handed it to her.

Lisa took the glass and reached for the nest of soft auburn curls that sat before her.

Annie quickly closed her legs. "Not yet, me luv."

Lisa watched as Annie poured the second glass. She turned toward Lisa and raised it in a toast.

"Here's to us and the Grammy's." She clinked Lisa's glass.

Lisa shot her glass straight down. "Good shit there." she winked.

Annie took the glass from Lisa and sat them both down. She stood up, still straddling Lisa. She inched closer to Lisa. She traced Lisa's lips with her tongue, and then lightly kissed her.

Lisa felt the intense heat starting to take over her body.

Annie reached for Lisa's shirt and started to unbutton it.

Lisa reached for Annie's breast.

She swatted it away. "Not yet." Annie smiled.

She slowly peeled off Lisa's shirt. She kissed her neck, sucking and biting, descending down Lisa's now bony frame.

Annie stopped and looked at Lisa. The woman she fell in love with, was now nothing more than a walking skeleton. She unbuttoned Lisa's jeans. "Get up." She instructed.

Lisa looked over Annie's shoulder at her monitors.

Annie grabbed her face. "I said get up." she said sternly. She grabbed the remote and turned off the monitors.

"What the fuck, Annie, I need-."

"Do what I said." Annie said, looking Lisa in the eye.

Lisa sighed. She stood up. She watched as Annie unzipped her jeans, and pulled them down.

With one sweep of her arm Annie cleared off the desk, sending its contents to the ground.

Lisa stared at Annie, half in a daze, half amazed.

Annie pulled Lisa onto the desk. She climbed onto Lisa straddling her. She took her robe off, staring at Lisa like a hungry wild cat.

Lisa reached for Annie; again her hand was pushed away.

Annie started planting little kisses on Lisa. She reached into Lisa's drawer and pulled out her vibrator. She held it up to Lisa. "You want this?" she asked, as she started to lick the head of Lisa's favorite toy.

Lisa could feel her wetness starting to flow. "Yes." she said faintly.

Annie turned on the toy and slowly rubbed it around her already errect nipples.

Lisa watched in excitement. She started to squirm, trying to keep herself in check.

Annie took the vibrator and started to dart it in and out of her mouth. She grinned as she took it and moved it across Lisa's breasts and around her stomach.

Lisa started to move into rhythm with the pleasurable torture Annie had her in. She moaned as she felt her build up growing more intense.

"Now." Lisa groaned looking at Annie.

"Now what?" Annie teased.

"Fuck me now!" Lisa yelled.

"Say please." Annie grinned.

Lisa looked at her.

"No? Ok, ave it yer own way," She smiled as she took the toy and slid it in-between her own legs.

Lisa was panting as she watched Annie.

"Say please." Annie looked at her again.

"Please." Lisa said, finally giving into Annie's game.

Annie slid her hand between Lisa's legs. "My how wet we are." She said, as she slowly slid her finger into her and back out of her lover.

Lisa was about to explode.

Annie rubbed Lisa's clit ever so slowly, gently teasing her.

Lisa arched hard almost throwing Annie off the desk.

Annie knew Lisa couldn't last much longer. She took the vibrator and rubbed it against her.

Lisa moaned.

Annie ran the toy on Lisa's swollen clit, as Lisa shuddered under her buildup.

In one swift motion, Annie ran it down and back up plunging the shaking dildo into her lover. She moved it in and out swiftly as Lisa rocked to keep up with the sensation, until she exploded, moaning and shaking, her back arched high to meet with her orgasm.

Now drenched in sweat, Lisa grabbed Annie and kissed her.

Annie smiled. She knew her lover approved. "We need to get going luv. You don't want to be late for the ceremony." She kissed Lisa again and rolled off the desk.

"Now where do ya think yer going?" Lisa said out of breath.

"To shower. You can join me if you want." Annie winked and walked out.

Lisa laid on the desk, still trying to catch her breath. She was coming down off her high and she was starting to feel like it. She sat up and looked around the room. She spotted her bottle of pills on the floor. She picked them up and opened it.

"Sod it! Only two left." She said as she popped them both into her mouth. She walked over to the bar and took a bottle of gin. She opened it and took a swig. "Kick in fast there." She said. She smiled as she headed for the staircase, Annie would certainly be rewarded for this, Lisa thought.

The limo pulled up top of the red carpet. Eddie looked around.

"You ok?" Sonata asked.

"Yeah. This is all such madness. It's only been a year, and here we are."

Sonata smiled. "But this time you are nominated."

Eddie smiled. "We are nominated."

The limo driver opened the door.

"Give us a moment will ya?" Eddie asked.

The driver smiled and shut the door.

"Sonata, I know yer worried about me. But I'll be ok. Everything is under control. You'll see, things will be different. After tonight, it will be you and me…and Bobcat. I know our luv is worth saving,"

Sonata smiled. "Oh Eddie, I think so too, but there has to be changes, a lot of changes."

"There will be, you'll see, luv. I promise ya." She leaned in and kissed Sonata.

Sonata could taste the bitterness from Eddie's drug use. They were eating her alive. She smelled different. Sonata only hoped that this time Eddie would keep her promise. Sonata looked at Eddie. She could no longer sit around and watch her destroy her life.

Like Lisa, Eddie was also burning through her money. Their business manager met with Sonata. The unpleasant news was all in black and white. Eddie's accounts were almost at the point of bankruptcy. Lisa and Annie would need to file by the end of the year. However, Linda and Pamela had invested wisely. They would be set for life, as would their son. Sonata also invested. She was glad she had a separate account from Eddie. She decided to wait to tell Eddie until after the awards.

"Yer head is driftin' again." Eddie chuckled. She kissed Sonata again. "Let's go, luv. Time fer some fun."

Sonata smiled as Eddie knocked on the glass.

The limo driver opened the door. Eddie stepped out to a roar of screams and applause. The flashes going off were blinding to say the least. She held out her hand for Sonata, who took it, and stepped out.

Hundreds of people were calling Eddie's name. She looked around and waved.

Amy Wilde spotted them and came over.

"I'd say this was your night." she said to Sonata, trying to be heard over the crowd.

Sonata hugged her friend. "I hope so."

"Hey, Amy." Eddie grinned as she hugged her. "Yer lookin' good."

"So are you. When are you gonna dump the redhead and take me away from all of this?"

Sonata and Eddie laughed.

The crowd started to chant Eddie's name. Reporters were calling for her and photographers were clamoring to get the best position for that money shot.

The Travelers were still hot, and they showed no signs of slowing down. Their CD's were selling; their tour merchandise was selling out at each show.

They had toy companies courting them for the doll rights, and there was even talk of a Saturday morning cartoon.

Eddie looked around. This was her party and she wasn't going to miss it. This was better than any drug, she thought. She stopped for a moment and watched Sonata talking to Amy. She knew she needed to do something, and she had too do it soon. She kicked her demons once before, and she could do it again.

The chants of "Eddie!" brought her back to reality.

She grinned. She leaned over to Sonata and kissed her cheek. "Be back in a bit, luv."

Eddie waved to the crowd and started to walk over to them. The closer she got, the louder the screams became.

The reporters and photographers all scrambled to switch their positions as Eddie jumped over the barricade to be with the fans.

"Here we go again." Sonata chuckled. She squeezed Amy's hand, "I'll call you," she said as she walked over to security.

Eddie signed autographs and posed for pictures.

Sonata watched as another limo quickly pulled up.

Linda and Pamela got out and looked around.

Again, the crowd went crazy. Linda spotted Sonata and walked over to her.

"Hey, good lookin'." Linda smiled, "Whatta ya say we dump the other two and make a break fer it."

Sonata giggled and hugged her.

"Where's Eddie?" Pamela asked.

Sonata pointed to the middle of the screaming frenzy of fans, behind the barricade.

"She has all the fun I tell ya." Linda looked at Pamela. "Shall we?"

"Why the hell not!" Pamela smiled.

Linda took Pamela's hand and led her over to the fans.

Sonata watched with delight as the fans approved of Linda and Pamela's decision.

"Sonata." The familiar voice came up from behind her.

She turned around to see Lee Reynolds and Kenny, flanked by their latest plastic surgery rejects.

"Hello Lee…Kenny, nice to see you." She played it up. She knew after tonight, that every major record label would be wanting to sign the Travelers.

"Let's be clear about some things, Sonata." Lee started.

"Hold it. Before you launch into one of your speeches, let me save you some time. Tonight is a night for the Travelers to enjoy the fruits of their labors, not to talk shop. Call me on Monday and we'll talk then." Sonata smiled and walked toward Eddie.

She was proud of herself. She stood up to Lee Reynolds, and left Kenny standing there with his mouth open. This was going to be a good night.

Everyone was inside now, mingling. The producer of the show, reminded everyone that this would be a live broadcast to the east coast. They were set to start in 15 minutes.

Eddie was introduced to The Osbournes, while Linda and Pamela chatted with Tina Turner.

Lisa and Annie were late as usual. Sonata stepped away to phone them, and as always, they didn't answer.

They announced that everyone needed to start taking their seats; Sonata turned and saw Lisa and Annie walking over to their row.

"There you are." Sonata said. "We were wondering if you were going to make it."

"You know us, we had to get up fer it." Lisa grinned.

Sonata frowned. Yeah she knew all too well. Because of Lisa getting up for things, she now had Eddie using. She hated it, and was starting to hate Lisa more than she already did.

Eddie couldn't remember the last time she had so much fun. This was her kind of party. She excused herself and went to the restroom. She had to level off so she could enjoy Sonata and the rest of the night.

It was a very rewarding night for the Travelers. They had won every award they were nominated for. They performed in a tribute to Marvin Gaye, where Eddie took the lead on "Let's Get It On." They got a standing ovation for their rendition.

Sonata was all smiles. Eddie was magic. She loved her so much.

They returned to their seats, just in time for the song of the year award. Eddie had wanted this one most of all. She and Sonata were up against Lisa for the writing honors. She wanted to share this night with Sonata, and she wanted to tell the world how she felt.

Rock and roll star Melissa Etheridge, and R&B legends the Pointer Sisters came out to announce the award.

Eddie took Sonata's hand and looked deep into her eye's.

Sonata smiled.

"I luv ya so much, Sonata." Eddie whispered.

Sonata smiled and squeezed her hand.

"It'll be different from now on, I promise. We'll make it."

"And the winner is…." Anita Pointer said, as Melissa opened the envelope. "Don't Tell My Heart It's Over, Eddie Sutcliffe and Sonata Williams." They yelled.

Sonata's mouth opened. She froze. She and Eddie just won the music industry's highest honor.

Eddie jumped up and hugged Linda and Pamela. She was thrilled.

Annie stood up and hugged her. "I knew you could do it." She whispered into her ear.

She looked at Lisa. She knew Lisa was hurt, and pissed. It was a dangerous combination. She held her hand out to Lisa. "No hard feelings mate."

Lisa shot her a look.

Eddie took Sonata's hand and helped her to her feet.

The ovation was deafening as they made their way to the stage to accept their award.

Eddie stepped up to the mike. "Oh my, I hope I don't piss meself." Eddie said as she looked back. "That's Melissa Etheridge. I think you're amazing, and the Pointer Sisters. What magical harmonies you have. It's been an honor learning from you all!" She turned back around to the audience. "I know I need to be brief, but please bear with me. First off I need to thank the lady standing next to me. She is an incredible force in me life. I never thought it possible to be luvd in the capacity she luvs me…even when I'm being a shit, which is a lot of the time. I do know that no matter what anyone thinks, it's all about luv, and I do luv ya, Sonata, very much…I want to share this award with me mates, Linny, Pam, and Annie, you make it so easy fer a bird to go to work…my assistant Karli, you are me right arm, and I luv ya. Ollie you are a great young man, and I am glad to know ya. To all the folks at Reynolds Records, thanks fer giving The Travelers a go…I also share this award with Lisa O'Brien." She looked at Lisa. "If it wasn't fer yer genius, there wouldn't ave been the Travelers…Ya found me working in a music store, and now look at us…not bad eh?…I know I've been rambling, but I have to thank me brothers back home in England, and I dedicate this to me mum. I miss her, but know she is lookin' down, watching out fer me…and to the fans, wow! You are the best! Thank you for overlooking the personal, and loving the music. Yer unconditional luv means the world to me and me mates…Thank you."

The crowd started to applaud. Eddie turned toward Sonata and kissed her. She took her hand and followed the others off stage.

Lisa looked around. "C'mon, I'm leaving." Lisa said to Annie.

"Lisa there's only one more award." Annie said.

"I don't give a flying fuck! I'm leaving, either ya come with me, or yer ass gets left behind."

"Lisa come on, just sit tight fer a few more minutes." Pamela said.

"Yeah, Lisa fer once don't spoil it fer the rest of us." Linda looked at her.

"Sod off!" Lisa growled. "This whole thing is a bunch of bullshit!"

"Funny, ya didn't think so when we won, the other six awards." Linda said.

"C'mon baby, one more award." Annie smiled, "Then we'll go back and celebrate."

Sonata and Eddie were backstage fielding the media's endless questions about being lesbians in mainstream music. An official came up to them and told them that the last award was being presented. They quickly excused themselves and made their way back to the side of the stage just in time to hear: "…And the album of the year goes to…The Travelers."

Eddie kissed Sonata, and then joined her friends onstage.

Lisa sauntered up to the microphone. "We're thankin' all the usuals. Ya heard yer names plenty tonight, so no need fer ya to hear em again. Mostly we want to thank the fans who know good shit when they hear it. Thanks fer the good times on and off the stage…you know who you are…" She chuckled.

Sonata frowned. Leave it to Lisa to bring down the decorum of the show.

The mike was turned off and the music started to play. They walked off stage.

"Nice, Lisa." Sonata said.

"I would ave thanked ya Sonata, but thought I'd save it for later," she grinned and licked her lips.

Eddie didn't like Lisa's attitude, and it was about time she put her in her place.

"Lay off her, Lisa." she said.

"Sssh…Keep it down." Pamela said.

"She's right, this isn't the time or place fer ya to start, Lisa." Linda added.

"Shut yer yap fer once, Linny. I am so sick of ya thinking yer the perfect one of us." She looked at Eddie, "Yer gonna crash Eddie, you'll need me then won't ya? Choose wisely."

Eddie looked at Lisa. She didn't need Lisa. Sonata showed her that she was worthy just as Eddie Sutcliffe. She no longer needed Lisa O'Brien. However, her addiction did. And right now, her addiction was stronger than her.

"Travelers, you are needed in the press room now." A voice called to them.

Sonata watched as Eddie took a step back.

"C'mon Lisa." Annie tugged on her sleeve.

Lisa smiled as she looked at Sonata, "The party is at our house. See ya there." She grinned.

The others walked to the pressroom. Eddie stayed behind. She looked at Sonata. She could see the sadness in her eyes. Sadness that her actions were causing.

"Sorry, me luv." she choked out. She brushed Sonata's cheek with her finger then turned and walked away.

Sonata rolled over to find Eddie's side of the bed still empty. She looked at the clock it was 1:00am. She told Eddie that she didn't want to go to Lisa's for their party. Eddie had told her they had to go for face sake. They had a fight, and Sonata came home. Her heart was broken to think that Eddie would chose to be with Lisa over her. She knew it was the drugs. She couldn't take it anymore. She had been down this path twice before. Once with her mother's drug addiction, and when she was with K.C. Reynolds. She couldn't do it again. She decided she was going to give Eddie an ultimatum and she was going to do it now.

"Ouch." Eddie said as she clinched her teeth. The needle found a sore spot. Eddie looked at her arm and she started to see the needle tracks, since she used more often. She looked up at Lisa who was helping her shoot up. What were they becoming? she thought.

Annie handed Eddie a drink.

"Thanks there, luv. Yer a good bird Annie."

Lisa looked up at the half naked super model who was trying to get her attention. She smiled.

"Lisa. That's too much." Annie yelled as she grabbed the syringe from Lisa. She eased it out of Eddie's arm.

Eddie's buzz was different this time. She was hot and her ears were ringing.

Lisa stood up and wandered over to the blonde. She took her hand and led her to the bedroom.

The party was starting to wind down when Karli came into the living room and looked around. "Eddie, Sonata called, she's on her way over."

"Huh?" Eddie stared at Karli; she couldn't get her into focus.

"Sonata…your girlfriend?…Hello? Earth to Eddie Sutcliffe come in please."

"That's great, Karli." Eddie mumbled.

"What's wrong with her?" Karli looked at Annie.

"I dunno. She was shootin' up with Lisa." Annie said nervously.

Sonata pulled up to the house in time to see the remaining few partygoers leaving. Karli had told her what was going on there and Sonata knew Eddie needed to get out.

She got out of the car and walked to the front of the house. She saw Lisa in the doorway kissing some tall blonde that was definitely not Annie.

"Eddie, wake up." Annie said to her.

"I'm good, luv." Eddie grinned. She looked at Annie. "Do ya know how beautiful ya are?"

"Eddie, you're stoned." Annie giggled.

"Maybe, but it's true. She took Annie's hand and pulled her onto her lap. "Ya smell good too. Like a rose."

Annie shivered. All of the time she was with Lisa, she secretly wanted Eddie. She knew that Lisa wouldn't let her go, and she knew she couldn't compete with Eddie's love for Sonata.

Eddie looked at Annie. She was cute. Too bad she was with Lisa. She had a lot to offer someone. She traced Annie's lips with her finger.

Annie stopped her finger and kissed it. She looked at Eddie.

Eddie took her face into her hands and kissed her.

Annie melted. It was just like she thought it would be. Eddie was so tender and romantic. What a turn on. She leaned in and kissed her again.

"I don't care what you think, Lisa, this little game of yours, it's…" Sonata froze as she reached the living room followed by Lisa and Karli.

"Eddie." Was all she could say.

Eddie broke off the kiss. Annie jumped up.

Sonata turned and started to walk out.

Eddie struggled to stand and catch her balance. "Luv, wait." she called to Sonata as they reached the door.

"Don't, Eddie."

"Sonata." Eddie grabbed her arm.

"Let go of me." She pulled her arm from Eddie's grasp, and turned to her. "It's over, Eddie." She choked out. "Don't bother coming home, cause you no longer have one with me." Tears started to stream down her face. She ran out.

"Sonata!" Eddie called to her.

The crashing glass from the living room turned Eddie around.

"Lisa, No!" Annie screamed.

Eddie moved toward the living room,

Lisa was standing over Annie. She had just hit her, and was holding a gun to her head. "Did ya forget who the fuck you belong to?" Lisa hissed.

"Lisa, please. It…it. was just a kiss." Annie pleaded.

Lisa cocked the gun. "Don't ya ever shit in me face like that!," she backhanded Annie.

"Stop it!" Eddie yelled.

Lisa turned and looked at Eddie.

"If ya know what's best fer ya, Eddie, you'll get the fuck out of here now!"

"Let her go." Eddie said again.

She was unstable, but she had one shot to take Lisa out. She had to try and save Annie. She lunged forward, trying to grab the gun. Lisa tried to pull away from Eddie.

"Annie, run!" Eddie yelled as she tried to hold Lisa off.

The gunshot rang loud in Eddie's ear as she fell backwards as her head hit the glass coffee table.

Lisa looked around.

Annie lay motionless on the floor. A puddle of blood staining the white carpet.

"This isn't fucking funny!" Lisa yelled. She walked over to Eddie. "This better not be a joke." She walked over to Annie and dropped to her knees. She listened for a heart beat…nothing. "Hey…this was a bloody accident!" She called looking around. "You can't pin this shit on me!" She looked down, the gun still in her hand. She thought how it was going to look. She would be blamed for Annie's death. There was no way she would go back to jail. She looked back at Eddie who was still face down bleeding from her head.

The approaching sounds of sirens brought Lisa back to reality. Tears now streaming from her eyes, she took the gun and cocked it.

❧   ❧   ❧

Sonata tossed and turned. She felt empty inside. She never thought she would lose Eddie, and especially not to Lisa or a drug habit. She prayed that Eddie would crash, and see that their love was worth saving, she needed to get help. She rolled back over and started to drift off, when there was a knock at the door.

Sonata felt a sense of relief. She tossed on her robe and went to the door. She was glad Eddie was home, but there was some things that needed to be dealt with. She looked through the peephole. It wasn't Eddie.

"Who is it?" She asked.

"The police." He held up his badge to the peephole.

Sonata felt her heart fall into her stomach. She unlocked the door.

"Sorry to bother you at such a late hour, Miss Williams. I'm detective Jordan. May I come in?"

"Ah, yes, sure." Sonata opened the door to let him in.

"Sorry to bother you so late. We have this listed as the home address of a Miss Eddie Sutcliffe. Is that correct?"

"Yes it is." Sonata swallowed hard. "Is there a problem?"

"Yes ma'am, there is. We responded tonight to shots fired at a home on Mapleton Drive. The residence is owned by a Lisa O'Brien, and Annie Sullivan. The two and Miss Sutcliffe were found at the residence."

Sonata turned pale. Instant guilt and nausea came to her. Why didn't she stay and try to talk to Eddie? She could have prevented it. "Is Eddie…?"

"Miss Sutcliffe was found overdosed, but alive. She had trauma to her head."

"And Lisa and Annie?"

"Deceased. Both from gun shot wounds, Miss Sullivan to the chest, and Miss O'Brien to the head.

"Where is Eddie?" Sonata asked.

"Detox. She is a 51-50. We are waiting for her to wake up, so we can question her."

Sonata took a breath. She was relieved that Eddie was still alive.

"I'd like to ask you a few questions if I can?" Detective Jordan smiled.

"Sure…of course."

"You are the manager of the deceased and Miss Sutcliffe.

"Yes sir, The Travelers."

"Were you and Miss Sutcliffe...close?"

Sonata looked at the detective. "Yes, we were close."

"How close?"

"What are you driving at detective? If you want to know if Eddie and I were lovers, then yes we were. In fact, it was more than that. We were soulmates and very much in love."

"Were?"

"We are having problems, life on the road, my new business. She started to hang around Lisa again...they used to be together. She started using again."

"That upset you?"

"Yes,. I don't do drugs, and I can't stand people who do. After the awards show tonight, I went over to Lisa and Annie's, to tell Eddie it was over."

"How did she take it?"

"Look, Detective Jordan, I love Eddie with all my heart. I can't be with her right now with all of her problems. I've been down that road before, and frankly, I won't go back to the past."

"Any idea where Eddie was getting her drugs from?"

"Lisa, as far as I know."

"Why didn't you say anything?"

"I tried."

"Do you think Eddie is capable of murder?"

Sonata laughed nervously. "You're kidding, right?"

"No, I'm not."

"Look detective, Eddie may not be perfect, but I can tell you, she didn't do this. She would never kill anyone."

"That remains to be seen, Miss Williams." He stood up.

"You'll see, you're wrong."

"For Eddie's sake I hope your right. Here's my card, just in case."

Sonata followed Detective Jordan to the door.

"Thank you for your time." he smiled politely at Sonata.

She watched him leave. Now what? She thought. Her first instincts told her to run to Eddie's side. She would need her. But Sonata didn't need this. The phone rang. She turned and looked at it. She couldn't talk to anyone. She let the answering machine pick it up.

"Sonata, it's Linda. The madness is on every channel of the telly. I hope yer with Eddie or on yer way. Karli called me; she said it wasn't Eddie's fault. I convinced her to go to the police and tell em what she knows, Pammy and I want ya ta know, that yer welcome to come stay with us. Give us a ring when ya get back, luv ya."

Sonata broke down, Tears came flowing down and she started to shiver. She sat on the couch and turned the TV on.

Every channel had breaking news coverage from outside Lisa and Annie's house. Sonata watched in horror as they kept re-enacting the events of the past night.

She watched, huddled up in a ball on the couch. Hoping that she would wake up in the morning with this having been nothing more than a bad nightmare.

Linda sat watching Eddie. It had been three days, since she was brought into the Strickland Rehab and Detox Center. Put there on a 51/50 by the police, she remained unconscious through the detoxification. The doctors said that it made the processes much easier and that her withdrawals, although not easy, would be more tolerable.

Linda looked at the paper. Everywhere she looked, it was there. Karli and Pamela walked in.

"Anything?" Karli asked.

"Some twitching, but nothing else."

"Well, it's official luv, they cleared Eddie of all the charges." Pamela smiled.

"Well, that is some good news, finally." Linda smiled. "Did you call Sonata?"

"Yeah she was happy to hear the news."

"But…?"

"But she won't come." Karli frowned.

"Bugger! She'll be the only one Eddie will want to see, when she comes to." Linda said.

"It's over Linda. I never thought I would hear myself say it, but it's over." Karli said.

"They had such a strong bond there too." Pamela added.

"I'll call her later, maybe I can get her head on straight." Linda said.

"Good luck, Linda." Karli sat down. "This will destroy Eddie."

"I knew this would happen. Lisa and her no good drugs."

A nurse came in and took Eddie's vitals. She smiled at the others and walked out.

"What did Sonata say when you saw her yesterday?" Pamela asked.

"Nothing really, just handed me a letter to give ta Eddie."

"Karli, Linda and I wanted to know if ya'd like to live with us and Ollie?"

"Aw, you guys are so great. But I can't leave Eddie. I think we kind of need one another."

"The offer is extended to her as well, as long as she's clean." Linda said.

Eddie heard the voices; she forced her eyelids open. The room was spinning. She felt the stirring in her stomach. "Don't ya all be talking about me now." she said weakly.

"Eddie!" Karli smiled, as she moved to her friend's bedside. "You're awake."

"Yeah, but right now I don't know if it's such a grand idea. Where am I?"

"I've said it before and I'll say it again. Sutcliffe, you are the klutzy one." Linda grinned. "Yer in the hospital, ya overdosed.

"Hey, Linny." Eddie half grinned, "I did?" She ran her hands through her hair.

"Hi, luv, how are ya?" Pamela asked.

"Hey, Pammy." Eddie slowly tried to sit up. She looked around the room. "Where's Sonata?"

They all exchanged glances.

"Ah, I think I'll let the nurses know yer awake." Pamela smiled as she walked out.

"Eddie, do you remember anything that happened?" Karli asked.

Eddie thought. She couldn't recall the details, but bit's and pieces were still there. "It's all still fuzzy in me head. We were at Lisa and Annie's celebrating the awards. Hey, where are they?"

Before anyone could answer, the doctor came in, followed by Karli and a nurse.

He checked Eddie and reassured her that everyday the symptoms would lessen, but she still had a very long road ahead of her. He advised the others not to stay too long. He excused himself and left with the nurse following in tow.

"So, where is Sonata?" Eddie asked her friends again.

"Ah…Eddie…" Karli started to say. She looked at Linda for help.

"Is she alright?" Eddie was concereined.

"Eddie…Sonata's not coming." Linda finally said.

"What do you mean?" Eddie looked confused.

"That night, the party at Lisa's…Well you and Sonata…Sonata found you with Annie on yer lap…you were kissing her."

Eddie looked puzzled. "What the hell fer?"

"That's what Sonata wanted to know, and ya didn't 'ave an answer fer her. You two had words, and she left."

"This is madness." Eddie carefully rubbed her head. "Wait a sec. I do recall Sonata leaving, I gave chase ta her."

"Do you remember what happened next?"

"No, me head was spinning and I was hot."

"Eddie listen to me, Annie and Lisa are dead." Karli said flatly.

Eddie tried to laugh. "Is this some kind of a joke?"

"No, Eddie, it's not." Linda said.

"What happened?"

"You walked in on Lisa holding a gun to Annie. She was in a rage about you two kissing. You tried to get the gun out of her hand, but you fell and hit your head on the coffee table. Lisa shot Annie, and then turned the gun on herself."

Eddie couldn't believe what she was hearing. She needed Sonata here with her. "I don't remember any of it." Eddie said as she started to cry. "I need to talk to Sonata." Eddie said as she looked around for a phone.

"Maybe we should let you rest." Pamela said looking at the others.

"Yes, good idea." Karli agreed.

Pamela leaned over and kissed Eddie. "You rest and we'll be back in a bit."

They started to walk out.

"Linny, hold up there a sec." Eddie called.

"I'll stay here with her. I'll catch up with you later." Linda kissed Pamela. She turned back and pulled up a chair next to Eddie's bed.

"This is pretty big news then, huh?"

"Bloody big. They had ta sneak us in the back, just ta get up here."

"I'm sorry this happened." Eddie looked at her friend. "I have ta see Sonata."

Linda reached into her pocket and pulled out the bulky envelope. She handed it to Eddie. "She asked me ta give ya this."

"Is she…?" Eddie looked at Linda.

"I'm sorry Eddie." Linda said.

Eddie started to cry.

Linda sat on the bed and held her friend. "Easy there."

"Why did ya even let me live? I can't go on if I don't have Sonata by me side."

"Don't talk like that, Eddie Sutcliffe!" Linda tried to play it down, even though it was breaking her heart as much as Eddie's. "First things first. Ya get yerslef better and get out of here. You and Karli can come stay with us. Pammy and I 'ave been talking, and were gonna sell everything here and move back home, we'll 'ave enough money fer all of us to live like queens!"

"I don't know if I can." Eddie said trying to wipe the tears from her eyes.

"You can do anything, Eddie Sutcliffe. We 'ave faith in ya." Linda smiled.

"Thanks, Linny, yer good people." Eddie half grinned.

"Anytime, I'm gonna catch up with the others and leave ya to rest fer a bit."

"You're coming back, right?"

"Of course me friend." Linda kissed Eddie. "See ya later."

She left, leaving Eddie holding the envelope from Sonata.

Feeling dizzy, she sank down in her bed and opened the letter. As she unfolded it, her mother's gold wedding band fell from it. Eddie's heart sank. She focused hard on the letter wiping tears away from her eyes, as she read it.

∾

My dear Eddie,

I'm just so relieved that you are ok. You should be proud that you tried to stop Lisa from such a horrible act of violence.

I know right now, you are wondering why I am not there with you. The truth is I can't be. I can't subject myself to the new way you have chosen to live your life. You have chosen your path...A path that has burned me before, and a path that I won't go down again. It is with that, that I think it best for us to go our separate ways. I do love you Eddie, and I believe in you and the glorious gift that God gave you. Please don't let drugs destroy it.

Thank you for the year plus, we shared together. I can finally say that I know what true love is.

With love and my best to you Eddie.

Sonata.

Eddie read the letter several times. She couldn't believe it. She threw the ring across the room. She rolled over and gave into the tears that had overcome her.

EPILOGUE

Eddie sat in front of the mirror of her dressing room.

It had been five years since she was last up on stage. Those five years had aged her. She stayed in rehab for two months. She called Sonata on occasion, hoping to speak to her, and maybe try to make amends. Words never came to her. She would often listen to Sonata in frustration until she would hang up. Her voice still captured her heart. She tried calling just last week, but the phone number was no longer in use. Eddie thought that was the final sign that things were over.

There was a knock at the door.

"It's open." she yelled.

"Are ya ready for the re-surgence of The Travelers?" Linda asked as she walked in.

"A bit nervous." Eddie smiled. She was so blessed that Linda, Pam, and Karli stood by her side.

After months of prodding by her brother, Eddie and the others decided to reform the band. This time Karli was on the drums, and Eddie took center stage.

They still had a huge fan base, and daily offers from the States for a reunion tour and a new CD. At first, Eddie wasn't up for it. She sat around in her pajamas, missing Sonata. Looking at photos, mementoes, and anything else that reminded her of the past. It wasn't until Linda kicked her ass and woke her up. They started writing again. Eddie loved it. It was her therapy.

"Oh my God! The place is packed." Karli yelled as she came in, followed by Pamela and Oliver.

Denny promised a full house." Eddie grinned.

"Did I hear me name?" Eddie's brother walked in.

Eddie smiled. She was thrilled to have both her brothers on board since they decided to take another go at the band. Denny was acting as manager and Ryan as security.

Eddie became inseparable with her brothers, and their families. They did everything together. They made a pact that to honor their mother; they would make sure she had new flowers at her grave every other day. Eddie often would sit and talk to her mother, down at the cemetery. She wouldn't date. There could never be anyone who could make her feel like Sonata. If she wasn't with her mother, she was walking the streets of England, tracing the steps of the magical times, she and Sonata once shared.

"Ok ladies, showtime." Ryan announced as he came in.

Eddie felt a bit shaky. It was almost seven years to the day that she walked out on this stage and fell in love with the beautiful redheaded American sitting in the front row.

The crowd was quiet with anticipation.

"Ya feel ok?" Denny asked his sister.

"Yeah, I'll be fine once I get out there."

"I'm proud of you, sis." he said, as he took Eddie into his arms. "We all are."

"Thanks, Denny." Eddie smiled. "I'm glad yer here fer the next go round."

"Me too."

"Ladies and gentleman, you are about to witness history." The announcer's voice boomed.

"This is it." Eddie said, as she ran to join her friends on stage. "Ok, mates let's kick some arse!"

"Please welcome back home to the Red Lion…. The fabulous Travelers!"

Eddie grinned as she heard the roar of the crowd.

The lights came up and the Travelers started to rock.

Denny watched as Eddie, as always, took total control over the audience. She hadn't lost a beat.

"The crowd is going mad." Ryan said as he walked up to Denny.

"Look at 'em Ryan, she has them in the palm of her bloody hand!"

Ryan looked out. "She is something quite special."

"Yes, she certainly is."

"Did you tell her about Stuart?"

"No, no need to. He was dead to her a long time ago, now it's for real. Just as long as he wasn't buried next to mum."

"I never realized how good Eddie really is." Ryan said, as he watched his sister.

"Still the best voice in music, about to make a huge comeback."

"Thank you all fer coming back out to see us. We've missed you all so much…Sometimes it takes a tragedy, to knock ya down and give ya a wake up call…I'm sure that Annie and Lisa are hearing ya too."

The crowd started to applaud.

"Here's a song that went to number one, cause of you folks. Yer a crazy lot and we thank ya fer it. This here's me favorite song…I want to tell ya all, when you find yer true luv, ya hang on to it. You cherish it and ya work hard ta keep it. Ya don't let nuthin' or no one, get in yer way…"

The crowd cheered.

"Don't let drugs take over yer mind. I did, and it cost me the world…This song is called Don't Tell My Heart It's Over."

You could have heard a pin drop as the crowd watched, mesmerized by Eddie's voice as she sat at the piano and played.

Pamela and Karli both had tears in their eyes, as Eddie played back the memories of her and Sonata.

The show was a huge success. Record people, friends and fans were all treated to a reception at the pub.

Eddie walked around mingling. Though her heart wasn't in it, she signed autographs and posed for pictures.

A pretty blonde walked up to her.

"Hi." she smiled.

"Hi, Eddie Sutcliffe." She held out her hand.

"Yes, I know." she smiled. "I'm Wendy, Wendy Ackerman." She took Eddie's hand.

"And why does that name ring a bell with me?"

"Cause I've been the one hounding you. I'm from UK Records Inc."

"Oh, ok, I've heard yer voice on the answer machine." Eddie smiled.

"Well, we would love to offer you a deal. We think you still have what it takes."

"Thank you. Sometimes I'm not so sure of that."

"Be sure, Eddie." Wendy winked.

What a flirt. Eddie thought. It was kind of nice. She was a beautiful woman. But a record executive, when would she learn?

"Here's my card, maybe we can get together fer a drink and talk about it."

"Well, Denny handles all that stuff now." Eddie said, taking the card.

"Well then, give him my number, but the other offer still stands fer you."

Wendy leaned into Eddie and whispered. "I hope ya call. I'd like to get to know you better." She smiled and walked away. Eddie watched her as she walked out of the pub. She looked down at the card. Maybe she should give Wendy a call. It was a sign of the new times ahead for her. A new career and a new life.

❦   ❦   ❦

The party lasted till the next morning. Eddie and Linda stayed to play darts with some of the fans. It was nice to be out and about again. The life was definitely coming back to Eddie Sutcliffe.

"Ya want a lift?" Linda asked, as they walked out of the pub.

"No thanks, I'm gonna head out to see me mum."

"Ah, tellin' her about the blonde I take it?"

"She was rather beautiful wasn't she?" Eddie grinned.

"A real knockout. I saw her slip ya her number." Linda teased.

"Ya make a good spy, Linny." Eddie laughed.

Linda laughed. "Ya gonna ring her up?"

"Seriously thinkin' I might."

"Well I think ya should, put the past in the bloody past, and make a new go of it."

"I'm thinkin' I'll just do that." she hugged Linda. "Thank ya so much, Linny, yer a grand one."

"Ya coming by fer supper later?" Linda asked as she got into her car.

"Count on it." Eddie smiled, as she watched Linda drive off.

The air was cool, and though Eddie was dog tired, she had a new found spring in her step. She was actually looking forward to calling Wendy and going out on a date. She decided that she would give Wendy a ring after she went to see her mother.

Eddie walked through the cemetery gates. As always, she took the same path counting plots, twenty-one, till she reached her mother. She excused herself to Wilfred Brighton, her mother's neighbor, as she sat on his tombstone.

"Good mornin' mum. I ave so much to tell ya…The show went great. But I'm sure ya knew that. I think I did ok too. Not too rusty. It felt right an all…We might take it to the studio and record again…I think I would like that, in fact I know I would. Karli was incredible. She really picked up her own drumming style. She doesn't beat em, like so many others…And Linny and Pam picked up right where they left off…Oh afterward, Denny had this reception, I met this bird there, her…" Eddie looked at the flowers. They were fresh roses. Not the same ones she had brought the day before. "Who brought you flowers? I must ave gotten me signals crossed with Denny and Ryan. Things are starting to get crazy, and their runnin' around like jackals."

"I brought them Eddie."

Eddie froze. The familiar voice sent chills through her. She looked up at the silhouette standing in front of her. She stood up to get a better look.

"I hope you don't mind?" Sonata smiled.

"This can't be true. It has to be a dream."

"No, no dream, it's me."

Eddie wanted so badly to take Sonata in her arms and kiss her. All of her feelings she pushed away came flooding back in an instant. "What are ya doing here, Sonata?"

"I came to see you, Eddie. I saw the show, you were incredible as always."

"Thanks." Eddie smiled.

There was an awkward silence as the two stared at one another.

"I wanted so badly to talk to you, but I just couldn't find the right words to tell you…"

"Please, Sonata, I was a daft arse to ever let drugs get between us. You tried to stop me, but I was spinning out of control."

"I wasn't any better with work, Eddie."

"Oh yeah, how is Savoy doing? I am sure it's huge." Eddie tried to make small talk.

"I sold the business and the house…Bob and I moved back to Venice Beach…"

"How is Bobcat doing?"

"Good. Sonata chuckled. He misses you. Amy is watching him for me now…Eddie, I don't want to take up anymore of your time, so let me just lay this out on the line…I miss you. I can't do anything without thinking about you. I have been so alone since we parted." Tears started to run down her cheeks. "I'm so alone, Eddie…. I still love you…I'm still in love with you."

Eddie moved closer and wiped her tears away. "I was the crazy one luv, I shouldn't 'ave left without a fight. I haven't been able to think of anyone or anything except you. I called you a few times, but I just listened to yer voice."

"That was you? Sonata chuckled. "I knew it was."

"You did?" Eddie said.

"I felt you, Eddie."

Eddie slowly took Sonata's face into her hands. She looked deep into Sonata's eyes. The magic was still there. She slowly and tenderly kissed Sonata.

Chills ran through Sonata. It was just like the night Eddie kissed her on the dance floor.

"Can we go somewhere?" Eddie asked.

"My hotel?" Sonata offered.

"Great. Where are ya staying?"

"The Savoy." Sonata grinned.

"Perfect! After we make luv fer a hundred times or so, we can 'ave room service and decide when ya want to move in. I've got a lot of things to tell ya"

Sonata kissed Eddie. "I want to hear every last word," she giggled. "Eddie are you sure about this? I mean us?"

Eddie reached for the gold chain around her neck, and took it off. "I think this belongs to ya luv." She slid the gold wedding band off the chain and put it on Sonata's ring finger. "There now, back home where it belongs." She kissed Sonata. "So are you luv. So are you."

They kissed one another and looked deeply into each other's eyes.

Eddie held out her hand for Sonata. "I luv you Sonata."

Sonata took her hand. "I love you Eddie."

Hand in hand they started to walk back to the hotel, to start over where their journey of love first began.

THE END

0-595-34298-1

Printed in the United Kingdom
by Lightning Source UK Ltd.
121584UK00002B/2/A